A DOG'S PURPOSE

A Dog's Purpose

W. BRUCE CAMERON

A TOM DOHERTY ASSOCIATES BOOK

NEW YORK

A DOG'S PURPOSE

A Forge Book
Published by Tom Doherty Associates, LLC
175 Fifth Avenue
New York, NY 10010

www.tor-forge.com

Forge® is a registered trademark of Tom Doherty Associates, LLC.

ISBN 978-0-7653-6676-4

First Edition: July 2010

Printed in the United States of America

S 0 9 8 7 6 5 4 3 2 1

{ ACKNOWLEDGMENTS }

So many people have helped me in so many ways to get me from where I started to where I am today, I hardly know where to begin the task of identifying them all—and where to *stop* is even more perplexing a choice. So let me state for the record that I know that as both a writer and a person I am a work in progress who thus far is a sum of all I've learned and experienced, and that I owe everything to the people who have taught me, helped me, and supported me.

I do want to make sure I acknowledge some of the writings I used in my research into how dogs think. *Dogwatching*, by Desmond Morris. *What the Dogs Have Taught Me*, by Merrill Markoe. *The Hidden Life of Dogs*, by Elizabeth Marshall Thomas. *Search and Rescue Dogs*, by the American Rescue Dog Association. The works of Cesar Millan, James Herriot, Dr. Marty Becker, and Gina Spadafori.

I wouldn't be anything without the support of my family, especially my parents, who have always believed in my writing despite a couple of decades' worth of rejection notices.

Also believing in me is my agent, Scott Miller, at Trident Media, who never gave up, not on this book, not on me.

Scott's efforts led me to Tor/Forge and my editor, Kristin Sevick, whose faith in *A Dog's Purpose*, combined with a careful eye and an expert touch, refined and improved this novel. She and everyone else at Tor/Forge have been a delight to work with.

As I write these words, this book hasn't yet gone to press, and already there are so many people working to support it. Sheryl Johnston, who is a great publicist and a terror behind the wheel. Lisa Nash, who reached out to her vast network to help validate the voice of this book. Buzz Yancey, who tried to create, well, buzz. Hillary Carlip, who took on the task of redesigning wbrucecameron.com and created adogspurpose.com and succeeded so fabulously. Amy Cameron, who applied her years of teaching experience to the task of writing a study guide for any educator who wants to use *A Dog's Purpose* in the classroom. Geoffery Jennings, bookseller extraordinaire, who gave an early draft his thumbs-up. Lisa Zupan, who gets it.

Thanks to all the editors who carry my column in their newspapers, despite the turmoil in the industry. Thanks especially to *The Denver Post*, which picked me up after the sad demise of the *Rocky Mountain News*. Thanks, Anthony Zurcher, for doing such a great job editing my column for all these years.

Thanks to Brad Rosenfeld and Paul Weitzman at Preferred Artists, for preferring me, and to Lauren Lloyd, for managing everything.

Thanks, Steve Younger and Hayes Michael, for all the legal work—I still think we should plead insanity.

Thanks, Bob Bridges, for continuing his volunteer work on my column's mistakes and typos. I wish I could afford to pay you one hundred times your current salary.

Thanks, Claire LaZebnik, for coming out on the ledge to talk to me about writing.

Thanks, Tom Rooker, for whatever the heck it is that you're doing.

Thanks to Big Al and Evie, for investing themselves in my "genius" career. Thanks, Ted, Maria, Jakob, Maya, and Ethan, for admiring my pants.

Thanks to everyone in the National Society of Newspaper Columnists, for trying to keep us all off the endangered species list.

Thanks, Georgia Lee Cameron, who introduced me to the world of dog rescue.

Thanks, Bill Belsha, for the work you did on my head.

Thanks, Jennifer Altabef, for being there when I needed you.

Thanks, Alberto Alejandro, for almost single-handedly making me a bestselling author.

Thank you, Kurt Hamilton, for motivating me to make sure there was nothing seriously wrong with the pipes.

Thanks to Julie Cypher, for loaning me everything she owns.

Thanks, Marcia Wallace, you are my favorite action figure.

Thanks, Norma Vela, for all the horse sense.

Thanks, Molly, for the car ride, and Sierra, for letting it happen.

Thanks, Melissa Lawson, for providing the final cut.

Thanks, Betsy, Richard, Colin, and Sharon, for showing up for everything and for trying to teach me how to dance the rumba.

The very first person I told this story to was Cathryn Michon. Thank you, Cathryn, for insisting that I write A Dog's Purpose immediately, and for everything else.

Now I understand why so many people are still talking when the music plays at the Academy Awards: the list of individuals I want to thank is simply endless. So let me just stop here, ending with one final note: I want to acknowledge the sacrifice and tireless hard work of the many men and women who work in animal rescue, helping lost, abandoned, and abused pets find new and happy lives with loving families. You are all angels.

A DOG'S PURPOSE

{ ONE }

One day it occurred to me that the warm, squeaky, smelly things squirming around next to me were my brothers and sister. I was very disappointed.

Though my vision had resolved itself only to the point where I could distinguish fuzzy forms in the light, I knew that the large and beautiful shape with the long wonderful tongue was my mother. I had figured out that when the chill air struck my skin it meant she had gone somewhere, but when the warmth returned it would be time to feed. Often finding a place to suckle meant pushing aside what I now knew was the snout of a sibling seeking to crowd me out of my share, which was really irritating. I couldn't see that my brothers and sister had any purpose whatsoever. When my mother licked my stomach to stimulate the flow of fluids from under my tail, I blinked up at her, silently beseeching her to please get rid of the other puppies for me. I wanted her all to myself.

Gradually, the other dogs came into focus, and I grudgingly accepted their presence in the nest. My nose soon told me I had one sister and two brothers. Sister was only slightly less interested in wresting with me than my brothers, one of whom I thought of as Fast, because he somehow always moved more quickly than I could. The other one I mentally called Hungry, because he whimpered whenever Mother was gone and would suckle her with an odd desperation, as if it were never enough. Hungry slept more than my siblings and I did, so we often jumped on him and chewed on his face.

Our den was scooped out underneath the black roots of a tree, and was cool and dark during the heat of the day. The first time I tottered out into the sunlight, Sister and Fast accompanied me, and naturally Fast shoved his way to the front.

Of the four of us, only Fast had a splash of white on his face, and as he trotted jauntily forward this patch of fur flashed in the daylight. *I'm special,* Fast's dazzling, star-shaped spot seemed to be declaring to the world. The rest of him was as mottled and unremarkably brown and black as I was. Hungry was several shades lighter and Sister shared Mother's stubby nose and flattened forehead, but we all looked more or less the same, despite Fast's prancing.

Our tree was perched on a creek bank, and I was delighted when Fast tumbled head over heels down the bank, though Sister and I plummeted with no more grace when we tried to make the same descent. Slippery rocks and a tiny trickle of water offered wonderful odors, and we followed the wet trail of the creek into a moist, cool cave—a culvert with metal sides. I knew instinctively that this was a good place to hide from danger, but

Mother was unimpressed with our find and hauled us unceremoniously back to the Den when it turned out our legs weren't powerful enough to enable us to scale back up the bank.

We had learned the lesson that we couldn't return to the nest on our own when we went down the bank, so as soon as Mother left the nest we did it again. This time Hungry joined us, though once he was in the culvert he sprawled in the cool mud and fell asleep.

Exploring seemed like the right thing to do—we needed to find other things to eat. Mother, getting impatient with us, was standing up when we weren't even finished feeding, which I could only blame on the other dogs. If Hungry weren't so relentless, if Fast weren't so bossy, if Sister didn't wiggle so much, I knew Mother would hold still and allow us to fill our bellies. Couldn't I always coax her to lie down, usually with a sigh, when I reached up for her while she stood above us?

Often Mother would spend extra time licking Hungry while I seethed at the injustice.

By this time, Fast and Sister had both grown larger than I— my body was the same size, but my legs were shorter and stubbier. Hungry was the runt of the litter, of course, and it bothered me that Fast and Sister always abandoned me to play with each other, as if Hungry and I belonged together out of some sort of natural order in the pack.

Since Fast and Sister were more interested in each other than the rest of the family, I punished them by depriving them of my company, going off by myself deep into the culvert. I was sniffing at something deliciously dead and rotten one day when right in front of me a tiny animal exploded into the air— a frog!

Delighted, I leaped forward, attempting to pounce on it with my paws, but the frog jumped again. It was afraid, although all I wanted to do was play and probably wouldn't eat it.

Fast and Sister sensed my excitement and came stampeding into the culvert, knocking me over as they skidded to a stop in the slimy water. The frog hopped and Fast lunged at it, using my head as a springboard. I snarled at him, but he ignored me.

Sister and Fast fell all over themselves to get at the frog, who managed to land in a pool of water and kick away in silent, rapid strokes. Sister put her muzzle in the pond and snorted, sneezing water over Fast and me. Fast climbed on her back, the frog—my frog!—forgotten.

Sadly, I turned away. It looked as though I lived in a family of dimwits.

I was to think of that frog often in the days that followed, usually just as I drifted off to sleep. I found myself wondering how it would have tasted.

More and more frequently, Mother would growl softly when we approached, and the day she clicked her teeth together in warning when we came at her in a greedy tumble I despaired that my siblings had ruined everything. Then Fast crawled to her, his belly low, and she lowered her snout to him. He licked her mouth and she rewarded him by bringing up food, and we rushed forward to share. Fast pushed us away, but we knew the trick, now, and when I sniffed and licked my mother's jaws she gave me a meal.

At this point we had all become thoroughly familiar with the creek bed, and had tracked up and down it until the whole area was redolent with our odors. Fast and I spent most of our time dedicated to the serious business of play, and I was beginning to understand how important it was to him for the game to wind up with me on my back, his mouth chewing my face and throat. Sister never challenged him, but I still wasn't sure I liked what everyone seemed to assume was the natural order of our pack. Hungry, of course, didn't care about his status, so when I was frustrated I bit his ears.

One afternoon I was drowsily watching Sister and Fast yank on a scrap of cloth they'd found when my ears perked up—an animal of some kind was coming, something large and loud. I scrambled to my feet, but before I could race down the creek bed to investigate the noise Mother was there, her body rigid with warning. I saw with surprise that she had Hungry in her teeth, carrying him in a fashion that we'd left behind weeks ago. She led us into the dark culvert and crouched down, her ears flat against her head. The message was clear, and we heeded it, shrinking back from the tunnel opening in silence.

When the thing came into view, striding along the creek bed, I felt Mother's fear ripple across her back. It was big, it stood on two legs, and an acrid smoke wafted from its mouth as it shambled toward us.

I stared intently, absolutely fascinated. For reasons I couldn't fathom I was drawn to this creature, compelled, and I even tensed, preparing to bound out to greet it. One look from my mother, though, and I decided against it. This was something to be feared, to be avoided at all costs.

It was, of course, a man. The first one I'd ever seen.

The man never glanced in our direction. He scaled the bank and disappeared from view, and after a few moments Mother slid out into the sunlight and raised her head to see if the danger had passed. She relaxed, then, and came back inside, giving each of us a reassuring kiss.

I ran out to see for myself, and found myself disheartened

when all that remained of the man's presence was a lingering scent of smoke in the air.

Over and over again the next few weeks, Mother reinforced the message we'd learned in that culvert: Avoid men at all costs. Fear them.

The next time Mother went to hunt, we were allowed to go with her. Once we were away from the security of the Den, her behavior became timid and skittish, and we all emulated her actions. We steered clear of open spaces, slinking along next to bushes. If we saw a person, Mother would freeze, her shoulders tense, ready to run. At these times Fast's patch of white fur seemed as obtrusive as a bark, but no one ever noticed us.

Mother showed us how to tear into the filmy bags behind houses, quickly scattering inedible papers and revealing chunks of meat, crusts of bread, and bits of cheese, which we chewed to the best of our ability. The tastes were exotic and the smells were wonderful, but Mother's anxiety affected all of us, and we ate quickly, savoring nothing. Almost immediately Hungry brought up his meal, which I thought was pretty funny until I, too, felt my insides gripped in a powerful spasm.

It seemed to go down easier the second time.

I'd always been aware of other dogs, though I'd never personally met any except those in my own family. Sometimes when we were out hunting they barked at us from behind fences, most likely jealous that we were trotting around free while they were imprisoned. Mother, of course, never let us approach any of the strangers, while Fast usually bristled a little, somehow insulted that anybody would dare call out to us while he lifted his leg on their trees.

Occasionally I even saw a dog in a car! The first time this happened I stared in wonderment at his head hanging out the window, tongue lolling out. He barked joyously when he spotted me, but I was too astounded to do anything but lift my nose and sniff in disbelief.

Cars and trucks were something else Mother evaded, though I didn't see how they could be dangerous if there were sometimes dogs inside them. A large, loud truck came around frequently and took away all the bags of food people left out for us, and then meals would be scarce for a day or two. I didn't like that truck, nor the greedy men who hopped off it to scoop up all the food for themselves, despite the fact that they and their truck smelled glorious.

There was less time for play, now that we were hunting. Mother snarled when Hungry tried to lick her lips, hoping for a meal, and we all got the message. We went out often, hiding from sight, desperately searching for food. I felt tired and weak, now, and didn't even try to challenge Fast when he stood with his head over my back, thrusting his chest at me. Fine, let him be the boss. As far as I was concerned, my short legs were better suited for the low, slinking run our mother had taught us anyway. If Fast felt he was making some sort of point by using his height to knock me over, he was fooling himself. Mother was the dog in charge.

There was barely room for all of us underneath the tree now, and Mother was gone for longer and longer periods of time. Something told me that one of these days she wouldn't come back. We would have to fend for ourselves, Fast always pushing me out of the way, trying to take my share. Mother wouldn't be there to look after me.

I began to think of what it would be like to leave the Den.

The day everything changed began with Hungry stumbling into the culvert to lie down instead of going on the hunt, his breathing labored, his tongue sticking out of his mouth. Mother nuzzled Hungry before she left, and when I sniffed at him his eyes remained shut.

Over the culvert was a road, and along the road we'd once found a large dead bird, which we'd all torn into until Fast picked it up and ran off with it. Despite the danger of being seen, we tended to range up and down this road, looking for more birds, which was what we were doing when Mother suddenly raised her head in alarm. We all heard it the same instant: a truck approaching.

But not just any truck—this same vehicle, making the same sounds, had been back and forth along our road several times the past few days, moving slowly, even menacingly, as if hunting specifically for us.

We followed Mother as she darted back to the culvert, but for reasons I'll never fully understand, I stopped and looked back at the monstrous machine, taking an extra few seconds before I followed Mother into the safety of the tunnel.

Those few seconds proved to make all the difference—they had spotted me. With a low, rumbling vibration, the truck came to a stop directly overhead. The engine clanked and went quiet, and then we heard the sounds of boots on gravel.

Mother gave a soft whimper.

When the human faces appeared at either end of the culvert, Mother went low, tensing her body. They showed their teeth at us, but it didn't seem to be a hostile gesture. Their faces were brown, marked with black hair, black brows, and dark eyes.

"Here, boy," one of them whispered. I didn't know what it meant, but the call seemed as natural as the sound of the wind, as if I had been listening to men speak my whole life.

Both men had poles, I now saw, poles with ropes looped on

the end. They appeared threatening, and I felt Mother's panic boil over. Her claws scrabbling, she bolted, her head down, aiming for the space between the legs of one of the men. The pole came down, there was a quick snap, and then my mother was twisting and jerking as the man hauled her out into the sunlight.

Sister and I backed up, cowering, while Fast growled, his fur bristling on the back of his neck. Then it occurred to all three of us that while the way behind us was still blocked, the tunnel mouth in front of us was now clear. We darted forward.

"Here they come!" the man behind us yelled.

Once out in the creek bed, we realized we didn't really know what to do next. Sister and I stood behind Fast—he wanted to be the boss, so okay, let him deal with this.

There was no sign of Mother. The two men were on opposite banks, though, each wielding his pole. Fast dodged one but then was snagged by the other. Sister took advantage of the melee to escape, her feet splashing in the water as she scampered away, but I stood rooted, staring up at the road.

A woman with long white hair stood there above us, her face wrinkled in kindness. "Here, puppy, it's okay. You'll be all right. Here, puppy," she said.

I didn't run; I didn't move. I allowed the loop of rope to slip over my face and tighten on my neck. The pole guided me up the bank, where the man seized me by the scruff of the neck.

"He's okay; he's okay," the woman crooned. "Let him go."

"He'll run off," the man warned.

"Let him go."

I followed this bit of dialogue without comprehension, only understanding that somehow the woman was in charge, though she was older and smaller than either of the two men. With a reluctant grunt, the man lifted the rope off my neck. The woman offered her hands to me: rough, leathery palms coated with a flowery smell. I sniffed them, then lowered my head. A clear sense of caring and concern radiated off of her.

When she ran her fingers along my fur I felt a shiver pass through me. My tail whipped the air of its own accord, and when she astonished me by lifting me into the air I scrambled to kiss her face, delighting in her laughter.

The mood turned somber when one of the men approached, holding Hungry's limp body. The man showed it to the woman, who clucked mournfully. Then he took it to the truck, where Mother and Fast were in a metal cage, and held it up to their noses. The scent of death, recognizable to me as any memory, wafted off of Hungry in the dry, dusty air.

We all carefully smelled my dead brother, and I understood the men wanted us to know what had happened to Hungry.

Sadness came from all of them as they stood there silently in the road, but they didn't know how sick Hungry had been, sick from birth and not long for the world.

I was put in the cage, and Mother sniffed disapprovingly at the woman's smell, which had been pressed into my fur. With a lurch, the truck started up again, and I was quickly distracted by the wonderful odors flowing through the cage as we moved down the road. I was riding in a truck! I barked in delight, Fast and Mother jerking their heads in surprise at my outburst. I couldn't help myself; it was the most exciting thing that had ever happened in my whole life, including almost catching the frog.

Fast seemed overcome with sadness, and it took me a moment to understand: Sister, his favorite companion, was gone, as lost to us as was Hungry.

There was, I reflected, much more complexity to the world than I had supposed. It wasn't just about Mother and my siblings hiding from people, hunting, and playing in the culvert. Larger events had the ability to change everything—events that were controlled by human beings.

I was wrong about one thing: though we didn't know it at the time, Fast and I would meet up with Sister again in the future.

{ T W O }

Wherever we were headed on our truck ride, I had the sense we'd see other dogs when we got there. The cage in which we were being held was positively flooded with the scent of other canines, their urine and feces and even their blood mixed with fur and saliva. While Mother cowered, her claws extended to keep her from sliding on the bouncing, jerking floor, Fast and I paced, our noses down, smelling one distinct dog after another. Fast kept trying to mark the corners of the cage, but every time he tried to stand on three legs a good jounce from the truck sent him sprawling. Once he even landed on Mother, earning him a quick nip. I gave him a disgusted look. Couldn't he see she was unhappy?

Eventually, bored with smelling dogs who weren't even there, I pressed my nose to the wire grate and pulled in great snootfuls of the wind. It reminded me of the first time I'd buried my face in the succulent garbage bins that represented our main source of food; there were thousands of unidentifiable odors out there, all of them coming up my nose with such force I kept sneezing.

Fast took up position on the other side of the cage and lay down, not joining me at the side of the cage, because it hadn't been his idea. He gave me a surly look every time I sneezed, as if warning me that next time I tried that I'd better ask him for permission. Each time his cold gaze met my eyes I would glance pointedly at Mother, who, though obviously cowed by this whole experience, was still in charge as far as I was concerned.

When the truck stopped, the woman came around and spoke to us, pressing her palms to the side of the cage for us to lick. Mother stayed where she was, but Fast was as beguiled as I was, and stood next to me, his tail wagging.

"You are so cute. You hungry, babies? You hungry?"

We were parked in front of a long, flat dwelling, sparse desert grasses poking up between the truck's tires. "Hey, Bobby!" one of the men yelled.

The response to his shout was astonishing. From behind the house came a chorus of loud barks, so many I couldn't count the sources. Fast rose up on his back legs and put his paws on the side of the cage, as if that would somehow help him see better.

The racket continued as another man emerged from around the side of the house. He was brown and weathered, walking with a slight limp. The way the two other men stood grinning at him carried an air of expectation. When he saw us, he stopped in his tracks, his shoulders slumping.

"Oh no, senora. Not more dogs. We have too many now." He

radiated resignation and regret, but there was nothing angry in what I felt coming off him.

The woman turned and approached him. "We have two puppies, and their mother. They are maybe three months old. One of them got away, and one of them died."

"Oh no."

"The mother was feral, poor thing. She's terrified."

"You know what they told you the last time. We have too many dogs and they will not give us a license."

"I don't care."

"But senora, we have no room."

"Now Bobby, you know that's not true. And what can we do, let them live as wild animals? They're dogs, Bobby, little puppies, you see?" The woman turned back to the cage, and I wagged my tail to show her I had been paying rapt, if uncomprehending, attention.

"Yeah, Bobby, what's another three more?" one of the grinning men asked.

"One of these days there will be no money to pay you; it will all go to dog food," the man called Bobby replied. The men just shrugged, grinning.

"Carlos, I want you to take some fresh hamburger and go back out there to that creek. See if you can find the one that got away," the woman said.

The man nodded, laughing at Bobby's expression. I understood that the woman was in charge of this family of humans, and gave her another lick on the hand so she would like me best.

"Oh, you're a good dog, a good dog," she told me. I jumped up and down, my tail wagging so hard it whipped Fast in the face, who irritably blinked it off.

The one called Carlos smelled of spicy meat and exotic oils that I couldn't identify. He reached in with a pole, snagging Mother, and Fast and I followed willingly as she was led around the side of the house to a large fence. The barking here was deafening, and I felt a slight flicker of fear—just what were we getting into?

Bobby's scent had a citrus quality, oranges, as well as dirt, leather, and dogs. He opened the gate a little, blocking the way with his body. "Get back! Get back now; get back! Go on!" he urged. The barking lessened just a little, and when Bobby pulled the gate all the way open and Carlos thrust Mother forward it ceased completely.

I was so astounded by what greeted me, I didn't even feel the foot in my back as Bobby pushed me inside the enclosure.

Dogs.

There were dogs everywhere. Several were as large as or even larger than Mother, and some were smaller, and all were milling freely around in a large enclosure, a huge yard surrounded by a high wooden fence. I scampered forward toward a knot of friendly-looking dogs not much older than myself, halting just as I got to them to pretend to be fascinated by something on the ground. The three dogs in front of me were all light colored and all females, so I seductively peed on a mound of dirt before joining them to sniff politely at their rear ends.

I was so happy at this turn of events I felt like barking, but Mother and Fast were not having as easy a time of it. Mother, in fact, was hunting along the perimeter of the fence, seeking a way out, her nose pressed to the ground. Fast had approached a group of males and now stood stiffly with them, his tail quivering, while each took a turn lifting a leg against a fence post.

One of the males moved to stand squarely in Fast's path

while another circled back to sniff him aggressively from the rear, and that's when my poor brother folded. His butt sagged, and as he turned to face the male behind him his tail curved and slid up between his legs. I wasn't at all surprised when, seconds later, he was on his back, squirming with a certain desperate playfulness. I guessed he was no longer the boss.

While all this was happening, another male, muscular and tall, his ears hanging long on the sides of his head, stood absolutely still in the center of the yard, watching Mother run around in desperate circumnavigation. Something told me that of all the dogs in the yard, this was the one to be careful of, and, sure enough, when he broke from his rigid stance and padded over toward the fence the dogs surrounding Fast stopped messing around and raised their heads alertly.

A dozen yards from the fence, the lone male broke into a full run, bearing down on Mom, who stopped, cringing. The male braced her with his shoulders, blocking her, his tail straight as an arrow. She let herself be sniffed up and down the length of her body, still crouched against the fence.

It was my impulse, and I am sure it was also Fast's, to rush to her aid, but I somehow knew this would be wrong. This was the Top Dog, this male, a thick-boned mastiff with a brown face and dark, rheumy eyes. Mother's submission was simply the natural order.

After his careful examination, Top Dog aimed an economical stream of urine against the fence, which Mother dutifully examined, and then he trotted off, paying her no more attention. Mother herself seemed deflated, and slid off unnoticed to hide behind a pile of railroad ties.

In due course, the pack of males came over to check me over as well, but I crouched low and licked them all in the face, letting them know in no uncertain terms that they'd have zero problems with me—it was my brother who was the troublemaker. All I wanted to do was play with the three girls and explore the yard, which was populated with balls and rubber bones and all sorts of wonderful smells and distractions. A clear trickle of water fell continuously into a trough, providing refreshment whenever we wanted it, and the man named Carlos came into the yard once a day to clean up our messes. At regular intervals we would all break out in loud barking, for no reason other than the sheer joy of it.

And the feedings! Twice a day, Bobby, Carlos, Senora, and the other man would wade into the pack, separating us out into groups based on age. They would pour bags of rich food into large bowls, and we would bury our faces, eating as much as we could hold! Bobby stood by, and whenever he thought one of the dogs (usually the smallest of the girls) didn't get enough he would pick her up and give her another handful, pushing the rest of us away.

Mother ate with the adult dogs and occasionally I'd hear a growl from over on their side, though when I looked all I could see was wagging tails. Whatever they were eating smelled wonderful, but if one of the juveniles tried to wander over there to see what was going on the men would step in and stop the pup.

The woman, Senora, would bend and let us kiss her face, and she would run her hands through our fur and laugh and laugh. My name, she told me, was Toby. She said it to me every time she saw me: Toby, Toby, Toby.

I was certain I was, by far, her favorite dog—how could I not be? My best friend was a fawn-colored female named Coco, who had greeted me on my first day. Coco's legs and feet were white, her nose pink, her fur coarse and wiry. She was small enough that I could keep up with her despite my short legs.

Coco and I wrestled all day long, usually joined by the other girls and sometimes by Fast, who always wanted to play the game where he wound up the Top Dog. He had to keep his aggressive play in check, though, because when he became too rambunctious one of the males would be dispatched to trot over and teach Fast a lesson. When this happened, I always pretended I had never seen him before in my life.

I loved my world, the Yard. I loved running through the mud by the water trough, my paws making a dirty spatter that flecked my fur. I loved when we'd all start barking, though I seldom understood why we were doing so. I loved chasing Coco and sleeping in a pile of dogs and smelling other dogs' poops. Many days I would drop dead in my tracks, exhausted from play, deliriously happy.

The older dogs played, too—even Top Dog could be seen tearing up the yard, a ragged piece of blanket in his mouth, while the other dogs pursued and pretended not to be able to quite catch up with him. Mother never did, though—she had dug herself a hollow behind the railroad ties and spent most of her time just lying there. When I went to see how she was doing, she growled at me as if she didn't know who I was.

One evening, after dinner when the dogs were drowsy and sprawled out in the Yard, I saw Mother stealthily emerge from her hiding place and creep toward the gate. I was gnawing on a rubber bone, addressing a constant ache in my mouth for something to chew, but I stopped and regarded her curiously as she sat in front of the gate. Was someone coming? I cocked my head, thinking if we were having a visitor the other dogs would have started barking by now.

Many evenings Carlos and Bobby and the other men would sit at a small table and talk, opening and passing a glass bottle from which came a sharp chemical smell. Not this night, though—the dogs were all alone in the Yard.

Mother lifted her forelegs off the ground, pressing them against the slats of the wooden gate, and took the metal knob in her mouth. I was baffled—why, I wondered, would she chew on such a thing when there were all these perfectly good rubber bones scattered about? She twisted her head left and right, apparently unable to get a good bite of the thing. I glanced over at Fast, but he was sound asleep.

Then, astoundingly, the gate clicked open. My mother had opened the gate! She dropped her paws to the ground and shouldered the gate aside, sniffing cautiously at the air on the other side of the fence.

Then she turned to look at me, her eyes bright. The message in them was clear: my mother was leaving. I stood to join her, and Coco, who was lying nearby, lazily lifted her head to blink at me for a moment before sighing and stretching back out in the sand.

If I left, I'd never see Coco again. I was torn between loyalty to Mother, who had fed me and taught me and taken care of me, and to the pack, which included my worthless brother, Fast.

Mother didn't wait for my decision. She slunk off silently into the gloom of the approaching night. If I wanted to catch up to her, I would have to hurry.

I scampered out the open gate, pursuing her into the unpredictable world on the other side of the fence.

Fast never saw us go.

THREE

I didn't get very far. I couldn't move as quickly as Mother to begin with, and anyway the front of the house had a stand of bushes that I felt compelled to mark. She didn't wait for me, never even looked back. The last I saw of my mother she was doing what she did best: sliding into the shadows, unnoticed, unseen.

There was a time not long ago when all I wanted out of life was an opportunity to snuggle up to Mother, when her tongue and her warm body meant more to me than anything else. But now, watching her disappear, I understood that by leaving me behind she was simply doing what all mother dogs must do eventually. The compulsion to follow had been the last reflexive gesture in a relationship that had forever changed the day our family arrived at the Yard.

My leg was still in the air when Senora came out on her porch, stopping when she saw me.

"Why, Toby, how did you get out?"

If I wanted to get away I needed to run *now*, which was, of course, not what I did. Instead I wagged my tail and jumped up on Senora's legs, trying to lick her face. Her flowery smell was enlivened with a wonderfully greasy chicken odor. She smoothed my ears back, and I followed her, addicted to her touch, as she strode rapidly around to the still-open gate, the dog pack slumbering inertly inside the Yard. She gave me a gentle nudge and followed me in.

The moment the gate shut, the other dogs were on their feet, racing over to us, and Senora petted them and talked soothingly while I seethed a little over the divided attention.

It seemed more than a little unfair; I'd given up Mother to be with Senora, and here she was acting as if I were no more special than anybody else!

When Senora left, the gate clanked into place with a solid metallic sound, but I would never again regard it as an impassible barrier.

I was wrestling with Coco when Mother returned a few days later. At least, I thought it was my mother—I was distracted by a new wrinkle in our continuous wrestling match, one where I would circle behind Coco and climb up on her back, gripping her with my forelimbs. It was a wonderful game, and I couldn't understand why Coco was so surly about it, twisting and snarling at me. It felt so right, how could she be so unreceptive?

I looked up when Bobby opened the gate, and there was Mother, standing uncertainly. Joyously I tore across the yard, leading a charge of dogs, but I slowed down when I got closer.

This female dog was marked the same as Mother, with a

splotch of black over one eye, and had the stubby snout and short coat, but it wasn't Mother. She squatted and urinated submissively at our approach. I circled the new dog with the others, though Fast marched right up to her to sniff at her rear end.

Bobby had the same defeated sag to his shoulders as when he'd loaded us all into the truck the first time, but he stood close to the dog, protecting her with his body.

"You'll be okay, girl," he said.

It was Sister. I had nearly forgotten all about her, and now, inspecting her, I realized how different life must be on the other side of the fence. She was thin, her ribs plainly visible, and a white, oozing scar tracked down her side. Her mouth smelled of rotten food, and when she squatted a sickly odor came from her bladder.

Fast was overjoyed, but Sister was too cowed by the rest of the pack to accept his offer of play. She groveled in front of Top Dog and let all of the canines sniff her without making a single move to establish any boundaries. When they contemptuously dismissed her, Sister furtively inspected the empty feeding trough and drank some water as if she were stealing.

This was what happened to dogs who tried to live in the world without people—they became beaten down, defeated, starved. Sister was what we all would have become if we'd stayed in the culvert.

Fast clung to her side the whole time. It occurred to me that Sister had always been his favorite, more important to him than even Mother. I watched him kiss Sister and bow toward her without jealousy—I had Coco.

What did make me jealous was the attention Coco was getting from some of the other males, who seemed to think they could wander over and play with her as if I weren't there, which

I suppose they could. I knew my position in the pack and was happy for the sense of order and security it provided me, but I wanted Coco for myself and didn't appreciate it when I was rudely shouldered out of the way.

The males all seemed to want to play the game I'd invented, circling behind Coco and trying to jump on her, but I noted with cold satisfaction that she had no interest in playing this game with them, either.

The morning after Sister arrived, Bobby came into the yard and took Fast, Sister, Coco, and one other young male, a frisky spotted hound the men called Down, and put them all with me in a cage in the back of the truck. It was crowded and noisy, but I loved the high-velocity airstream and the expression on Fast's face when I sneezed on him. Astoundingly, a long-haired female dog from the pack rode in the cab with Carlos and Bobby. *Why did she get to be a front-seat dog?* I wondered. And why, when her scent flowed from the open windows, did a shiver pass through me, making me feel an urgent wildness?

We parked next to an old, gnarly tree that provided the only visible shade in a hot parking lot. Bobby went inside the building with the female from the cab while Carlos came around to the cage door. All of us except Sister surged forward.

"Come on, Coco. Coco," Carlos said. I could smell peanuts and berries on his fingers, plus something sweet I couldn't identify.

We all barked jealously as Coco was led into the building, and then we barked because we were barking. A large black bird landed in the tree above us and stared down at us as if we were idiots, so we barked at it for a while.

Bobby came back out to the truck. "Toby!" he called.

Proudly I stepped forward, accepting a loop of leather around my neck before jumping down onto the pavement, which was so hot it hurt my feet. I didn't even glance back at the losers in the cage as I entered the building, which was astoundingly cool and redolent with the smells of dogs and other animals.

Bobby led me down a hallway and then picked me up and dropped me on a shiny table. A woman entered and I thumped my tail as she put her soft, gentle fingers in my ears and probed under my throat. Her hands smelled of a strong chemical, though her clothes smelled of other animals, including Coco.

"What's this one?" she asked.

"Toby," Bobby said. I wagged harder when I heard my name.

"How many did you say, today?" While she and Bobby spoke, she lifted back my gums to admire my teeth.

"Three males, three bitches."

"Bobby," the woman said. I wagged my tail because I recognized his name.

"I know; I know."

"She's going to get into trouble," the woman said. She was feeling me up and down, and I wondered if it would be okay if I groaned with pleasure.

"There are no neighbors to complain."

"Still, there are laws. She can't just keep taking on more dogs. There are already too many. It's not sanitary."

"She says otherwise, the dogs all die. There are not enough people to take them on."

"It is against the law."

"Please don't tell, Doctor."

"You put me in a bad position, Bobby. I have to be concerned with their welfare."

"We bring them to you if they are sick."

"Someone is going to file a complaint, Bobby."

"Please, don't."

"Oh, not me. I'm not going to say anything without telling you first, give you a chance to find a solution. Okay, Toby?"

I gave her a lick on the hand.

"Good boy. We're going to get you into surgery now, fix you right up."

Bobby chuckled.

Soon I was in another room, brightly lit but deliciously cool, full of the strong chemical smell that came off the nice lady. Bobby held me tightly and I lay still, somehow sensing this was what he wanted. It felt good to be held like that, and I thumped my tail. I felt a brief, sharp pain, behind my neck, but I didn't complain, wagging vigorously to show that I didn't mind.

The next thing I knew, I was back in the Yard! I opened my eyes and tried to stand up, but my back legs weren't working. I was thirsty but too tired to go get water. I put my head down and went back to sleep.

When I awoke, I was instantly aware that there was something around my neck, a white cone of some kind, so stupid looking I worried I might be dismissed from the pack. I had an aching, itchy feeling between my back legs, though I couldn't get at it with my teeth because of the silly collar. I stumbled over to the faucet and drank a little, my stomach queasy and my underside very, very sore. I could tell by the smells in the Yard that I had missed supper, but I couldn't have cared less, at that point. I found a cool patch of earth and flopped down with a groan. Fast was lying there, and he looked over at me—he, too, was wearing the ridiculous collar.

What had Bobby done to us?

The three females who had gone with us to the building with the nice lady were nowhere to be seen. The next day I limped around the Yard, sniffing for signs of Coco, but there was no evidence that she had come back with us.

Aside from the humiliation of the stupid collar, I also had to suffer the indignity of an inspection of the sore area by every male in the pack. Top Dog flipped me over on my back with a not-so-gentle shove, and I lay there in misery as first he and then the other males sniffed me with undisguised contempt.

They didn't try the same thing with the females, who bounded into the yard a few days later. I was overjoyed to see Coco, who also wore the strange collar, and Fast did his best to comfort Sister, who plainly felt the entire process had been traumatizing.

Carlos eventually removed the collars, and from that point on I found myself somehow less interested in the game where I climbed on Coco's back. Instead, I had a new game, where I would strut up to Coco with a rubber bone and chew it right in front of her, tossing it up in the air and dropping it. She would pretend she didn't want it, looking away, but her eyes always came back to the bone when I nudged it toward her with my nose. Finally she would lose control and lunge, but I knew her so well I could snatch the bone away before she closed her jaws on it. I would dance back, wagging joyfully, and sometimes she would chase me and we'd run in big circles, which was my favorite part of the game. Other times she would yawn in fake boredom, so I'd come close again, tantalizing her with the rubber bone until she simply couldn't take it anymore and made another grab for it. I loved this game so much that when I slept I dreamed about it.

Sometimes there were real bones, though, and these were handled differently. Carlos would come into the yard with a greasy bag, handing out charred treats and calling our names as he did so. Carlos didn't understand that he should always give one to Top Dog first, which was okay by me. I didn't always get a bone, but when I did, Carlos would say, "Toby, Toby," and hand it to me right past some other dog's nose. There were different rules when humans were involved.

Once when Fast got a bone and I didn't, I saw something extraordinary. Fast was hunkered down across the yard, chewing frantically, intoxicating odors wafting up from his prize. I'd slid over to watch enviously, so I was standing right there when Top Dog walked up.

Fast tensed, spreading his legs a little as if getting ready to stand, and as Top Dog came forward Fast stopped chewing and loosened a deep growl. No one *ever* growled at Top Dog. I sensed, though, that Fast was right—this was his bone, given to him by Carlos, and not even Top Dog could take it.

But the bone was so delicious, Top Dog couldn't seem to help himself. He shoved his nose forward, and that's when Fast struck, a sharp click of his teeth right in Top Dog's face! Fast's lips were drawn back and his eyes were slits. Top Dog stared at him as if dumbfounded at this open rebellion, and then, with his head raised regally, he turned and lifted his leg on the fence, paying Fast no further attention.

I knew that if Top Dog wanted to, he could have taken Fast's prize. Top Dog had that power, and he'd exerted it before. I'd seen what happened when, right around the time we took the truck ride to visit the nice lady in the cool building, the male dogs had assembled around one of the females, sniffing at her and lifting their legs with a certain frantic purpose. I was in the group, I'm sorry to say; there was just something so compelling about her, I can't even describe it.

Every time a male tried to smell her from behind, the female sat in the dirt. Her ears were back in humility, but she also growled a few times, and when she did the males backed off as if she had just been elected Top Dog.

We were all gathered so close together, it was impossible not to bump into one another, and that's when a fight erupted between Top Dog and the largest male in the pack, a huge black and brown dog whom Bobby called Rottie.

Top Dog fought with expert efficiency, seizing Rottie by the back of the neck and dragging the dog's shoulders down to the ground. The rest of us gave the fight a wide berth, and it was over in seconds, really, Rottie flipping over on his back subserviently. The noise had drawn Carlos, though, who called, "Hey! Hey! That's enough." Carlos stood in the yard, ignored by the males, while Coco trooped over to him to be petted. After watching us a few minutes, Carlos called for the female who had been getting all the attention and took her outside the gate.

I didn't see her again until we were all in the truck the next morning, headed out to see the nice lady in the cool room, and she was a front-seat dog with the men.

After Fast was finished with his bone, he seemed to have second thoughts about nipping at Top Dog. My brother hung his head, tail wagging low, and shambled over to where Top Dog was standing. Fast made several play bows, which Top Dog ignored, and then Fast licked Top Dog in the mouth. This seemed to be sufficient apology, so, with that, Top Dog played with Fast a little, rolling my brother over and letting Fast chew at his neck before he abruptly walked away.

This was how Top Dog maintained order, by keeping us all in our places but not taking advantage of his position to steal food that was given to us by the men. We had a happy pack, right up until the day that Spike arrived.

After that, nothing was the same.

FOUR

It was starting to seem to me that just when I had life all figured out it changed. When we were running with Mother, I learned to fear humans, I learned to scavenge for food, I learned how to placate Fast so he would be in what, for him, was a good mood. And then the men came and took us to the Yard and everything was different.

In the Yard I adjusted quickly to life in the pack, I learned to love Senora and Carlos and Bobby, and just when my play with Coco was starting to assume a different, more complex character we were taken to visit the nice lady in the cool room and the urgency I'd been feeling went completely away. I still spent most of my day chewing on, and being chewed by, Coco, but without the odd compulsions that had occasionally seized me.

In between the two worlds—the one outside and the Yard—stood the gate Mother had opened. I thought about the night of her escape so many times I could practically feel the metal knob in my mouth. Mother had shown me a way to freedom, if I wanted it. But I was a different dog than Mother. I loved the Yard. I wanted to belong to Senora. My name was Toby.

Mother, however, was so anti-social that no one seemed to notice she was gone. Senora had never even given Mother a name. Fast and Sister sniffed every so often at the depression behind the railroad ties where Mother had lain but never showed any outward concern about her disappearance beyond that. Life went on, just as before.

And then, with everyone's status in the pack settled, with me feeding at the adult trough, with Carlos sneaking us bones and Senora handing out treats and kisses, in came a new dog.

His name was Spike.

We'd heard the doors on Bobby's truck slam, so we were all barking, though it was so hot that day that some of us who were lying in the shade didn't even get off our bellies. The gate opened and Bobby entered, leading a large, muscular male on the end of his pole.

Having the entire pack rush you at the gate was intimidating, but the new dog didn't budge. He was as dark and broad as Rottie and as tall as Top Dog. Most of his tail was missing, but what little stub he possessed wasn't wagging, and he stood with his weight balanced on all four legs. A low rumble emitted from his chest.

"Easy, Spike. Okay there," Bobby said.

The way Bobby said "Spike," I knew that was his name. I decided to let everyone else have a turn at inspecting him before I did anything.

Top Dog had, as usual, hung back, but now he emerged from the cool shadows near the waterspout and trotted forward to meet the new arrival. Bobby slipped the loop off Spike's neck. "Easy, now," Bobby said.

Bobby's tension rippled through the pack, and I could feel the fur on my back rising up, though I wasn't sure why. Top Dog and Spike were stiffly examining each other, neither one backing down, the pack in a tight circle. Spike's face was covered with scars—teardrop-shaped pits and lumps colored a pale gray against his dark fur.

Something about the way Spike seemed to take us all in, every single one of us arrayed against him, made me afraid, though the result was as it should be. Spike allowed Top Dog to put his head over his back, though he didn't bow or lower his stomach to the ground. Instead, Spike went over to the fence, carefully sniffed at it, and then lifted his leg. The males immediately lined up after Top Dog to do the same thing on the same spot.

Senora's face appeared over the top of the gate, then, and a lot of the anxiety I'd been feeling went away. Several of us broke from the circle and ran over to her, putting our legs on the fence so she could reach our heads.

"See? He'll be okay," Senora said.

"A dog like him's been bred to fight, senora. He is not like the rest of 'em, no ma'am."

"You be a good dog, Spike!" Senora called over to him. I looked jealously in the new dog's direction, but his reaction to having his name spoken was to glance over as if it were nothing at all.

Toby, I wanted her to say. *Good dog, Toby.* Instead she said, "There are no bad dogs, Bobby, just bad people. They just need love."

"Sometimes they're broke inside, senora. And nuthin' will help 'em."

Senora's hand absently reached down and scratched behind Coco's ears. I frantically shoved my nose underneath Senora's fingers, but she didn't even seem to know I was there.

Later Coco sat down in front of me with a rubber bone, gnawing on it industriously. I ignored her, still hurt that I, Senora's favorite, had been treated so dismissively. Coco flipped on her back and played with the bone with her paws, lifting it out of her mouth and dropping it, holding it so lightly that I knew I could take it, so I lunged! But Coco was rolling away from me, and then I was chasing her in the yard, furious that she had gotten the game all backward.

I was so preoccupied with getting the stupid bone back from Coco because I was supposed to have it, not her, that I didn't see how it started; I just registered that suddenly the fight I think we'd all known was coming was already happening.

Normally a fight with Top Dog was over quickly, the lower-status dog accepting his punishment for challenging the order. But this horrible battle, loudly joined and viciously savage, seemed to last and last.

The two dogs clashed with their forelegs off the ground, each vying to obtain the higher position, their teeth flashing in the sun. Their yowling was the most ferocious and terrifying thing I had ever heard.

Top Dog went for his usual grip on the back of the neck, where control could be exerted without doing permanent damage, but Spike shook and snapped and bit until he had Top Dog's snout in his mouth. Though it had cost Spike a bloody tear under his ear, he now had the advantage over Top Dog, forcing our leader's head lower and lower toward the ground.

The pack did nothing, could do nothing but pant and circle anxiously, but the gate swung open and Bobby came running in, pulling a long hose behind him. A jet of water hit both dogs.

"Hey! Cut it out! Hey!" he shouted.

Top Dog went limp, acceding to Bobby's authority, but Spike held on, ignoring the man. "Spike!" Bobby yelled. He thrust his nozzle forward and blasted Spike right in the face with it, blood flying into the air. Finally Spike broke away, shaking his head to get it out of the spray, and the look he turned on Bobby was murderous. Bobby backed away, holding the hose out in front of him.

"What happened? Was it the new one? *El combatiente?*" Carlos called, coming into the yard.

"*Sí. Este perro será el problema,*" Bobby replied.

Senora joined the men in the Yard and, after much conferring, they called Top Dog over and tended to his wounds with a sharp-smelling chemical that I instantly associated with the nice lady from the cool room. Top Dog squirmed and licked and panted, his ears back, when Carlos dabbed something on the small cuts along his face.

I never thought Spike would allow the same treatment, but he stood without protest when they worked on the cut under his ear. He seemed accustomed to it, somehow, accepting the chemical smell as something that happened after a fight.

The next several days were agony. None of use knew where we stood anymore, especially the males.

Spike was unquestionably the leader now, a message he enforced by challenging every single one of us, head-to-head in the Yard. Top Dog had done the same, but not like this—for Spike, the most minor infraction was cause for discipline and most punishment included a swift, painful nip. When play became too boisterous and too intrusive on Top Dog's area, he had always is-sued a cold warning in the form of a stare, perhaps a growl. Spike spent his day on patrol and would snap at us for no reason whatsoever—there was a black energy in him, something strange and mean.

When the males jockeyed for new positions in the pack, chal-lenging each other, Spike was there and, too often, would him-self get involved, seemingly unable to hold back from plunging into the fray. It was unnecessary and distracting, causing so much tension that minor skirmishes began breaking out among us, fights for things that had been long ago decided, such as posi-tion at the food trough, or who would next get to lie in the part of the Yard turned cool by the leaky water faucet.

When Coco and I played our game where I had the rubber bone and she'd try to steal it, Spike would come over, growling, and force me to drop the prize at his feet. Sometimes he would carry the bone back to his corner, ending the play until I could find another toy, and other times he would sniff at it contemp-tuously and leave it lying in the dirt.

And when Carlos brought in his sack of bones, Spike didn't even bother to run over to see if he'd be given one. He'd wait until there were no men in the yard and then simply take what he wanted. Spike left some of the dogs alone, such as Rottie and Top Dog and, oddly, Fast, but whenever I was lucky enough to sink my teeth into one of Carlos's delicious treats I was resigned to the fact that Spike would soon be chewing on it instead.

It was the new order. We might be having trouble figuring out the rules, but we knew who made them, and we all accepted them, which was why I was so surprised when Fast took Spike on.

It was, of course, because of Sister. In a rare coincidence, the three siblings—Fast, Sister, and I—were standing by ourselves in the corner, investigating a bug that had crawled in from under the fence. Being in such free and simple association with my old family was so relaxing, especially after the stress-filled past few days, that I pretended that I had never seen anything more fascinating than a tiny black insect raising microscopic pincers as if daring the three of us to fight.

Thus distracted, none of us noticed Spike until he was upon us, and his quick, silent attack on Sister's haunches drew an instant frightened whelp from her.

I instantly slunk to the ground—we'd been doing nothing wrong!—but Fast couldn't take any more and he lashed back at Spike, teeth flashing. Sister darted away but I, propelled forward by a rage I'd never felt before, joined Fast in battle, the two of us snarling and biting.

I tried to leap up and grab a hunk of Spike's back, but he turned and slashed at me, and as I stumbled backward his jaws clamped down on my foreleg, and I let out a scream.

Fast soon found himself pinned to the ground, but I wasn't paying attention—the pain in my leg was agonizing, and I limped off, still crying. Coco was there, licking at me anxiously, but I ignored her, making a beeline for the gate.

Just as I knew he would, Bobby opened the gate and came into the Yard, his hose in his hand. The fight was over; Fast had made peace, and Sister was hiding behind the railroad ties. So it was my leg that drew his attention.

Bobby knelt in the dirt. "Good dog, Toby. Okay, boy," he told me. I gave my tail a feeble wag, and when he touched my paw, sending a searing pain all the way up to my shoulder, I licked him in the face to let him know I knew he hadn't done it on purpose.

Senora went with us to see the nice lady in the cool room.

Bobby held me down while she poked me with the same chemical-smelling needle she'd used on me before, and then the pain in my leg didn't bother me anymore. I lay drowsily on the table while the lady tugged on my leg, listening to her voice as she spoke to Bobby and Senora. I could feel her concern, her caution, but couldn't make myself care as long as Senora stroked my fur and Bobby leaned into me to hold me still. Even as Senora drew in her breath when the nice lady in the cool room said "permanent damage," I didn't so much as raise my head. I just wanted to lie on the table forever or at least until dinner.

When I got back to the Yard I was wearing the stupid cone collar again and I sported a hard lump of something encasing my wounded foot. I wanted to tear into the lump with my teeth, but not only did the collar look ridiculous, it also prevented me from getting at my foot! I could only walk on three legs, which Spike seemed to find amusing, because he came over to me and knocked me down with his chest. *Fine, Spike, go ahead; you are the ugliest dog I've ever seen.*

My leg hurt all the time and I needed to sleep, and usually Coco came over and rested her head on me as I did so. Twice a day Bobby came in and gave me a treat, and I pretended not to notice that there was something bitter inside the roll of meat, though sometimes instead of swallowing it I waited a bit and then spat it out: a small white thing the size of a pea.

I was still wearing the stupid collar the day all the men came. We heard several doors slamming in the driveway, so we took up our usual chorus of barking, though many of us went quiet when we heard Senora shriek.

"No! No! You can't take my dogs!"

The grief in her voice was unmistakable, and Coco and I nuzzled each other in alarm. What was going on?

The gate swung open, and several men cautiously entered the Yard, carrying the familiar poles with them. Several held metal canisters out in front of them and were braced as if expecting an attack.

Well, whatever this game was, most of us were willing to play. Coco was one of the first to approach, and she was snagged and pulled without resistance out through the gate. Most of the rest of the pack followed, lining up willingly, though several hung back—Sister, Fast, Spike, Top Dog, and myself, because I just didn't feel like limping over to them. If they wanted to play, let them play with Spike.

Sister broke into a run around the perimeter of the yard, as if expecting a hole to open. Fast went with her at first and then stopped in despair, watching her panicked, pointless flight. Two men closed in on her and captured her with a rope. Fast let them take him right away, so that he'd go with Sister, and Top Dog stepped forward with dignity when they called to him.

Spike, though, fought the loop, growling savagely and snapping at them. The men yelled, and one of them directed a thin stream of liquid from his canister at Spike's face, the scent instantly burning my nose from all the way across the Yard. Spike stopped fighting and fell to the ground, his paws over his snout. They dragged him out and then came to me.

"Nice doggy. You hurt your leg, boy?" one of the men asked. I gave my tail a feeble wag and ducked my head a little to make it easier for him to slip the loop over my head, which took a bit of doing because of my stupid plastic collar.

Once outside the fence, I was upset to see Senora crying, struggling against Carlos and Bobby. Her sadness came off her and washed into me, and I pulled against the noose, wanting to go comfort her.

One of the men tried to hand Senora a paper, but she threw it on the ground.

"Why do you do this? We're not hurting anyone!" Bobby shouted. His anger was clear and frightening.

"Too many animals. Poor conditions," the man with the paper said. He, too, radiated anger, and everyone was very tense and stiff. I noticed that his clothes were dark and that he had metal flashing on his chest.

"I love my dogs," Senora wailed. "Please don't take them from me." Senora was not angry; she was sad and afraid.

"Inhumane," the man replied.

I was mystified. Seeing the entire pack outside the Yard, led one by one to cages on the trucks, was very disorienting. Most of us had our ears back and our tails submissively low. I was next to Rottie, whose deep, heavy woofing filled the air.

My comprehension did not improve when we arrived at our destination, which smelled a little like the place with the nice lady in the cool room but was hot and filled with loud, anxious dogs. I followed willingly and was somewhat disappointed to find myself shoved into a cage with Fast and Top Dog—I would have preferred Coco or even Sister, though my fellow males were as cowed as I was and regarded me without hostility.

The barking was deafening, yet above it all I heard the unmistakable snarl of Spike in full attack, followed by a sharp squeal of pain from some unfortunate canine. Men yelled, and then a few minutes later Spike was led past us at the end of a pole, disappearing down a hallway.

A man stopped in front of our cage. "What happened here?" he asked.

The other man, the one who had just led Spike away, stopped and regarded me without interest. "Dunno."

From the first man I sensed a caring tinged with sadness, but from the second man there was nothing but disinterest. The first man opened the door and gently probed my leg, pushing Fast's face away. "This is ruined," he said.

I tried to communicate to him that I was a much better dog without the stupid collar on.

"Unadoptable," the first man said.

"We got too many dogs," the second man said.

The first man reached inside the cone and smoothed my ears back. Though I felt disloyal to Senora, I licked his hand. He mostly just smelled of other dogs.

"Okay," the first man said.

The second man reached in and helped me jump to the ground. He slipped the loop of rope around me and led me back to a tiny, hot room. Spike was there, in a cage, while two other dogs I'd never met paced loose outside Spike's cage, giving it a wide berth.

"Here. Wait." The first man was at the door. He reached down and unsnapped the collar, and the air that rushed at my face was like a kiss. "They hate those things."

"Whatever," the second man said.

They shut the door behind them. One of the new dogs was an old, old female, who sniffed my nose without much interest. Spike was barking, making the other dog, a younger male, nervous.

With a groan, I slid down to lie on the floor. A loud hiss filled my ears, and the young male began to whine.

Suddenly Spike toppled to the floor with a crash, his tongue sliding out of his mouth. I regarded him curiously, wondering what he was up to. The old female slumped nearby, her head coming to rest against Spike's cage in a manner I was astounded he would allow. The young male whined, and I regarded him blankly, then shut my eyes. I felt overwhelmed with a fatigue as heavy and oppressive as when I was a small puppy and my brothers and sister would lie on top of me, crushing me. That's what I was thinking about as I began to sink into a dark, silent sleep—being a puppy. Then I thought of running wild with Mother, and of Senora's caresses, and of Coco and the Yard.

Unbidden, the sadness I'd felt from Senora washed through me, and I wanted to squirm up to her and lick her palms and make her happy again. Of all the things I'd ever done, making Senora laugh seemed the most important.

It was, I reflected, the only thing that gave my life any purpose.

{ FIVE }

At once, everything was both strange and familiar.

I could clearly remember the loud, hot room, Spike filling the air with his fury and then abruptly falling into a slumber so deep it was as if he'd opened a gate with his mouth and run away. I remembered becoming sleepy, and then there was the sense that much time had passed, the way a nap in the afternoon sun will span the day and suddenly it will be time for the evening feed. This nap, though, brought me not just to a new time but to a new place.

Familiar was the warm, squirming presence of puppies on either side of me. Familiar, too, was the shoving clamber for a turn at the teat and the rich, life-giving milk that was the reward for all the pushing and climbing. Somehow, I was a puppy again, helpless and weak, back in the Den.

But when I took my first bleary look at the face of my mother, she wasn't the same dog at all. Her fur was a light color, and she was larger than, well, than Mother. My brothers and sisters—seven of them!—shared the same light-colored fur, and when I examined my forelegs I realized that I matched the rest of the litter as well.

And not only were my legs no longer dark brown—they stretched out from me in perfect proportion to the rest of my body also.

I heard a lot of barking and smelled many dogs nearby, but this wasn't the Yard. When I ventured from the Den, the surface beneath my pads was rough and hard and a wire fence abruptly ended my exploration after half a dozen yards. It was a cage with a wire top and a cement floor.

The implications of all this made me weary, and I stumbled back to the Den, climbed up on top of a pile of siblings, and collapsed.

I was a little puppy again, barely able to walk. I had a new family, a new mother, and a new home. Our fur was uniformly blond, our eyes dark. My new mother's milk was far richer than what had come from my first mother.

We lived with a man, who came by with food for my mother, which she gulped down quickly before returning to the Den to keep us warm.

But what about the Yard, and Senora, and Fast and Coco? I could remember my life very clearly, and yet everything was different now, as if I had started over. Was that possible?

I recalled Spike's outraged barking and how, as I fell asleep in that hot room, I was seized with an inexplicable question, a question of *purpose*. This didn't seem like the sort of thing a dog should think about, but I found myself returning to the issue often, usually as I was just dozing off for an irresistible nap. Why? Why was I a puppy again? Why did I harbor a nagging feeling that as a dog there was something I was supposed to *do*?

Our enclosure didn't offer much to look at, and there was nothing fun to chew on except each other, but as my brothers and sisters and I became more aware, we discovered there were more puppies in a kennel to the right: tiny, energetic little guys with dark markings and hair that stuck up all over the place. On the other side was a slow-moving female, all alone, with a hanging belly and distended teats. She was white with black spots, and her coat was very short. She didn't walk around much and seemed pretty uninterested in us. About a foot of space separated the two kennels, so all we could do was smell the little puppies next to us, though they looked like they'd be fun to play with.

Straight ahead was a long strip of lawn that beckoned with sweet odors of moist earth and rich, green grass, but we were prevented from going out there by the locked door to the cage. A wooden fence encircled both the grassy area and the dog cages.

The man wasn't anything like Bobby or Carlos. When he ventured into the kennel area to feed the dogs, he didn't speak much to any of us, radiating a bland indifference so at odds with the kindness of the men tending the dogs in the Yard. When the puppies in the kennel next to us rushed over to greet him, he pushed them away from the dinner bowl with a grunt, letting the mother have access to her food. We were less coordinated in our attack and usually didn't manage to tumble our way to the cage door before he'd already moved on and our mother let us know we were not to share her meal.

Sometimes the man would be talking when he moved from cage to cage, but not to us. He spoke softly, focused on a piece of paper in his hands.

"Yorkshire terriers, week or so," he said one time, looking in at the dogs in the cage to our right. He stopped in front of our pen and peered inside. "Golden retrievers, probably three weeks yet, and got a Dalmatian ready to pop any day."

I decided my time in the Yard had prepared me to dominate the puppies in my family, and was irritated they didn't feel the same way. I'd maneuver to grab one the way Top Dog had grabbed Rottie, and then two or three of my siblings would jump on top of *me*, not understanding the point of the whole thing at all. By the time I'd fought them off, the original target of my attentions would be off wrestling with someone else, as if it were all some kind of game. When I tried a menacing growl, though, I sounded ridiculously nonthreatening, my brothers and sisters joyously growling back.

One day the spotted dog next to us drew our attentions—she was panting and pacing nervously—and we instinctively hung close to our mother, who was watching our neighbor intently. The spotted dog ripped up a blanket, shredding it with her teeth, and circled around several times before lying down with a gasp. Moments later, I was shocked to see a new puppy lying by her side, covered in spots and cloaked in a slippery-looking film, some kind of sac that the mother immediately licked off. Her tongue pushed the little puppy over, and after a minute it groggily crawled toward its mother's teats, which reminded me that I was hungry.

Our mother sighed and let us feed awhile before she abruptly stood up and walked away, one of my brothers dangling along for a second before dropping off. I jumped on him to teach him a lesson, which wound up taking a lot of time.

When next I glanced over at the spotted dog, there were six more puppies! They looked spindly and weak, but the mother didn't care. She licked them, guiding them to her side, and then lay quietly while they fed.

The man came and entered the cage where the newborns lay sleeping, looking them over before turning and walking away. Next he opened the door for the furry-looking puppies in the kennel to the right of ours and released them into the grassy area!

"No, not you," he said to the mother, blocking her way as she tried to follow. He shut her in and then put bowls of food down for the puppies, which they climbed in and licked off of each other—these idiots wouldn't last a day in the Yard. The mother sat behind her cage door and whimpered until her brood had quit feeding, and then the man let her out to join her pups.

The hairy little dogs came over to our cage door to sniff us, finally going nose-to-nose with us after living next door for these past few weeks. I licked at the goop on their faces while one of my brothers stood on my head.

The man left the puppies running free while he departed out a gate in the wooden fence that was exactly like the one Carlos and Bobby always accessed to enter the Yard. I watched jealously as the puppies ranged up and down the tiny patch of grass, sniffing hello to the other caged dogs and playing with each other. I was tired of being inside the pen and wanted to get out and explore. Whatever was my purpose in my new life, this didn't feel like it.

After a few hours, the man returned, carrying another dog who looked exactly like the mother of the hairy puppies who were running free, except that he was a male. The man shoved the mother back into her pen and dropped the male in with her before shutting the gate, locking them in together. The male seemed pretty glad to see the mother, but she snarled at him when he jumped on her from behind.

The man left the fence gate open behind him, and I was surprised at the feeling of longing that swept through me as I peered at the tiny sliver of outside world visible on the other side of the fence. If I were ever running free in the grass, I knew I would head right out that open gate, but naturally the puppies who currently had that option didn't do anything about it; they were too busy wrestling.

The mother raised her paws up on the cage door and cried softly as the man methodically rounded up her puppies and carried them out the gate. Soon they were all gone. The mother dog paced back and forth in her cage, panting, while the male in the cage with her lay there and watched. I could feel her distress, and it unsettled me. Night fell, and the mother dog let the male lie with her—they seemed to know each other, somehow.

The male was only in there for a few days before he, too, was taken away.

And then it was our turn to be let out! We tumbled out joyously, lapping up the food that was set out for us by the man. I ate my fill and watched my brothers and sisters go crazy, as if they'd never seen anything so exciting before as a bunch of dog food bowls.

Everything was wonderfully moist and rich, not at all like the dry and dusty dirt in the yard. The breeze was cool and carried with it the tantalizing scent of open water.

I was sniffing the succulent grass when the man returned to release our mother. My siblings bounded over to her, but I didn't because I'd found a dead worm. Then the man left, and that's when I started thinking about the gate.

There was something wrong with this man. He didn't call me Toby. He didn't even talk to us. I thought of my first mother, the very last time I saw her, escaping the Yard because she couldn't live with humans, not even with someone as loving as Senora. But the man didn't love us at all.

My gaze focused on the doorknob in the gate.

There was a wooden table next to the door. By climbing up on a stool I was able to get on the table, and from there I was just able to stretch out and put my mouth on the metal knob, which instead of being round was a strip of metal, a handle.

My tiny teeth weren't very useful in getting a purchase on the thing, but I did my best to manipulate it the way Mother had the night she fled from the Yard. Soon I lost my balance and toppled to the ground, the gate still locked. I sat and barked at it in frustration, my voice a tiny yip. My brothers and sisters raced over to jump on me in their usual fashion, but I turned from them in irritation. I was in no mood to play!

I tried it again. This time I put my front paws on the knob to keep from tumbling to the ground, and as I did so it fell away beneath me, so that my whole body hit the lever on my way down. I landed on the sidewalk with a grunt.

To my astonishment, the gate edged ajar. I shoved my nose into the crack and pushed, and it swung wider. I was free!

I eagerly scampered out into the open, my little legs tripping over themselves. A dirt path lay right in front of me, two tracks dug into sandy soil. I instinctively knew that was the way to go.

After I'd run a few feet I stopped, sensing something. I turned and looked back at my new mother, who was sitting just inside the open gate, watching me. I remembered Mother back in the Yard, glancing once at me before heading back out into the world. My new mother wouldn't be joining me, I realized. She was staying with the family. I was on my own.

Yet not for a moment did I hesitate. I knew from past experience that there were better yards than this, with loving people who would stroke my fur with their hands. And I knew that the time for suckling at my new mother's teat was at an end. It was just how it was supposed to work—a dog eventually separated from his mother.

But mostly I knew an opportunity was in front of me that was irresistible, a whole new world to be explored with long, if somewhat clumsy, legs.

The dirt track eventually led to a road, which I decided to follow, if for no other reason than the fact that it led straight into the wind, which was bringing me wonderful new scents. Unlike the Yard, which had always been parched, I smelled damp, rotting leaves, and trees, and pools of water. I skipped forward, the sun in my face, happy to be free, off on an adventure.

I heard the truck coming long before I saw it but was so busy trying to catch an amazing winged bug I didn't even look up until the door slammed. A man with wrinkled, tanned skin and muddy clothes knelt down, his hands out in front of him.

"Hey there, little fella!" he called.

I regarded him uncertainly.

"You lost, fella? You lost?"

Wagging, I decided he must be okay. I trotted over to him and he picked me up, holding me high over his head, which I didn't appreciate very much.

"You're a pretty little fella. You look like a purebred retriever; where did you come from, fella?"

The way he was speaking to me reminded me of the first time Senora called me Toby. I instantly understood what was happening—just as the men had pulled my first family from the culvert, this man had taken me from the grass. And now my life would be what he decided it would be.

Yes, I decided. *My name could be Fella.* I was thrilled when he sat me down inside the front of the truck, right beside him. The front seat!

The man smelled like smoke and had an eye-watering tang to him that reminded me of when Carlos and Bobby would sit out in the Yard at a small table and talk and hand a bottle to each other. He laughed when I tried to climb up to lick his face, and continued to chuckle as I squirmed around in the narrow places of the truck, taking in rich, strange odors.

We bumped along for a while, and then the man stopped the truck. "We're in the shade here," he told me.

I looked around blankly. A building with several doors was directly in front of us, and from one of them came strong chemical smells exactly like those coating the man.

"I'm just going to stop for one drink," the man promised, rolling up the windows. I didn't realize he was leaving until he'd slipped out and shut the door behind him, and I watched in disillusionment as he entered the building. What about me?

I found a cloth strap and chewed on it for a little while, until I got bored and put my head down to sleep.

When I awoke, it was *hot*. The sun now came full force into the truck, the cab airless and humid. Panting, I started whimpering, putting my paws up so I could see where the man had gone. There was no sign of him! I dropped my feet, which were literally burning from the windowsill.

I had never felt such heat. An hour or so went by as I paced back and forth across the scorching front seat, panting harder than I ever had in my life. I began to quiver, and my vision was swimming. I thought of the faucet in the yard; I thought of my mother's milk; I thought of the spray from the hose Bobby used to break up dogfights.

Blearily I noticed a face staring in the window at me. It

wasn't the man; it was a woman with long black hair. She looked angry, and I backed away from her, afraid.

When her face vanished, I lay back down, nearly delirious. I didn't have the energy to pace anymore. I had an odd heaviness in my limbs, and my paws were beginning to twitch of their own accord.

And then there was a hard crash, rocking the truck! A rock tumbled past me, bouncing off the seat and falling to the floor. Clear pebbles showered down on me, and a cool kiss of air swept in over my face. I lifted my nose to it.

I was limp and helpless when I felt hands slide around my body and raise me into the air, too exhausted to do anything but hang slackly in her hands.

"You poor puppy. You poor, poor puppy," she whispered.

My name is Fella, I thought to myself.

{ SIX }

Nothing in my life has ever felt as good as the cool, clear flow of liquid that pulled me out of my dreamless sleep. The woman stood over me with a water bottle and was carefully showering me with the sweet spray. I shuddered with pleasure as the trickle painted my back, and raised my mouth to lap and bite at the stream the way I'd often attacked the drizzle that fell from the faucet above the trough in the Yard.

A man stood nearby, and both he and the woman were watching me with concerned expressions.

"Do you think he'll be okay?" the woman asked.

"Looks like the water is doing the job," he replied.

From both of them came the sort of open adoration I often felt pouring out of Senora when she stood at the fence to watch us play. I rolled on my back so the water would wash over my hot tummy, and the woman laughed.

"Such a cute puppy!" the woman exclaimed. "Do you know what kind it is?"

"Looks like a golden retriever," the man observed.

"Oh, puppy," the woman murmured.

Yes, I could be Puppy, I could be Fella, I could be whatever they wanted, and when the woman swept me up in her arms, heedless of the wet splat I made against her blouse, I kissed her until she closed her eyes and giggled.

"You're coming home with me, little guy. I've got someone I want you to meet."

Well, it looked like I was a front-seat dog now! She held me in her lap while she drove, and I gazed up at her in gratitude. Curious about my new surroundings, I finally crawled off and explored the inside of the car, astounded at the rich, cold air coming from two vents in front of me. Against my wet fur the air was so chilly I actually began to tremble, and wound up climbing onto the flat floor on the other side of the car, where a soft warmth, just like Mother, quickly lured me back into another nap.

I woke up when the car stopped, sleepily regarding the woman as she reached down and picked me up.

"Oh, you are so cute," she whispered. As she held me against her chest and stepped out of the car I could feel her heart beating strongly and I sensed something like alarm coming off of her. I yawned off the last vestiges of my nap and, after a quick squat in some grass, was ready to face whatever challenge had her so worked up.

"Ethan!" she called. "Come here; I want you to meet someone."

I looked up at her curiously. We were in front of a big white house, and I wondered if there were kennels in the back, or maybe a big yard. I couldn't hear any barking, though, so maybe I was the first dog here.

Then the front door of the house banged open and a human being like I'd never seen before ran out on the porch, jumped down the cement steps, and stopped dead in the grass.

We stared at each other. It was, I realized, a human child, a male. His mouth broke into a huge grin and he spread his arms. "A puppy!" he sang, and we ran to each other, instantly in love. I could not stop licking him and he could not stop giggling, and we rolled together in the grass.

I guess I had never bothered to consider that there might be such a thing as a boy, but now that I had found one, I thought it was just about the most wonderful concept in the world. He smelled of mud and sugar and an animal I'd never scented before, and a faint meaty odor clung to his fingers, so I licked them.

By the end of the day I would know him not just by smell but also by sight, sound, and gesture. His hair was dark, like Bobby's, but very short, and his eyes were much lighter. He had a way of turning his head to look at me as if he were trying to hear me more than see me, and his voice bubbled with joy whenever he talked to me.

For the most part, though, I was drinking in his scent, licking his face, chewing his fingers.

"Can we keep him, Mom? Can we keep him?" the boy gasped between giggles.

The woman squatted down to pet my head. "Well, you know your dad, Ethan. He's going to want to hear that you'll take care of him—"

"I will! I will!"

"And that you'll walk him and feed him—"

"Every day! I'll walk him and feed him and brush him and give him water—"

"And you'll have to clean up when he poops in the yard."

The boy didn't answer that one.

"I bought some puppy food at the store; let's give him some dinner. You won't believe what happened, I had to run to the gas station and get a jug of water; the poor thing was nearly dead with heat exhaustion," the woman said.

"Want some dinner? Huh? Dinner?" the boy asked.

Sounded pretty good to me.

To my amazement, the boy picked me up and carried me right into the house! I had never in my life imagined such a thing was even possible.

I was going to like it here just fine.

Some of the floors were soft and embedded with the same animal odor I'd picked up on the boy, while other floors were slick and hard, causing my feet to skitter out from underneath me as I pursued the boy through the house. When the boy picked me up, the flow of love between us was so strong it gave me a hollow feeling in my tummy, almost like hunger.

I was lying on the floor with the boy, wrestling over a cloth, when I felt a vibration rumble through the house and heard the sound I'd learned meant the closing of a car door.

"Your father's home," the woman, whose name was Mom, told the boy, who was called Ethan.

Ethan stood up and faced the door, and Mom came to stand beside him. I grabbed the cloth and gave it a victorious shake but found it much less interesting without a boy attached to the other end of it.

A door opened. "Hi, Dad!" the boy yelled.

A man stepped into the room, looking back and forth between the two of them. "Okay, what is it?" he asked.

"Dad, Mom found this puppy . . . ," Ethan said.

"He was locked in a car, nearly dead from heatstroke," Mom said.

"Can we keep him, Dad? He's the best puppy in the world!"

I decided to take advantage of the lapse in security and dove onto the boy's shoes, biting his laces.

"Oh. I don't know; this is not a good time," the father said. "Do you know how much work a puppy is? You're only eight years old, Ethan. It's too much responsibility."

I yanked on one of the boy's laces and it gave, sliding away from his shoes. I tried to run off with it, but it remained attached to his feet so that it yanked me back, tumbling me head over heels. Snarling, I dove back onto the laces, grabbing them and giving them a furious shake.

"I'll take care of him, and I'll walk him and feed him and wash him," the boy was saying. "He's the best puppy in the world, Dad. He's already housebroken!"

Having wrestled the shoes into submission, I decided this would be a good time to take a little break, and squatted, depositing a stool along with my urine.

Wow, did *that* get a reaction!

Soon the boy and I were sitting on the soft floor. Mom would say, "George?" and then Ethan would say, "George? Here, George! Hi, George!" and then Dad would say, "Skippy?" and Ethan would say, "Skippy? Are you Skippy? Here, Skippy!"

It was exhausting.

Later, playing out in the backyard, the boy called me Bailey. "Here, Bailey! Here, Bailey!" he would call, slapping his knees.

When I trotted over to him he would dash away, and we ran around and around in the backyard. As far as I was concerned, it was an extension of the game inside, and I was prepared to respond to "Hornet" and "Ike" and "Butch," but it seemed like this time "Bailey" would stick.

After another meal, the boy took me into the house. "Bailey, I want you to meet Smokey the cat."

Holding me tightly against his chest, Ethan turned so I could see, sitting in the middle of the floor, a brown and gray animal whose eyes grew big when he spotted me. This was the smell I'd been tracking! The thing was larger than me, with tiny ears that looked like they'd be fun to bite. I struggled to get down to play with this new friend, but Ethan held me tight.

"Smokey, this is Bailey," Ethan said.

At last he placed me on the floor and I ran over to kiss the cat, but he drew his lips back from a set of really wicked-looking teeth and spat at me, arching his back and thrusting his puffy tail straight up into the air. I stopped, puzzled. Didn't he want to play? The musty smell coming from under his tail was delicious. I tried to inch in and give Smokey's butt a friendly sniff, and he hissed and spat and raised a paw, nails extended.

"Aw, Smokey, be a nice cat. Be a nice cat."

Smokey gave Ethan a baleful glare. I picked up on the boy's encouraging tone and yipped in a very welcoming fashion, but the cat remained unapproachable, even batting at my nose when I tried to lick his face.

Okay, well, I was ready to play with him whenever he wanted, but I had more important things to care about than some snotty cat. Over the next several days, I learned my place in the family.

The boy lived in a small room full of wonderful toys, while

Mom and Dad shared a room with no toys whatsoever. One room had a basin of water I could only drink from if I climbed into it, and also had no toys unless you counted the white paper that I could pull from the wall in a continuous sheet. The rooms for sleeping were at the top of some steps that were impossible for me to climb despite my full-sized dog legs. The food was all kept hidden in one part of the house.

Every time I decided I needed to squat and relieve myself, everyone in the house went crazy, scooping me up and racing out the door with me, setting me in the grass and watching me until I'd recovered from the trauma of it all enough to continue with my business, which earned me so much praise I wondered if this was my main function in the family. Their praise was inconsistent, though, because there were some papers they'd set out for me to rip up and if I squatted on them I was called a good dog, too, but with relief, not joy. And, as I mentioned, sometimes when we were all in the house together they became upset with me for doing *exactly the same thing*.

"No!" Mom or Ethan would shout when I wet the floor. "Good boy!" they'd sing when I peed in the grass. "Okay, that's good," they'd say when I urinated on the papers. I could not understand what in the world was wrong with them.

Dad mostly ignored me, though I sensed he liked it when I got up in the morning to keep him company while he ate. He regarded me with mild affection—nothing like the berserk adoration flooding out of Ethan, though I could feel that was how much Dad and Mom loved the boy. Occasionally Dad would sit at the table in the evenings with the boy and they would talk quietly, concentrating, while sharp, pungent fumes filled the air. Dad would let me lie on his feet, since the boy's feet were too far off the ground for me to reach.

"Look, Bailey, we built an airplane," the boy said after one of these sessions, thrusting a toy at me. It made my eyes water with the chemical odors, so I didn't try to take it away. Making noises, the boy ran around the house holding the toy, and I chased after him and tried to tackle him. Later he put the thing on a shelf with other toys that faintly smelled of the same chemicals, and that was it until he and Dad decided to build another one.

"This one is a rocket, Bailey," Ethan told me, offering me a toy shaped like a stick. I turned up my nose at it. "We're going to land one on the moon one day, and then people will live there, too. Would you like to be a space dog?"

I heard the word "dog" and sensed there was a question, so I wagged. *Yes,* I thought. *I would be happy to help clean the dishes.*

Cleaning the dishes was where the boy would put a plate of food down and I would lick it. It was one of my jobs, but only when Mom wasn't watching.

Mostly, though, my job was to play with the boy. I had a box with a soft pillow in it where the boy put me at night, and I came to understand that I was to stay in the box until Mom and Dad came in and said good night and then the boy would let me up into his bed to sleep. If I got bored in the night, I could always chew on the boy.

My territory was behind the house, but after a few days I was introduced to a whole new world, the "neighborhood." Ethan would burst out the front door in a dead run, me at his heels, and we'd find other girls and boys and they'd hug me and wrestle with me and tug toys from my mouth and throw them.

"This is my dog, Bailey," Ethan said proudly, holding me up. I squirmed at the sound of my name. "Look, Chelsea," he said, offering me to a girl his size. "He is a golden retriever. My mother rescued him; he was dying in a car from heat exhaust-station. When he gets old enough I'm going to take him hunting on my grandpa's farm."

Chelsea cuddled me to her chest and gazed into my eyes. Her hair was long and lighter than even mine, and she smelled like flowers and chocolate and another dog. "You are sweet, you are so sweet, Bailey, I love you," she sang to me.

I liked Chelsea; whenever she saw me she would drop to her knees and let me pull on her long blond hair. The dog scent on her clothing came from Marshmallow, a long-haired brown and white dog who was older than I but still a juvenile. When Chelsea let Marshmallow out of her yard we would wrestle for hours and sometimes Ethan would join us, playing, playing, playing.

When I lived in the Yard, Senora loved me, but I now realized it was a general love, aimed at all the dogs in the pack. She called me Toby, but she didn't say my name the way the boy whispered, "Bailey, Bailey, Bailey," in my ear at night. The boy loved *me*; we were the center of each other's worlds.

Living in the Yard had taught me how to escape through a gate. It had led me straight to the boy, and loving and living with the boy was my whole purpose in life. From the second we woke up until the moment we went to sleep, we were together.

But then, of course, everything changed.

One of my favorite things to do was to learn new tricks, as the boy called them, which consisted of him speaking to me in encouraging tones and then feeding me treats. "Sit," for example, was a trick where the boy would say, "Sit, Bailey! Sit!" and then he would climb on my rear end, forcing it to the ground, and then he would feed me a dog biscuit.

"Dog Door! Dog Door!" was a trick where we would go out to the "garage," where Dad kept his car, and the boy would shove me through a plastic flap in the side door to the backyard. Then he'd call for me and I'd push my nose through the flap and he'd feed me a dog biscuit!

My legs, I was gratified to see, kept growing with the rest of me, so that as the nights grew cooler I was able to keep up with the boy, even at a sprint.

One morning, the dog door trick took on an entirely different meaning. The boy was up early, barely after sunrise, and Mom was running in and out of different rooms.

"Take care of Bailey!" Mom called at one point. I looked up from where I was giving a chew toy a serious working over, taking note of Smokey the cat, who sat on the counter and gazed down upon me with insufferable haughtiness. I picked up the chew toy and shook it to demonstrate to Smokey what a great time he was missing out on by being so snooty.

"Bailey!" the boy called. He was carrying my bed, and, intrigued, I followed him out to the garage. What was this game?

"Dog Door," the boy said to me. I sniffed his pockets but couldn't smell any biscuits. Since the whole point of playing Dog Door was, in my opinion, the dog biscuits, I decided to turn away and lift my leg on a bicycle.

"Bailey!" I felt impatience from the boy and regarded him in puzzlement. "You sleep here, okay, Bailey? You be a good dog. If you need to go to the bathroom, you go out the dog door, okay? Dog Door, Bailey. I have to go to school now. Okay? I love you, Bailey."

The boy gave me a hug, and I licked him in the ear. When he turned, I naturally followed, but at the door to the house he barred me from entry. "No, Bailey, you stay in the garage until I get home. Dog Door, okay, Bailey? You be a good dog."

He shut the door in my face.

"Stay"? "Dog Door"? "Good dog"? How were these terms, which I'd heard so often, even remotely related, and which one was "Stay" again?

None of this made any sense to me. I sniffed around the garage, which was full of wonderful smells, but I wasn't in the mood to explore; I wanted my boy. I barked, but the door to the house remained shut, so I scratched it. Still nothing.

I heard some children yelling from the front of the house and ran to the big garage doors, hoping they would lift up as they sometimes did when the boy stood in front of them, but nothing happened. A loud truck of some kind swept up the voices of the children and carried them away. A few minutes later, I heard Mom's car drive off, and then the world, which had been so full of life and fun and noise, became intolerably quiet.

I barked for a while, but that did nothing at all, though I did smell Smokey just on the other side of the door, smugly taking note of my predicament. I scratched the door. I chewed on some shoes. I ripped up my dog bed. I found a trash bag full of clothing, tore it open the way Mother had when we were scavenging for garbage, and strewed the clothes around the garage. I peed in one corner and pooped in the other corner. I tipped over a metal container and ate some pieces of chicken and some spaghetti and a waffle, and licked out a can of fish that smelled like Smokey's breath. I ate some paper. I knocked over my water dish and chewed on it.

There was nothing to do.

After what seemed like the longest day of my life, I heard Mom's car pull into the driveway. Her car door slammed, and I heard running feet pound through the house.

"Bailey!" the boy shouted, opening the door.

I tackled him, overjoyed that we had ended this madness forever. But he stood staring at the garage.

"Oh, Bailey," he said, sounding sad.

Full of manic energy, I burst past him and skittered around in the house, leaping over furniture. I spotted Smokey and took off in pursuit, chasing him up the stairs and barking when he dove under Mom and Dad's bed.

"Bailey!" Mom called to me sternly.

"Bad dog, Bailey," the boy said crossly.

I was astounded at this false accusation. Bad? I'd been accidentally locked in the garage but was more than willing to forgive *them*. Why were they scowling at me like that, shaking their fingers at me?

Moments later I was back in the garage, helping the boy, who picked up everything I'd played with and put most of it into the trash container I'd knocked over. Mom came out and sorted through the clothing, taking some into the house with her, but no one praised me for discovering where the items had been hiding.

"Dog Door," the boy said crossly, but he didn't give me any treats. I was beginning to think that "Dog Door" was the same as "bad dog," which was very disappointing, to say the least.

Obviously, this had been a very upsetting day for everybody, and I was certainly willing to put the whole incident behind us, but when Dad came home Mom and the boy talked to him and he yelled, and I knew he was mad at me. I slunk off into the living room and ignored Smokey's snide expression.

Dad and the boy left right after dinner. Mom sat at the table and stared at papers, even when I approached and put a wonderful wet ball in her lap. "Oh, yuck, Bailey," she said.

When the boy and Dad came home, the boy called me out into the garage and showed me a big wooden box. He climbed inside, so I joined him, though the space was hot and tight with the two of us in there. "Doghouse, Bailey. This is your doghouse."

I didn't see how the box related to me, but I was certainly happy to play "Doghouse" when treats were introduced into the mix. "Doghouse" meant "go inside the doghouse and eat the dog biscuit." We did the doghouse trick and the dog door trick while Dad moved around the garage, placing things up on shelves and tying a rope on the big metal container. I was overjoyed that "Dog Door" had treats associated with it again!

When the boy grew tired of tricks, we went inside and wrestled on the floor. "Time for bed," Mom said.

"Oh, Mom, please? Can I stay up?"

"We both have school tomorrow, Ethan. Time for you to say good night to Bailey."

While conversations like this took place in the house all the time, I rarely bothered to pay attention, but this time I lifted my head at my name, sensing a shift in the boy's emotions. A sadness and regret wafted off him and he stood, his shoulders slumped.

"Okay, Bailey. Time for bed."

I knew what bed was, but apparently we were going to take a detour along the way, because the boy led me out to the garage for another rousing game of Doghouse. I was perfectly fine with this but shocked when, moments later, the boy sealed me back in the garage, all by myself.

I barked, trying to make sense of it all. Was it because I'd chewed up my dog bed? I never slept in the thing anyway; it was just for show. Did they really expect me to remain outside in the garage all night? No, that couldn't be it.

Could it?

I was so distressed, I couldn't help but whimper. The thought of the boy lying in bed without me, all alone, made me so sad I wanted to chew shoes. My cries grew louder, my heartbreak unrestrained.

After ten or fifteen minutes of relentless grief, the garage door cracked. "Bailey," the boy whispered.

I ran to him in relief. He eased out, carrying a blanket and a pillow. "Okay. Doghouse, Doghouse," he told me. He crept over to the doghouse and arranged the blanket on the thin pad inside. I climbed in next to him—we both had two feet sticking out the door. I put my head on his chest, sighing, while he stroked my ears.

"Good dog, Bailey," he murmured.

A little while later, Mom and Dad opened the door from the house and stood there, watching us. I flapped my tail but didn't get up, not wanting to wake the boy. Finally, Dad came out and picked up Ethan and Mom gestured to me and the two of us were put to bed inside the house.

The next day, as if we hadn't learned anything from our mistakes, I was out in the garage again! This time there was far less for me to do, though I did, with some effort, manage to tear the pad out of the doghouse and shred it up pretty well. I knocked over the trash container but couldn't get the lid off. Nothing on the shelves was chewable—nothing I could reach, anyway.

At one point I went over and assaulted the flap over the dog door, my nose picking up the rich scent of an oncoming rainstorm. Compared to the Yard, where a dry, sandy dust had coated our parched tongues every day, the place the boy lived was wetter and colder, and I loved the way scents would blur together and re-form when it rained. Wonderful trees, laden with leaves, sheltered the ground everywhere we went, and they would harbor raindrops and release them later when tossed by breezes. It was all so deliciously moist—even the hottest days were usually broken by cooler air at night.

The tantalizing odors drew my head farther and farther through the dog door until suddenly, quite by accident, I was out in the yard, without the boy having to push me!

Delighted, I tore around the backyard, barking. It was as if the dog door had been put there to let me out into the backyard from the garage! I squatted and relieved myself—I was finding I much preferred doing my business outdoors instead of in the house, and not just because of the lack of drama. I liked to wipe my paws on the lawn after I went, trailing the scent from the sweat on my pads onto the blades of grass. It was also much more gratifying to lift my leg and mark the edge of the yard than, say, the corner of the couch.

Later, when the cold rain turned from mist to serious drops, I discovered the dog door worked both ways! I wished the boy were home so he could see what I had taught myself.

After the rain ended, I dug a hole, chewed the hose, and barked at Smokey, who sat in the window and pretended not to hear me. When a large yellow bus pulled up in front of the house and disgorged the boy and Chelsea and a bunch of other kids from the neighborhood, I was in the backyard, my paws up on the fence, and the boy ran up to me, laughing.

I didn't really go into the doghouse after that, except when Mom and Dad yelled at each other. Ethan would come out into the garage and get into the doghouse with me and put his arms around me, and I would sit perfectly still for however long he wanted me to. This was, I decided, my purpose as a dog, to comfort the boy whenever he needed me.

Sometimes families would leave the neighborhood and new families would arrive, so when Drake and Todd moved in a few houses down I considered it nothing but good news—and not just because Mom made delicious cookies to take to the new neighbors, feeding me a couple as a reward for keeping her company in the kitchen. New boys meant more children to play with.

Drake was older and bigger than Ethan, but Todd was the same age and he and Ethan became fast friends. Todd and Drake had a sister named Linda who was even younger; she fed me sugary treats when no one was watching.

Todd was different from Ethan. He liked to play games in the creek with matches, burning plastic toys, like Linda's dolls. Ethan would participate, but he didn't laugh as much as Todd; mostly Ethan just watched the things burn.

When Todd announced he had firecrackers one day, Ethan got pretty excited. I had never seen anything like a firecracker and was pretty startled at the flash and the noise and the way the plastic doll instantly had a smoky smell—or at least the part I could find after the explosion. At Todd's urging, Ethan went into his house and came back with one of the toys he had built with his father and the boys put a firecracker in it and threw it in the air, and it blew up.

"Cool!" Todd yelled. But Ethan just grew quiet, frowning at the little shards of plastic floating away in the creek. I sensed a jumble of confused emotions from him. When Todd tossed firecrackers up into the air and one came down near me, the percussion snapped against my side. I ran over to the boy for reassurance, and he hugged me and took me home.

Having such easy access to the backyard had some advantages. Ethan wasn't always particularly attentive to the fence gate, which meant I sometimes was free to stroll the neighborhood. I'd trot out and go over to visit the brown and white dog named Marshmallow, who lived in a big wire cage on the side of her house. I marked her trees pretty well, and sometimes, caught by a scent that was both foreign and familiar, I would skip off, nose to the air, and wander far from home on an adventure. During those wanderings I sometimes forgot about the boy altogether and I was reminded of the time several of us were taken from the Yard to the cool room with the nice lady, how the front-seat dog had a provocative odor similar to the one luring me onward.

Usually I lost the scent and then would remember who I was and turn and trot home. The days that the bus brought Ethan home, I would go with him over to Chelsea and Marshmallow's house and Chelsea's mother would feed Ethan snacks, which he always shared with me. Other days Ethan came home in Mom's car. And some days no one in the house got up for school and I would have to bark to wake them all up!

It was a good thing they no longer wanted me to sleep in the garage. I would hate for them to miss the morning!

One day I wandered farther than usual, so that when I headed back toward home it was getting late in the afternoon. I was anxious, my inner clock telling me that I had already missed Ethan's arrival on the bus.

I cut through the creek, which took me right past Todd's backyard. He was playing on the muddy bank, and when he saw me he called to me.

"Hey, Bailey. Here, Bailey." He held out his hand to me.

I regarded him with open suspicion. There was just something different about Todd, something inside of him I didn't trust.

"Come on, boy," he said, slapping his hand against his leg. He turned and walked toward his house.

What could I do? I was compelled to do what a person told me. I lowered my head and followed.

EIGHT

Todd let me in his house through the back door, shutting it noiselessly behind him. Some of the windows were covered, giving the place a dark, gloomy feel. Todd led me past the kitchen, where his mother was sitting and watching a flickering television. I knew from Todd's behavior that I was supposed to be quiet, but I thumped my tail a little when I smelled the mother, who carried a strong chemical odor similar to the man who had found me by the road and named me Fella.

The mother didn't see us, but Linda sure did. She sat upright when we walked past her in the living room. She, too, was watching television, but she slid off the couch and made to follow us down the hallway.

"No," Todd hissed at her.

I certainly knew *that* word. I cringed a little at the venom in Todd's voice.

Linda held her hand out and I licked it, and Todd pushed it away. "Leave me alone." He opened a door and I went inside, sniffing at the clothes on the floor. It was a small room with a bed in it. He locked the door behind us.

I found a crust of bread and ate it quickly, just performing a quick cleanup. Todd pushed his hands into his pockets. "Okay," he said. "Okay, now . . . now . . ."

He sat at his desk and opened a drawer. I could smell fire-crackers in there; the pungent odor was unmistakable. "I don't know where Bailey is," he was saying quietly. "I haven't seen Bailey."

I wagged at my name, then yawned and collapsed on a soft pile of clothing. I was tired from my long adventure.

A tiny knock on the door electrified Todd, who leaped to his feet. I jumped up, too, and stood behind him while he whispered angrily out his door at Linda, whom I could smell more than see in the dark hallway. She seemed both scared and concerned, for some reason, making me anxious. I started to pant a little, yawning nervously. I felt too tense to lie back down.

The conversation ended with Todd slamming his door and locking it again. I watched as he went to his drawer, fished around, and brought out a small tube. He was emanating an agitated excitement. He removed the top and took a tentative sniff while heavy chemical vapors instantly filled the room. I knew the astringent odor from when the boy and Dad would sit at the table and play with their airplane toys.

When Todd shoved it at me I already knew I didn't want my nose anywhere near the tube, and I jerked my head away. I sensed the flash of rage in Todd, and it frightened me. He picked up a cloth and dripped a lot of clear liquid from the tube onto it, folding and squeezing the cloth so that the sticky coating was all over it.

Just then I heard Ethan, a plaintive cry from outside the window. "Bayleeeee!" he was calling. I ran to the window and jumped up, but it was too high for me to see out, so I barked in frustration.

My rear end stung as Todd struck it with an open palm. "No! Bad dog! No barking!"

Again, the heat of his fury flowed off of him as strong as the vapors coming from the cloth in his hand.

"Todd?" a woman called from somewhere in the house.

He gave me a mean look. "You stay here. You *stay*," he hissed. He backed out of the room, shutting the door behind him.

My eyes watering at the fumes that still filled the air, I paced around apprehensively. The boy was calling me, and I couldn't figure out how Todd had the right to keep me locked up in here as if it were the garage.

Then a small sound alerted me: Linda was opening the door, holding out a soggy cracker. "Here, Bailey," she whispered. "Good dog."

What I really wanted was out of there, but I was no idiot; I ate the cracker. Linda held the door open wider. "Come on," she urged, and that was all I needed. I bounded down the hallway after her, turning down some stairs and trotting to the front door. She pushed it open and the cool air washed those horrible fumes right out of my head.

Mom's car was down the street, and the boy was leaning out of it, calling, "Bailey!" I took off as fast as I could, in hot pursuit. The car's taillights flashed brightly and Ethan was out on the street, running to me. "Oh, Bailey, where have you been?" he said, burying his face in my fur. "You are a bad, bad dog."

I knew being a bad dog was wrong, but the love pouring out of the boy was so strong, I couldn't help but feel that in this case, being a bad dog was somehow good.

It wasn't long after my adventure at Todd's house that I was taken on a car ride to see a man in a clean, cool room. I realized I'd been to a similar place before. Dad drove Ethan and me to the place, and from Dad's attitude I got the sense that I was somehow being punished, which hardly seemed fair. If anyone belonged in the cool room, in my opinion, it was Todd. He was mean to Linda and he kept me apart from my boy—it wasn't my fault I had been a bad dog. Nonetheless, I wagged and lay quietly when a needle was slipped into my fur behind my head.

When I awoke I was stiff, sore, and itchy, with a familiar ache low in my belly, and I was wearing a stupid plastic collar, so that my face lay at the bottom of a cone again. Smokey clearly felt this was hilarious, so I did my best to ignore him. In fact, nothing felt better than lying on the cold cement floor of the garage for a few days, my rear legs splayed.

After the collar came off and I was back to my old self, I found that I was less interested in pursuing exotic odors outside the fence, though if the gate was left open I was always happy to explore the neighborhood and see what all the other dogs were up to. I stayed away from Todd's end of the street, though, and if I saw him or his brother, Drake, playing in the creek, I usually shied away from them, slinking into the shadows the way my first mother had taught me.

I was learning new words every day. Besides being a good dog, and sometimes a bad dog, I was being told more and more that I was a "big" dog, which to me mostly meant that I was finding it harder and harder to arrange myself comfortably on the boy's bed. I learned that "snow," which sounded so much like "no," but was shouted joyously, meant that the world was coated in a cold, white coat. Sometimes we went sledding down a long, steep road, and I usually tried to stay on the sled with Ethan until we crashed. And "spring" meant warm weather and longer days and that Mom spent all weekend digging in the backyard and planting flowers, the dirt smelling so wonderful that when everyone went to school I dug the flowers up, chewing the bittersweet blossoms out of a sense of loyal obligation to Mom, though I eventually spat them all out.

That day I was a bad dog again, for some reason, and even had to spend the evening out in the garage instead of lying at Ethan's feet while he worked on his papers.

Then one day the kids on the big yellow bus were so loud I could hear them shrieking five minutes before the thing stopped in front of the house. The boy was full of joy when he burst out and ran up to me, his mood so high that I ran around and around in circles, barking extravagantly. We went to Chelsea's house and I played with Marshmallow, and Mom was happy when she came home, too. And from that time on, the boy didn't go to school anymore and we could lie in bed quietly instead of getting up for breakfast with Dad. Life had finally gotten back to normal!

I was happy. One day we took a long, long car ride and when we were done we were at the "Farm," a whole new place with animals and smells I'd never before encountered.

Two older people came out of a big white house when we pulled into the driveway. Ethan called them Grandma and Grandpa and Mom did, too, though later I also heard her call them Mom and Dad, which I dismissed as mere confusion on her part.

There were so many things to do on the Farm that the boy

and I spent the first few days on a dead run. An enormous horse stared at me from over a fence when I approached, though she was unwilling to play or do anything but look blankly at me, even when I climbed under the fence and barked at her. Instead of a creek there was a pond, big and deep enough for Ethan and me to swim in. A family of ducks lived on its banks and drove me crazy by taking to the water and paddling away when I approached, but then the mother duck would swim back toward me whenever I grew tired of barking at them, so I'd bark some more.

In the scheme of things, I put ducks right down there with Smokey the cat when it came to their value to the boy and myself.

Dad left after a few days, but Mom stayed with us on the Farm that whole summer. She was happy. Ethan slept on the porch, a room on the front of the house, and I slept right with him and no one even pretended the arrangement should be different. Grandpa liked to sit in a chair and scratch my ears, and Grandma was always slipping me little treats. The love from them made me squirm with joy.

There was no yard, just a big open field with a fence designed to let me in and out at any point I desired, like the world's longest dog door, only without a flap. The horse, whose name was Flare, stayed inside the fence and spent the day eating grass, though I never saw her throw up once. The piles she left in the yard smelled as if they'd taste pretty good but were actually dry and bland, so I only ate a couple of them.

Having the run of the place meant I could explore the woods on the other side of the fence, or run down and play in the pond, or do just about anything I pleased. I mostly stuck close to the house, though, because Grandma seemed to be cooking delicious meals almost every minute of every day and needed me to be on hand to taste her concoctions to make sure they were acceptable. I was glad to do my part.

The boy liked to put me in the front of the rowboat and push it out in the pond, drop a worm into the water, and pull out a small, wriggling fish for me to bark at. He would then let it go.

"It's too little, Bailey," he always said, "but one of these days we'll catch a big one; you watch."

Eventually I discovered (much to my disappointment) that the Farm had a cat, a black one, who lived in an old, collapsing building called the barn. She always watched me, crouched in the darkness, whenever I took it into my head to go in there and try to sniff her out. This cat seemed afraid of me and therefore was a major improvement over Smokey, just like everything at this place.

And one day I thought I saw the black cat in the woods and took off in hot pursuit, though she was waddling slowly and, as I got closer, revealed that she was something else entirely, a whole new animal, with white stripes down her black body. Delighted, I barked at her, and she turned and gave me a solemn look, her fluffy black tail held high up in the air. She wasn't running, which I figured meant she wanted to play, but when I jumped in to paw at her, the animal did a most curious thing, turning away from me, her tail still in the air.

The next thing I knew, a plume of horrid smell enveloped my nose, stinging my eyes and lips. Blinded, yelping, I retreated, wondering what in the world had just happened.

"Skunk!" Grandpa announced when I scratched at the door to be let in. "Oh, you're not coming in, Bailey."

"Bailey, did you get into a skunk?" Mom asked me through the screen door. "Ugh, you sure did."

I didn't know this word "skunk," but I knew that something very odd had occurred out there in the woods, and it was followed by something odder still—wrinkling up his nose at me, the boy took me out into the yard and wetted me down with a hose. He held my head while Grandma carted up a basket of tomatoes from the garden and squeezed the tart juices all over my fur, turning it red.

I couldn't see how any of this helped matters any, particularly since I was then subjected to the indignity of what Ethan informed me was a bath. Perfumed soap was rubbed into my wet fur until I smelled like a cross between Mom and a tomato.

I had never been so thoroughly humiliated in my life. When I was dry, I was consigned to the porch, and though Ethan slept out there with me, he kicked me out of his bed.

"You stink, Bailey," he said.

The assault on my person thus complete, I lay on the floor and tried to sleep despite the riot of odors wafting around the room. When morning finally came I ran down to the pond and rolled in a dead fish that had washed up onshore, but not even that helped, much—I still smelled like perfume.

Eager to figure out what had happened, I went back into the woods to see if I could find that catlike animal and get an explanation. Now that I knew her scent, she wasn't hard to locate, but I'd hardly begun to sniff at her when the same exact thing happened, a blinding spray that hit me from, of all places, the animal's rear end!

I couldn't figure out how to resolve this misunderstanding and wondered if I wouldn't be better off just ignoring the animal altogether, making her suffer for all the ignominy she had put me through.

In fact, that's exactly what I decided to do once I trotted

home and was put through the entire cycle of washings and tomato juice dunkings again—was this my life, now? Every day I'd be slathered in vegetables, have stinky soaps rubbed into me, and be barred from entry into the main part of the house, even when Grandma was cooking?

"You are so stupid, Bailey!" the boy scolded me while he scrubbed me out in the yard.

"Don't use the word 'stupid'; it is such an ugly word," Grandma said. "Tell him . . . tell him he's a doodle; that's what my mother always called me when I was a little girl and I did something wrong."

The boy faced me sternly. "Bailey, you are a doodle dog. You are a doodle, doodle dog." And then he laughed and Grandma laughed, but I was so miserable I could barely move my tail.

Fortunately, around about the time that the smells faded from my fur the family stopped behaving so strangely and allowed me to rejoin them. The boy sometimes called me a doodle dog, but never angrily, more as an alternative to my name.

"Want to go fishing, doodle dog?" he'd ask, and we'd shove out in the rowboat and pull tiny fish out of the water for a few hours.

One day toward the very end of summer it was colder than usual and we were out in the boat, Ethan wearing a hood that was attached to his shirt at the neck. And suddenly he jumped up. "I've got a big one, Bailey, a big one!"

I responded to his excitement, leaping to my feet and barking. He wrestled with his rod for more than a minute, grinning and laughing, and then I saw it, a fish the size of a cat, coming to the surface right next to our boat! Ethan and I both leaned forward to see it, the boat rocked, and then with a yell the boy fell overboard!

I leaped to the side of the boat and stared down into the dark green water. I could see the boy vanishing from sight, and the bubbles rising to the surface carried his scent to me, but he showed no signs of resurfacing.

I didn't hesitate; I dove right in after him, my eyes open as I pushed against the water and struggled to follow the trail of bubbles down into the cold darkness.

NINE

I couldn't see much of anything down there in the water, which pressed against my ears and slowed my desperate descent. I could sense the boy, though, sinking slowly ahead of me. I swam even harder, finally catching blurry sight of him—it was almost like my first vision of Mother, a smeared image in murky shadows. I lunged, jaws open, and when I was right up to him I was able to seize the hood of his sweatshirt in my mouth. I lifted my head and, dragging him with me, rose as quickly as I could toward the sunlit surface of the pond.

We burst up into the air. "Bailey!" the boy shouted, laughing. "Are you trying to save me, boy?" He reached out and snagged the boat with his arm. Frantically I tried to claw my way up his body and into the boat, so I could pull him the rest of the way to safety.

He was still laughing. "Bailey, no, you doodle dog! Stop it!" He pushed me away, and I swam a tight circle.

"I have to get the rod, Bailey; I dropped the rod. I'm okay! Go on; I'm okay. Go on!" The boy gestured toward the shore, as if he were throwing a ball in that direction. He seemed to want me to leave the pond, so after a minute I did, aiming for the small area of sand next to the dock.

"Good boy, Bailey," he said encouragingly.

I looked around and saw his feet go up in the air, and then an instant later he vanished under the water. With a whimper I turned right around and swam as hard as I could, my shoulders lifting clear out of the pond with the effort. When I got to the trail of bubbles, I followed the scent. It was much harder to get myself down this time because I hadn't dived out of the boat, and as I was headed toward the bottom of the pond I sensed the boy coming up and I switched directions.

"Bailey!" he called delightedly. He tossed his rod into the boat. "You are such a good dog, Bailey."

I swam beside him as he pulled the boat over to the sand, so relieved I licked his face when he bent over to haul the boat onto the shore.

"You really tried to save me, boy." I sat, panting, and he stroked my face. The sun and his touch warmed me in equal measure.

The next day, the boy brought Grandpa down to the dock. It was much hotter than it had been the day before, and, racing ahead of the two of them, I made sure the duck family was out in the middle of the pond where it belonged. The boy was wearing another shirt with a hood, and the three of us trotted to the end of the dock and looked down into the green water. The ducks swam over to see what we were looking at, and I pretended I knew.

"You watch, he'll dive underwater; I promise," the boy said.

"I'll believe it when I see it," Grandpa replied.

We walked back to the shore side of the dock. Grandpa grabbed my collar. "Go!" he shouted.

The boy took off running, and after only a second Grandpa released me so I could follow. Ethan sailed off the end of the dock and made a huge splash, which the ducks complained about to each other, bobbing in the waves. I ran to the end of the dock and barked, then looked back at Grandpa.

"Go get him, Bailey!" Grandpa urged.

I looked down at the frothy water where the boy had gone in, then back at Grandpa. He was old and moved pretty slow, but I couldn't believe he was so daft that he wasn't going to do anything about this new situation. I barked some more.

"Go on!" Grandpa told me.

I suddenly understood and looked at him in disbelief. Did I have to do everything in this family? With one more bark I dove off the end of the dock, swimming down toward the bottom, where I could sense Ethan lying motionless. I gripped his collar in my jaws and headed for air.

"See! He saved me!" the boy called when we both surfaced.

"Good boy, Bailey!" Grandpa and the boy shouted together. Their praise pleased me so much I took off after the ducks, who quacked stupidly as they swam away. I got so close to being able to nip off a few tail feathers that a couple of them flapped their wings and briefly took flight, which meant I won, in my opinion.

The rest of the afternoon was spent playing "Rescue Me," and my anxiety gradually dissipated as I learned that the boy could pretty much fend for himself in that pond, though it so delighted him whenever I hauled him to the surface I dove after him every single time. The ducks eventually climbed out of the water and sat by the edge of the pond and watched us without comprehension. Why they didn't fly up into the trees with the other birds I'd never understand.

I could see no reason to ever leave the Farm, but when Dad arrived a few days later and Mom started walking from room to room, opening drawers and pulling things out, I had a feeling we were going to move yet again and began pacing anxiously, afraid I'd be left behind. It wasn't until the boy called, "Car ride!" that I was allowed to climb in and hang my head out the window. The horse, Flare, stared at me with what I assumed was unrestrained jealousy, and both Grandma and Grandpa hugged me before we drove away.

We wound up going back home, and I was delighted to reacquaint myself with the kids and dogs in the neighborhood, but not Smokey. We played games and I chased balls and wrestled with my friend Marshmallow, so busy having fun I was completely unprepared for the morning a few days later when we all got up early and I found myself being unceremoniously led out to the garage. I immediately ran out the dog door and confirmed that Ethan and Mom were both leaving, Ethan taking off with the rest of the children in the same yellow bus.

Well, this was intolerable. I barked for a while, and from down the street Marshmallow answered, so we barked at each other, but that didn't help as much as you'd think. I moodily went back into the garage, sniffing with disdain at the doghouse. I would *not* spend my day in there, I decided, even though it was the softest place around.

I saw Smokey's feet underneath the door and put my nose to the crack and inhaled his scent, letting out a frustrated sigh. I didn't sense a lot of sympathy coming from him.

Because I was a big dog now, the doorknob was easily within

reach, and it occurred to me that there was something I could do about my predicament. I put my paws on the door, took the knob in my mouth, and twisted it.

Nothing happened, but I kept trying, and eventually, with a small click, the door fell open!

Smokey had been sitting on the other side, probably laughing, but when I saw him he sure wasn't laughing anymore. His pupils grew dark and he turned and fled, so naturally I followed him, skittering around the corner and barking when he leaped up on the counter.

It was much better in the house. The night before, pizza dinner had arrived at the front door in a long, flat box, which was still sitting on the counter and therefore easily accessible. I pulled it onto the floor and ate the delicious cardboard, shredding the less flavorful parts, while Smokey watched in feigned disgust. Then I ate a can of his cat food, licking the metal clean.

Normally, I wasn't allowed to sleep on the couch, but I couldn't see any reason to follow that rule, since clearly everything had changed now that I was inside the house by myself. I settled in for a nice nap, my head on a soft pillow, the sun warm on my back.

Sometime later, I realized the sun had moved, which was most inconvenient, and I changed positions on the couch, groaning.

Not long after that, I heard the distinctive sound of one of the kitchen cupboards opening and raced in to see what was happening. Smokey was on the counter and had reached up and opened a door, which I thought was extremely enterprising of him. I watched intently as he leaped inside the cupboard, his tiny nose sniffing at the delicious items inside. He looked down at me, calculating something.

I decided to bite at the base of my tail a bit, and when I

turned back I was intrigued to see that Smokey was batting at a bag of food. He hit it once, twice, and on the third smack toppled the thing out of the cupboard and onto the floor!

I bit through the plastic and into some salty crunchy things, which I ate hurriedly in case Smokey tried to come down for his share. He watched impassively from his perch and then smacked down another bag, full of sweet, doughy rolls.

I decided then and there that I had been wrong about Smokey all along. I almost felt bad about eating his cat food earlier, though it was hardly my fault that he didn't finish his meal when it was served. What did he expect would happen?

I couldn't open the cupboards myself; the science somehow escaped me. I did, however, manage to snag a loaf of bread and pull it off the counter, carefully removing it from the package, which I chewed separately. The trash can in the kitchen didn't have a lid, so it was easy to access, though a few of the items—some bitter black grit that coated my tongue when I gave it an experimental lick, along with eggshells, and plastic containers—were inedible. I chewed the plastic anyway.

I was outside waiting when the bus pulled up, and although Chelsea and Todd both got off, there was no sign of the boy, which meant he would be arriving home with Mom. I went back into the house and pulled some shoes out of Mom's closet, though I didn't chew on them much because I was feeling pretty lethargic from all of the snacks Smokey had given me. I stood in the living room, trying to decide whether to lie on the couch, which no longer had any sun on it at all, or lie in the patch of sun on the carpet. It was a tough decision, and when I finally chose the sun I lay down uneasily, not sure I'd picked the right thing.

When Mom's car door slammed I tore through the house

into the garage and was out the dog door in an instant, wagging at the fence so no one would be the wiser. Ethan ran straight over to me and came into the yard to play with me while Mom went up the walk, her shoes clicking.

"I missed you, Bailey! Did you have fun today?" the boy asked me, scratching under my chin. We gazed at each other in adoration.

"Ethan! Come look what Bailey did!"

At the sound of my name, pronounced so sternly, my ears fell. Somehow, Smokey and I had been found out.

Ethan and I went into the house and I approached Mom with my tail in full wag so she'd forgive me. She was holding one of the shredded bags in her hand.

"The door to the garage was open. Look what he did," Mom said. "Bailey, you are a bad dog. A bad dog."

I hung my head. Though I'd technically done nothing wrong, I realized that Mom was mad at me. Ethan was, too, particularly when he started to pick up the bits of plastic off the floor.

"How in the world did he even get up on the counter? He must have jumped," Mom said.

"You are a bad dog, a bad, bad dog, Bailey," Ethan told me again.

Smokey strolled in, leaping languidly onto the counter. I gave him a glum look—he was a bad cat, a bad, bad cat.

Amazingly, no one said anything to Smokey about his role as instigator. Instead, they gave him a fresh can of food! I sat expectantly, figuring I should at least get a dog biscuit, but everyone was still giving me cross looks.

Mom pushed a mop around on the floor, and the boy carried a bag of trash out into the garage.

"Bailey, that was bad," the boy whispered to me again. Apparently, everyone was having a much harder time getting over the incident than I was.

I was still in the kitchen when I heard Mom shriek, "Bailey!" from the back of the house.

I guessed she had found her shoes.

Over the course of the next year or two, I noticed that when the children all played together Todd was often excluded. When he came around, an uneasiness went through the children, a mood change that Marshmallow and I could sense as easily as if one of them had screamed. Girls usually turned their backs on Todd, and the boys accepted him into their games with a noticeable reluctance. Ethan never went over to Todd's house anymore.

Todd's older brother, Drake, rarely came outside except to get in his car and drive away, though Linda soon learned to ride a bicycle and pedaled it down the street to be with little girls her age almost every day.

I took my cue from Ethan and never went near Todd again, though one snowy night when I was out in the backyard doing my business before bed I could smell him standing on the other side of the fence, back in some trees. I let out a warning bark and was pretty pleased when I heard him turn around and run away.

I didn't much care for the concept of school, which was what happened most mornings at home. I liked it better when summer came and Mom and Ethan no longer had school and we would go to the Farm to live with Grandpa and Grandma.

Whenever I arrived at the Farm I took off at a run, checking to see what was different and what was the same, marking my territory, and reacquainting myself with Flare the horse, the mysterious black cat in the barn, and the ducks, who had irresponsibly decided to produce another batch of ducklings. I often could smell the skunk in the woods but, mindful of the unpleasantness of our last meetings, elected not to chase her down. If she wanted to play, she knew where to find me.

One summer night the whole family sat with me in the living room far past normal bedtime and everyone was excited, though Mom and Grandma were also afraid. And then they yelled and cheered and Grandpa cried and I barked, swept up in all the emotions. Humans are so much more complex than dogs, with such a broad range of feelings—though there were many times I missed the Yard, for the most part I was now living a far richer life, even though I often didn't know what was going on. Ethan took me out into the night and gazed at the sky. "There's a man on the moon right now, Bailey. See the moon? Someday, I'll go there, too."

He radiated such happiness I raced over and got a stick for him to throw for me. He laughed.

"Don't worry, Bailey. I'll take you with me when I go."

Sometimes Grandpa would go for a car ride into town and

the boy and I would accompany him. Before long I had memorized a scent map of the entire trip—there was a moist smell that carried with it the distinct odor of stupid ducks and delicious rotting fish, followed a few minutes later by a powerfully pungent scent that filled the car.

"Phew," Ethan often said.

"That's the goat ranch," Grandpa would always reply.

With my head out the window I often spied the goats who were responsible for all the wonderful smells, and I would bark at them, though they were so dumb they never once fled in terror but just stood there, staring like Flare the horse.

Soon after the goat ranch a great rattle would seize the car as we drove over a wooden bridge and I would start wagging then, because I loved car rides to town and the banging rumble noise meant we were almost there.

Grandpa liked to go to a place where he sat in a chair and a man played with his hair, and Ethan would get bored and we'd wind up walking up and down the streets, looking at windows and hoping to meet other dogs, which I assumed was the reason we were in town in the first place. The best location for dogs was in the park, which was a big grassy area where people sat on blankets. There was a pond, but the boy didn't want me to swim in it.

Everywhere in town I could smell the goat ranch—if I ever needed to catch my bearings, I would just turn my nose until the scent was the strongest, and that way lay home.

One day we were in the park and an older boy was throwing a plastic toy for his dog to catch. The dog was a black female, short, and all business—when I trotted up to her she completely ignored me, her eyes on the plastic toy, which was a thin, brightly colored disk. It would soar through the air and she would run and leap and snag it before it even touched the ground, which I suppose was a pretty impressive trick if you liked that sort of thing.

"What do you think, Bailey? Do you want to do that, boy?" Ethan asked me. His eyes were shining as he watched the little dog catch the plastic disk, and when we got home he went right to his room and got busy making what he called the "flip."

"It's like a cross between a boomerang, a Frisbee, and a base-ball," he told Grandpa. "It will fly twice as far, because the ball gives it weight, see?"

I sniffed at the object, which had been a perfectly good football before Ethan cut it up and asked Grandma to put new stitches in it. "Come on, Bailey!" the boy shouted.

We raced outside. "How much money can you make on an invention like this?" the boy asked his grandpa.

"Let's just see how she flies," Grandpa observed.

"Okay, ready, Bailey? Ready?"

I took this to mean that something was about to happen and stood alertly. The boy cranked his arm back and flung the flip into the air, where it twisted and fell from the sky as if it had hit something.

I trotted off the porch and went over to sniff it.

"Bring the flip, Bailey!" the boy called.

Gingerly I picked the thing up. I remembered the short dog chasing the elegant flying disk in the park and felt a pang of envy. I took it back over to where the boy was standing and spat it out.

"Not aerodynamic," Grandpa was saying. "Too much resistance."

"I just need to throw it right," the boy said.

Grandpa went back inside, and for the next hour the boy practiced throwing the flip out into the yard and I brought it back. I could sense a building despair in him, so one time when he threw the flip and it flopped to the ground I brought him back a stick instead. "No, Bailey," he said sadly. "The flip. Get the flip."

I barked, wagging, trying to get him to see just how fun the stick could be if he would give it a chance.

"Bailey! The flip!"

And then someone said, "Hi."

It was a girl Ethan's age. I trotted over to her, wagging, and she petted me on the head. In one hand she carried a covered basket containing some sweet-smelling breads, which really got my attention. I sat down, looking as attractive as possible so she'd hand over what was in her basket. "What's your name, girl?" she asked me.

"He's a boy," Ethan said. "Name is Bailey."

I looked over at the boy because he said my name and saw that he was acting strange. It was almost as if he were afraid, but not exactly, though he had taken a half step back when he saw her. I looked back at the girl, who I really liked because of the rich-smelling biscuits in her basket.

"I live down the road. My mom made some brownies for your family. Uh," the girl said, gesturing to her bicycle.

"Oh," the boy said.

I kept my attention on the basket.

"So, um," the girl said.

"I'll get my grandma," the boy said. He turned and walked inside the house, but I elected to stay with the girl and her dog biscuits.

"Hi, Bailey, are you a good dog? You're a good dog," the girl told me.

Good, but not so good as to get a dog biscuit, I discovered, even though after a minute I gave the basket a nudge with my nose to remind her of the business at hand. Her hair was light colored and she brushed at it while she waited for Ethan to come back. She, too, seemed the tiniest bit afraid, though I could see nothing that would give anybody anxiety except a poor starving dog who needed a treat.

"Hannah!" Grandma said, coming out of the house. "It's so good to see you."

"Hi, Mrs. Morgan."

"Come in, come in. What have you got there?"

"My mom made some brownies."

"Well, isn't that wonderful. Ethan, you probably don't remember, but you and Hannah used to play together when you were just babies. She's a little more than a year younger than you."

"I don't remember," Ethan said, kicking at the carpet.

He was still acting oddly, but I felt duty bound to guard the basket of dog biscuits, which Grandma set on a side table. Grandpa was sitting in his chair holding a book, and now he reached into the basket, looking over the tops of his glasses.

"Do not spoil your dinner!" Grandma hissed at him. He snatched his hand back, and he and I exchanged grieving looks.

For the next several minutes nothing much happened, biscuit wise. Grandma did most of the talking while Ethan stood with his hands in his pockets and Hannah sat on the couch and didn't look at him. Finally, Ethan asked Hannah if she wanted to see the flip, and at the sound of the dreaded word I whipped my head around and stared at him in disbelief. I had assumed we had ended that chapter of our lives.

The three of us went out into the yard. Ethan showed Hannah the flip, but when he threw it, it still fell to the ground like a dead bird.

"I need to make some design changes to it," Ethan said.

I walked over to the flip but didn't pick it up, hoping the boy would decide to end this embarrassment once and for all.

Hannah stayed for a while, going over to the pond to look at the stupid ducks, petting Flare on the nose, and taking a couple of turns with the flip. She got on her bicycle and as she steered down the driveway I trotted beside her, then when the boy whistled for me returned at a dead run.

Something told me we'd be seeing that girl again.

Later that summer, too early in the season to go back home and go to school, in my opinion, Mom packed up the car. Ethan and I stood next to it as Grandma and Grandpa eased into their seats.

"I'll navigate," Grandpa said.

"You'll fall asleep before we cross the county line," Grandma replied.

"Now, Ethan. You are a big boy. You be good. You call if you have any problems."

Ethan squirmed under his mother's hug. "I know," he said.

"We'll be back in two days. You need anything, you can ask Mr. Huntley next door. I made you a casserole."

"I know!" Ethan said.

"Bailey, you take good care of Ethan, okay?"

I wagged my tail in cheerful noncomprehension. Were we going for a car ride or what?

"I stayed by myself all the time when I was his age," Grandpa said. "This will be good for him."

I could feel worry and hesitation in Mom, but eventually she got behind the wheel. "I love you, Ethan," Mom said.

Ethan muttered something, kicking at the dirt.

The car rolled off down the driveway, and Ethan and I

solemnly watched it go. "Come on, Bailey!" he shouted when it was out of sight. We ran into the house.

Everything was suddenly more fun. The boy ate some lunch and when he was done he put the plate on the floor for me to lick! We went into the barn and he climbed up on the rafters while I barked, and when he jumped into a pile of hay I tackled him. An inky shadow from the corner told me the cat was watching all of this, but when I trotted over to investigate she slid off and vanished.

I became uneasy when Ethan unlocked the gun cabinet, something he had never done without Grandpa being there. Guns made me nervous; they reminded me of when Todd threw a firecracker and it banged so close to me I felt a percussion against my skin. But Ethan was so excited, I couldn't help but prance around at his feet. He put some cans on a fence and shot the gun and the cans went flying. I couldn't quite understand the connection between the cans and the loud bang of the gun but knew it was somehow all related and, judging from the boy's reaction, gloriously fun. Flare snorted and trotted to the far end of her yard, distancing herself from all the commotion.

After that the boy made dinner by warming up some succulent chicken. We sat in the living room and he put on the television and ate off of a plate in his lap, tossing me pieces of skin. Now *this* kind of fun I understood!

At that moment, I didn't care if Mom ever came back.

After I licked the plate, which the boy left on the floor, I decided to test the new rules and climbed up in Grandpa's soft chair, looking over my shoulder to see if I'd draw the expected "Down!" command. The boy just stared at the television, so I curled up for a nap.

I drowsily registered the telephone ringing and heard the

boy say "bed," but when he hung up he didn't go to bed; he sat back down to watch more television.

I was in a solid sleep when a sudden sense of something wrong roused me with a jolt. The boy was sitting stiffly upright, his head cocked.

"Did you hear a noise?" he whispered at me.

I debated whether the urgency I sensed in his voice meant that my nap was over. I decided that what was needed was a calming influence, and lowered my head back on the soft cushion.

From within the house there was a light thump. "Bailey!" the boy hissed.

Okay, this was serious. I got off the chair, stretched, and looked at him expectantly. He reached down and touched my head, and his fear leaped from his skin. "Hello?" he called. "Is someone there?"

He froze, and I emulated his posture, on high alert. I wasn't at all sure what was happening, but I knew there was a threat. When another thump caused him to jump, fright rippling over his skin, I prepared myself to face whatever or whoever was the problem. I could feel the fur rising on my back, and I gave a low growl of warning.

At the sound of my growl, the boy moved soundlessly across the room. I shuffled after him, still alert, and watched as he opened the gun cabinet for the second time that day.

ELEVEN

Holding Grandpa's rifle in his trembling hands, the boy crept up the stairs, down the hall, and into Mom's bedroom. I was right on his heels. Ethan checked her bathroom and under the bed, and when he whipped the closet door open he yelled, "Ha!" scaring me half to death. We repeated this examination in the boy's room, Grandma and Grandpa's room, and the small room with the couch where Grandma slept when Grandpa made his loud rumbling noises at night. Before leaving on the car ride, Grandma had been in this room doing more work on the flip, trying to fix it at Ethan's direction, and it was called the sewing room.

The boy checked the whole house, Grandpa's gun out in front of him, and he rattled every knob and tested every window. Passing through the living room, I walked hopefully over to Grandpa's chair, but the boy still wanted to explore the house, so with a weary sigh I accompanied him on a check of the shower curtains.

Finally he returned to Mom's room. He worked the doorknob, and then he dragged her dresser over in front of the door. He set the rifle down next to the bed and called me up to lie with him. When he clung to me, I was reminded of how he sometimes came out to the doghouse in the garage when Mom and Dad were shouting. He felt full of the same lonely terror. I licked him as comfortingly as I knew how—we were together; how could anything be wrong?

The next morning we slept in and then had a fabulous break-fast. I ate toast crusts and licked scrambled eggs and finished his milk for him. What a great day! Ethan put more food in a bag, along with a bottle that he filled with water, and slid the whole thing in his backpack. Were we going for a walk? Sometimes Ethan and I would go for a walk and he'd take sandwiches for us to share. Lately, his walks always seemed to take us down by where the girl lived; I could smell her scent on the mailbox. The boy would stand and look at the house, and then we'd turn around and go back home.

The fear from the night before was totally gone. Whistling, the boy went out to take care of Flare, who wandered over to eat the bucket of dry, tasteless seeds or whatever they were that she munched on when she wasn't trying to make herself sick with grass.

I was surprised, though, when the boy fetched a blanket and a shiny leather saddle from the barn and affixed them to the horse's back. We'd done this a few times before, with Ethan climbing up to sit high on Flare's back, but always with Grandpa there, and always with the gate to Flare's yard firmly closed.

Now, though, the boy opened the gate, hoisting himself up with a grin.

"Let's go, Bailey!" he called down to me.

I followed, feeling surly. I didn't like that Flare suddenly was getting all the attention and that I was so far away from the boy, forced to walk beside the huge creature, who I had come to conclude was just as dumb as the ducks. I especially didn't appreciate it when, with a flick of her tail, Flare dropped a smelly pile of poo on the road, narrowly missing me. I lifted my leg on it because it now, after all, belonged to me, but I felt fairly certain the horse had meant the thing as an insult.

Soon we were off-road, in the woods, walking along a trail. I chased down a rabbit and would have caught it if it hadn't cheated by suddenly changing direction. I smelled more than one skunk and haughtily refused to take even a single step in that direction. We stopped at a small pool and Flare and I drank, and later the boy ate his sandwich, tossing me the crusts.

"Isn't this great, Bailey? Are you having a good time?"

I watched his hands, wondering if his questioning tone indicated he was going to feed me some more sandwich.

Aside from the fact that we had Flare with us, I was really enjoying myself. Of course, just getting away from the stupid flip was reason in and of itself to celebrate, but after several hours we were so far from home I could no longer smell any sign of it.

I could tell that Flare was getting weary, but from the boy's attitude I concluded we still had a way to go to reach our destination. At one point, Ethan said, "Do we go this way? Or that way? Do you remember, Bailey? Do you know where we are?"

I looked up at him expectantly, and, after a moment, we continued on, picking up a trail that had many, many animal scents on it.

I'd marked so much territory my leg was sore from being lifted into the air. Flare stopped and let loose with a huge gush of urine, which I felt was entirely inappropriate behavior, since her scent would obliterate mine and I was the dog. I wandered up ahead to clear the smell from my nose.

I topped a small rise and that's when I saw the snake. It was coiled in a patch of sun, sticking its tongue out rhythmically, and I stopped dead, fascinated. I'd never seen one before.

I barked, which caused no reaction whatsoever. I trotted back to the boy, who had Flare underway again.

"What is it, Bailey? What did you see?"

I decided that whatever the boy was saying, it wasn't *go bite the snake.* I slid in next to Flare, who was plodding along expressionlessly, and wondered how she would react when she saw the snake curled up in front of her.

At first she *didn't* see it, but then as she approached, the snake suddenly pulled back, lifting its head, and that's when Flare screamed. Her front legs came off the ground and she spun, kicking, and the boy went flying off her back. I ran to him at once, of course, but he was okay. He jumped to his feet. "Flare!" he shouted.

I watched sourly as the horse retreated at a full gallop, her hooves pounding the dirt. When the boy took off running I understood what was needed and ran ahead in hot pursuit, but the horse kept going and soon the gap between me and my boy was too great and I turned back to be with him.

"Oh no!" the boy was saying, but the "no" wasn't for me. "Oh God. What are we going to do, Bailey?"

To my utter dismay, the boy started crying. He did this less and less as he had gotten older, which made it all the more upsetting now. I could feel his utter despair, and I shoved my face into his hands, trying to comfort him. The best thing, I decided, would be for us to go home and eat more chicken.

The boy eventually stopped crying, looking blankly around the woods. "We're lost, Bailey." He took a drink of water. "Well, okay. Come on."

Apparently the walk wasn't over, because we set out in an entirely new direction, not at all the way from which we'd come.

We went a long way into the woods, at one point crossing our own scent, and still the boy plodded on. I grew so weary that when a squirrel darted out right in front of me I didn't even bother to chase it; I just followed the boy, who I could tell was also getting tired. When the light began to fade from the sky, we sat down on a log and he ate the last of the sandwiches, carefully feeding me a hunk. "I'm really sorry, Bailey."

Just before dark, the boy became interested in sticks. He began dragging sticks over to a tree that had blown over, stacking them up against the wall of mud and gnarly roots. He piled pine needles on the ground underneath this canopy and stacked more sticks on top. I watched curiously, ready despite my fatigue to chase one if he threw it, but he just stayed focused on his task.

When it became too dark to see, he climbed in on the pine needles. "Here, Bailey! Come here!"

I crawled in beside him. It reminded me of the doghouse. I ruefully remembered Grandpa's chair, wondering why we couldn't just go home and sleep there. But the boy soon started to shiver, and I put my head on top of him and eased my belly onto his back the way I used to lie on my brothers and sisters when we were cold.

"Good dog, Bailey," he told me.

Soon his breathing became deep and he stopped shivering. Though I wasn't exactly perfectly comfortable, I carefully lay in a position to keep him warm as possible through the night.

We were up when the birds started to call and before it was even fully light were already walking again. I sniffed hopefully at the sack, fooled by the smells, but when the boy let me put my head inside I found nothing to eat.

"We'll save it in case we need to make a fire," he told me. I translated this to mean "we need more sandwiches" and thumped my tail in agreement.

The nature of our adventure changed that day. The hunger in my belly grew to be a sharp pain, and the boy cried again, sniffling for about an hour. I could feel anxiety wafting through him, followed by a sullen, lethargic apathy that I found just as alarming. When he sat down and stared at me with glassy eyes, I licked him full in the face.

I was worried about my boy. We needed to go home, now.

We came to a small stream and the boy flopped down on his stomach and we drank thirstily. The water gave the boy both energy and purpose; when we set off again, we were following the stream, which twisted and turned through the trees and, at one point, through a meadow full of singing bugs. The boy turned his face to the sun and increased his pace, hope surging through him, but his shoulders slumped when after an hour or so the stream reentered the dark woods.

We spent that night clinging to each other as before. I smelled a carcass nearby, something old but probably edible, but I didn't leave the boy. He needed my warmth more than ever. His strength was leaving him; I could feel it ebbing away.

I had never been so afraid.

The next day the boy stumbled a few times while he walked. I smelled blood; his face had been whipped by a branch. I sniffed at it.

"Go away, Bailey!" he yelled at me.

I felt anger and fear and pain coming from him, but I didn't back away, I stayed right there, and knew I had done the right thing when he buried his face in my neck and cried some more.

"We're lost, Bailey. I'm so sorry," the boy whispered. I wagged at my name.

The little stream wandered into a boggy area, losing all definition and making for mucky travels. The boy sank up to his calves, so that his feet made a sucking sound as he pulled them out. Bugs descended on us, landing in our eyes and ears.

Midway across the swamp the boy just stopped. His shoulders sagged, his chin dropping. The air left his lungs in a long, deep sigh. Distressed, I picked my way across the slimy area as quickly as I could, putting a paw on his leg.

He was giving up. An overwhelming sense of defeat was building within him, and he was surrendering to it. He was losing his very will to live. He was like my brother Hungry, lying down that last time in the culvert, never to get back up again.

I barked, startling both the boy and me. His dull eyes blinked at me. I barked again.

"Okay," he muttered. Lethargically he drew his foot out of the mud and tentatively set it down, sinking again.

It took us more than half the day to cross that swamp. When we picked up the stream on the other side of the bog, it moved water with more purpose, becoming deeper and faster. Soon another trickle joined it, and then another, so that the boy had to make a running start to leap across it when a downed tree blocked his path on one side or another. Each leap seemed to make him tired, and we wound up taking a nap for a few hours. I lay with him, terrified the boy wouldn't wake up, but he did, rousing himself slowly.

"You're a good dog, Bailey," he told me, his voice hoarse.

It was late in the afternoon when the stream joined a river. The boy stood and looked blankly at the dark water for a long time, then aimed us downstream, pushing through grasses and thickly choked trees.

Night was just starting to fall when I picked up the scent of men. At this point Ethan seemed to be walking without purpose, his feet scuffing numbly in the dirt. Each time he fell, he took longer and longer to get back up, and he registered nothing when I darted ahead, my nose to the ground.

"Come on, Bailey," he mumbled. "Where you going?"

I think he didn't even notice when we crossed the footpath. He was squinting in the fading light, trying to keep from tripping, and I sensed nothing from him for several seconds when the grasses underfoot became a well-trod trail of dirt. I could smell several different men—all of them old scents but as clear to me as the track of children up and down the streets back home. Then suddenly the boy straightened, taking in a breath. "Hey!" he said softly, his gaze sharpening on the path.

Now that I had a firm sense of where we were going, I trotted on ahead a few yards, my fatigue lifting with the boy's rising excitement. Both the trail and the river were bending in parallel to the right, and I kept my nose down, noticing how the man smell was becoming both more strong and more recent. Someone had been here not long ago.

Ethan stopped, so I went back to him. He was standing, staring, his mouth open.

"Wow," he said.

I realized there was a bridge across the river, and, as I watched, a figure broke out of the gloom and walked along the railing, peering at the water. Ethan's heart rate ticked up; I could hear it. His excitement, though, faded into a fear, and he shrank back, reminding me of my first mother's reaction when we would come across men while we were hunting.

"Bailey, be quiet," he whispered.

I didn't know what was going on, but I sensed his mood—it was the same thing that had happened at home, the night he got the gun out and poked it into all of the closets. I looked at him alertly.

"Hey!" the man on the bridge called. I felt the boy stiffen, getting ready to run away.

"Hey!" the man shouted again. "Are you Ethan?"

TWELVE

The man on the bridge gave us a car ride. "We've been searching the whole state of Michigan for you, son," he said. Ethan looked down, and from him I sensed sadness and shame and a little fear. We drove to a big building, and as soon as we stopped Dad opened the car door and he and Mom hugged Ethan and Grandma and Grandpa were there and everyone was happy, though there were no dog treats of any kind. The boy sat in a chair with wheels and a man pushed him into the building, and just before he went inside the boy turned and waved at me, and I thought he would probably be okay, though I felt pretty anxious to be separated from him. Grandpa held tight to my collar, so I didn't have any choice in the matter.

Grandpa took me for a car ride and I was a front-seat dog. We went to a place where they handed Grandpa a delicious-smelling sack through his window and he fed me dinner right there in the car, unwrapping hot sandwiches and handing them to me one at a time. He ate one, too.

"Don't tell Grandma about this," he said.

When we got home I was startled to see Flare standing in her usual place in her yard, regarding me with a slack expression. I barked at her through the car window until Grandpa told me to stop barking.

The boy was only gone one night, but it was the first time since we'd been together that I had slept without him, and I paced the hallway until Dad shouted, "Lie down, Bailey!" I curled up in Ethan's bed and fell asleep with my head on the pillow, where his scent was the strongest.

When Mom brought Ethan home the next day I was overjoyed, but the boy's mood was somber. Dad told him he was a bad boy. Grandpa talked to him in front of the gun cabinet. Everyone was tense—and yet nobody so much as mentioned the name Flare, and it was Flare who was the cause of the whole thing! I realized that because no one else had been there they didn't know what had really happened and were mad at the boy instead of the horse.

I was angry enough to want to go outside and bite that horse, but I didn't, of course, because the thing was huge.

The girl came over to see the boy, and the two of them sat on the porch and didn't talk much, just sort of mumbled and looked away from each other.

"Were you scared?" the girl asked.

"No," the boy said.

"I would have been scared."

"Well, I wasn't."

"Did you get cold at night?" she pressed.

"Yeah, pretty much."

"Oh."

"Yeah."

I alertly followed this exchange, sifting carefully for words such as "Bailey," "car ride," and "treats." Hearing none of them, I put my head down and sighed. The girl reached down and petted me, so I rolled on my back for a tummy rub.

I decided I liked the girl, and wished she visited more often and brought more of those biscuits and gave me some.

Then, before I was ready, Mom packed and we took the big long car ride that meant school was coming. When we pulled in the driveway at home, several of the children came running over, and Marshmallow and I got reacquainted on the lawn, slipping right into our ongoing wrestling match.

There were other dogs in the neighborhood, but I liked Marshmallow the best, probably because I saw her nearly every day when the boy went to stay with Chelsea's mother after school. Often when I would head out through the open gate on an adventure Marshmallow would be out, too, and would accompany me while we explored the issue of other people's trash cans.

So I was alarmed to hear Chelsea leaning out of her mother's car one day, calling, "Marshmallow! Marshy! Here, Marshmallow!" Chelsea came over to talk to Ethan, and before long all the kids in the neighborhood were calling Mashmallow's name. It was clear to me that Marshmallow had been a bad dog and had gone off somewhere on her own adventure.

Her scent was most recent in the area of the creek, but there were so many children and dogs, I didn't have a good sense of what direction she'd taken. Chelsea was sad and cried, and I felt bad for her and put my head in her lap, and she hugged me.

Todd was one of the children who were helping to look for Marshmallow, and curiously, her scent was on his pants. I sniffed him carefully, and he frowned and pushed my head away. His shoes were muddy and Marshmallow's scent was strong there, too, plus other things I couldn't identify.

"Come on, Bailey," Ethan said when he saw Todd's reaction to my examination.

Marshmallow never did come home. I remembered my first mother, running out the gate and into the world without a look back. Some dogs just want to be free to wander, because they don't have a boy who loves them.

Eventually Marshmallow's scent faded from the wind, but I never seemed to stop sniffing for her. When I remembered playing with Marshmallow I found myself thinking of Coco, back in the Yard. I would have loved to see Coco again, and Marshmallow, but I was beginning to understand that life was far more complicated than it had appeared to be in the Yard and that it was people who were in charge of it, not dogs. What mattered was not what I wanted; what mattered was that I was there in the woods when Ethan was cold and hungry, keeping him warm at nights, being his companion.

That winter, around the time when Dad put a tree in the living room for Merry Christmas, Chelsea got a new puppy. They named her Duchess. She was relentlessly playful, to the point where I'd get annoyed at her sharp teeth digging into my ears and would give her a quick growl to make her stop. She'd blink at me innocently and back off for just a few seconds before deciding I couldn't have meant it, and then she'd come right back at me. It was very irritating.

In the spring, the word "go-kart" swept through the neighborhood, and all up and down the street the children were sawing and hammering on wood, totally ignoring their dogs. Dad would come out to the garage every evening and talk to the boy while he fussed over whatever he was doing. I even went so far as to go into the boy's closet and bring out the loathsome flip, thinking I could tantalize him with that, but he remained totally focused on playing with pieces of wood that he never once threw for me to chase and bring back.

"See my go-kart, Bailey? It's going to go fast!"

Finally the boy opened the garage door, sat on the go-kart, and rode it like a sled down the short driveway. I trotted beside him, thinking we'd both been through a lot of bother for such a pointless ending, but when the go-kart reached the bottom of the driveway he picked it up and carried it back into the garage to play with it some more!

At least with the flip you had something you could chew on.

On a sunny day when there was no school, all of the kids in the neighborhood took their go-karts to a long, steep street several blocks away. Duchess was too young to accompany the procession, but I went along with my boy, though I had no enthusiasm for his initial idea that he should sit in the go-kart and I should pull him down the street by a leash.

Todd and his older brother, Drake, were among the kids and laughed and said things about Chelsea's go-kart, and I could sense that her feelings were hurt. When they lined up the go-karts at the top of the hill, Todd's was next to Ethan's.

I was not at all prepared for what happened next: someone yelled, "Go!" and then the go-karts were off, rolling down the hill, gathering speed. Drake ran up behind Todd and gave his go-kart a big push, and it leaped ahead.

"Cheating!" Chelsea yelled. Her go-kart was moving very slowly, but Ethan's was gaining speed and soon I had to run to keep up. The other go-karts fell away, and after a little bit it was just Ethan's go-kart, steadily closing in on Todd's.

I ran with abandonment, an exuberant freedom, galloping down the hill after my boy. At the bottom a boy named Billy stood with a flag on a stick, and I sensed that he was somehow part of what was happening. Ethan was hunched over, his head low, and it was all so much fun I decided I wanted to be on the go-kart with him. I put on an extra burst of speed and leaped through the air, landing on the back of his go-kart and nearly toppling off again.

The force of my impact threw us forward, so that we were now passing Todd! Billy waved his stick and I could hear yelling and cheering behind us as the go-kart, now on the flat part of the road, rolled to a stop.

"Good dog, Bailey," the boy told me, chuckling.

All the other go-karts rolled up behind us, followed by the rest of the children, who were all yelling and laughing. Billy came over and held Ethan's hand up into the air, dropping his stick with the flag on it. I picked up the stick and pranced around with it, daring someone to try to take it and have some real fun.

"Not fair, not fair!" Todd shouted.

The crowd of children grew quiet. A hot fury poured off of Todd, who stood facing Ethan.

"The damn dog jumped on the kart; that's why you won. You're disqualified," Drake said, standing behind his brother.

"Well, you pushed your brother!" Chelsea shouted.

"So?"

"I would have caught you anyway," Ethan said.

"Everyone who says Todd's right, say 'aye!'" Billy called.

Todd and his brother shouted, "Aye!"

"Everyone who says Ethan won, say 'nay.'"

"Nay!" all of the other children shouted. I was so startled at this loud outburst, I dropped my stick.

Todd took a step forward and hit Ethan, who ducked and tackled Todd. They both fell to the ground.

"Fight!" Billy yelled.

I started to surge forward to protect my boy, but Chelsea put a firm hand on my collar. "No, Bailey. Stay."

The boys rolled around, the two of them tied together in a tight knot of anger. I twisted around, trying to slip my collar, but Chelsea held fast. Frustrated, I barked.

Ethan was soon sitting up on top of Todd. Both boys were panting. "You give?" Ethan demanded.

Todd looked away, his eyes squeezed shut. Humiliation and hate wafted off of him in equal amounts. Finally, he nodded. The boys stood up warily, beating at the dirt on their pants.

I felt the sudden rage from Drake at the exact moment he lunged forward, slamming Ethan with both hands. Ethan rocked back but didn't fall.

"Come on, Ethan. Come on," Drake snarled.

There was a long pause while Ethan stood looking up at the older boy, and then Billy stepped forward. "No," Billy said.

"No," Chelsea said.

"No," some of the other children said. "No."

Drake looked at us all for a minute, and then he spat on the ground and picked up the go-kart. Without a word, the two brothers walked away.

"Well, we sure showed everybody today, didn't we, Bailey?" Ethan said to me. Everyone hauled their go-karts to the top of the hill and rolled them back down, all day long. Ethan allowed Chelsea to ride his go-kart, since hers had lost a wheel, and she had me ride behind her every time.

That night Ethan was excited at dinner, talking rapidly to Mom and Dad, who smiled as they listened. It took the boy a long time to fall asleep, and after he did so his restlessness made me slide off the bed and lie on the floor. This meant I wasn't really asleep when I heard a huge crash from downstairs.

"What was that?" the boy asked me, sitting bolt upright in bed. He jumped down onto the floor as the lights came on in the hallway.

"Ethan, stay in your room," Dad told him. He was tense, angry, and afraid. "Bailey, come."

I obediently eased down the stairs with Dad, who moved cautiously and turned on the lights in the living room. "Who's there?" he asked loudly.

Wind blew the curtains on the front window—a window that was normally never opened. "Don't come down with bare feet!" Dad shouted.

"What is it?" Mom asked.

"Someone threw a rock through our window. Stay back, Bailey."

I sensed Dad's concern and sniffed around the room at all the glass. On the floor was a rock, little shards of the window clinging to it. When I put my nose to it, I instantly recognized the smell.

Todd.

THIRTEEN

A year or so later, in the spring, Smokey the cat got sick. He lay around moaning and didn't protest when I put my nose down in his face to investigate this new behavior. Mom became very worried and took Smokey for a car ride. When Mom came home, she was sad, probably because cats are no fun in a car.

A week or so later, Smokey died. After dinner the family went into the backyard, where Ethan had excavated a big hole, and they wrapped Smokey's body in a blanket and put it in the hole and covered it with dirt. Ethan hammered a piece of wood into the soil next to the mound of wet dirt, and he and Mom cried a little. I nuzzled them both to remind them that there was really no need to grieve, since I was okay and really a much better pet than Smokey ever was.

The next day, after Mom and the boy left for school, I went out into the yard and dug Smokey back up, figuring they couldn't have meant to bury a perfectly good dead cat.

That summer we didn't go to the Farm at all. Ethan and some friends in the neighborhood would get up every day and go to people's houses and cut grass with loud lawn mowers. The boy would take me along with him but always tied me to a tree. I loved the smell of the newly cut grass, but I did not care for lawn mowing in general and felt this activity was somehow involved in us not visiting the Farm. Grandpa and Grandma did drive in for a week, but it wasn't nearly as much fun, especially when Dad and Grandpa exchanged some harsh words when they were alone in the backyard peeling husks off of corn. I felt the anger in both of them and wondered if it was a reaction to the fact that the corn husks were inedible, something I'd verified by both smelling and chewing. After that day, Dad and Grandpa were very uneasy in each other's company.

When school started again, several things were different. The boy no longer went to Chelsea's house when he got home—in fact, he usually was the last one to arrive, smelling of dirt, grass, and sweat as he raced up the driveway after a car dropped him off in the street. And some nights we'd go on a car ride to what I came to understand was a football game, where I would sit on a leash at the end of a long yard next to Mom and people would yell and scream for no reason. Boys wrestled and threw a ball to each other, sometimes running down close to where I was standing and other times playing all the way at the far end of the big yard.

I could smell Ethan in the group of boys sometimes. It was a little frustrating to just sit there and not go out and enhance the game—at home, I'd learned to get my mouth around a football.

One time I was playing with the boy and I bit too hard and the football collapsed until it was a saggy flat wad of leather, sort of like the flip. After that, Ethan didn't want me chewing on footballs, but I was still allowed to play with them as long as I was careful. Mom didn't know this and held me tight by the leash. I knew if she would just let me go get the football, the boys would have a lot more fun chasing me than each other, because I was faster than any of them.

Chelsea's puppy, Duchess, grew up, and we became good friends, once I demonstrated to her how she was to behave around me. One day when the gate was open I trotted over to see her and she was wearing a plastic cone around her neck and seemed very out of sorts. She thumped her tail a little when she saw me outside her cage, but she didn't bother to get up. The sight made me uneasy—I hoped no one was planning to put one of those things on me again.

When it snowed Ethan and I played with sleds, and when the snow melted we played with bouncy balls. A couple of times the boy pulled the flip out of the closet and stared at it while I glanced away in dread. He'd hold it up and look it over, feeling its heft, and then put it away with a sigh.

That summer was another one without a Farm visit, and once again the boy cut grass with his friends—I would have thought he'd gotten it out of his system, but he apparently still enjoyed it. That year, Dad left for several days and while he was gone Grandpa and Grandma visited. Their car smelled like Flare and hay and the pond, and I stood and sniffed it for several minutes and raised my legs on the tires.

"My goodness, you are such a big boy!" Grandma told Ethan.

There was more football when the days turned cool, plus a wonderful surprise: Ethan could take his own car rides! This changed everything, because now I went almost everywhere with him, my nose out the window as I stood in the front seat, helping him drive. It turned out that the reason he stayed out so late was that he played football every night after school, leaving me tied up by the fence with a dish of water. It was boring, but at least I got to be with the boy.

Sometimes when Ethan took a car ride he forgot me, so I'd sit in the yard and yip for him to come back. Usually when this happened, Mom would come to see me.

"Want to go for a walk, Bailey?" she'd ask over and over until I was so excited I was dancing around in circles. She'd put the leash on my collar and we'd patrol the streets, stopping every few feet so I could mark the territory. Often we'd pass groups of children playing and I'd wonder why Ethan didn't do that as much anymore. Mom sometimes unsnapped the leash and let me run with the children a little bit.

I liked Mom a lot. My only complaint was that when she exited the bathroom she would close the lid on my water bowl. Ethan always left the lid up for me.

When school ended that summer, Ethan and Mom took us on a car ride to the Farm. I was overjoyed to be back. Flare pretended not to recognize me and I wasn't sure if they were the same ducks or different ones, but everything else seemed exactly the same.

Nearly every day Ethan would work with Grandpa and some men, hammering and sawing boards. I assumed at first that the boy was building another go-kart, but after a month or so it became clear that they were putting together a new barn, right next to the old one, which had a big hole in the roof.

I was the first one to spot the woman coming up the driveway, and ran down to enforce any needed security. When I got close enough to smell her I realized it was the girl, all grown up now. She remembered me, and I squirmed in pleasure as she scratched behind my ears.

"Hi there, Bailey; did you miss me? Good dog, Bailey."

As the men noticed the girl they stopped working. Ethan was coming out of the old barn and stopped in surprise.

"Oh. Hi. Hannah?"

"Hi, Ethan."

Grandpa and the other men were grinning at each other. Ethan looked over his shoulder at them and flushed, then came over to where Hannah and I were standing.

"So, hi," he said.

"Hi."

They looked away from each other. Hannah stopped scratching me and I gave her a little nudge to remind her to keep at it.

"Come on in the house," Ethan said.

The rest of that summer, whenever I went for a car ride it smelled like the girl had been sitting in my seat. Sometimes she would come over and have dinner with us, and then she and Ethan would sit on the porch and talk and I would lie at their feet to give them something interesting to talk about.

One time I was awakened from a well-deserved nap by a little alarm coming off the both of them. They were sitting on the couch and their faces were really close together and their hearts were beating and I could sense fear and excitement. It sounded a little like they were eating, but I couldn't smell any food. Not sure what was happening, I climbed up on the couch and forced my nose into the place where their heads were together, and they both burst out laughing at me.

The day Mom and Ethan drove back home for school, the smell of paint from the new barn was in the air and the girl came over and she and Ethan went down to the dock and sat with their feet in the water and talked. The girl cried, and they hugged a lot and didn't throw sticks or do any of the things people normally do at a pond, so I wasn't quite sure what was going on. There was more hugging at the car, and then we drove away, Ethan honking.

Things were different at home. For one thing, Dad had his own room now, with a new bed in it. He shared the bathroom with Ethan, and frankly, I didn't like to go in there after Dad had been in it. For another, when Ethan wasn't playing football with his friends he spent a lot of time in his room talking on the phone. He said the name Hannah often during these calls.

The leaves were falling from the trees on the day Ethan took me for a car ride to a place with big silver school buses full of people, and there, coming off of one of them, was the girl! I don't know who was more happy to see her, me or the boy—I wanted to play with her, but all he wanted to do was hug. I was so excited at this development I didn't mind that I was automatically a backseat dog for the return trip.

"Coach says there will be scouts from U of M and Michigan State tonight, to see me, Hannah," the boy said. I understood the word "Hannah," of course, but I also picked up a surge of fear and excitement from the boy. From Hannah there was happiness and pride. I looked out the window to see if I could figure out what was going on but didn't see anything unusual.

That night, I was proud to stand with Hannah while Ethan played football with his friends. I felt fairly certain she had never been to such a place as wonderful as the big yard, and I led her over to where Mom usually took me and showed Hannah where to sit.

We'd only been there a little while when Todd came walking

up. I hadn't seen much of Todd lately, though his sister, Linda, still rode up and down the street on a bicycle all the time. "Hi, Bailey," he said to me, really friendly, but there was still something very wrong about him and I just sniffed at his hand when he offered it to me.

"Do you know Bailey?" the girl asked. I wagged at the mention of my name.

"We're old pals, aren't we, boy. Good dog."

I did not need to be called good dog by someone like Todd.

"You don't go to school here; do you go to East?" Todd asked.

"No, I'm just visiting Ethan's family."

"What are you, a cousin or something?"

The people in the crowd all shouted and I jerked my head around, but there was nothing happening but more wrestling. It fooled me every time they did that.

"No, just . . . a friend."

"So you want to party?" Todd asked her.

"Sorry?"

"Want to party? Some of us are getting together. This game's going nowhere."

"No, I . . . I'd better wait for Ethan." I cocked my head at the girl. I could sense her getting anxious for some reason, and I could feel Todd's anger building inside him like it always did.

"Ethan!" Todd turned and spat in the grass. "So are you two a couple, or what?"

"Well . . ."

"'Cause you should know, he's pretty much going out with Michele Underwood."

"What?"

"Yeah. Like, everybody knows it."

"Oh."

"Yeah. So if you're thinking, you know, him and you, that's not, you know, that's not going to happen." Todd moved closer to the girl, and when she stiffened I saw that his hand was touching her shoulder. Her rising tension brought me back to my feet. Todd looked down at me and we locked eyes, and I felt the fur lifting on the back of my neck. Almost involuntarily, a low growl emerged from deep in my throat.

"Bailey!" The girl leaped to her feet. "What's the matter?"

"Yeah, Bailey, it's *me*, your pal." He turned to the girl. "I'm Todd, by the way."

"I'm Hannah."

"Why don't you tie up the dog and come with me? It'll be fun."

"Um, no, uh-uh. I couldn't do that."

"Why not? Come on."

"No, I have to take care of Bailey."

Todd shrugged. He stared at her. "Yeah. Well, whatever."

The force of his anger was so strong I growled again, and this time the girl didn't say anything to me about it. "Fine," Todd said. "You ask Ethan about Michele. Okay?"

"Yes, okay."

"You ask him." Todd jammed his hands in his pockets and walked away.

Ethan was pretty happy and excited when he ran over to see us an hour or so later. "Michigan State, here we come. Spartans!" he shouted. I wagged and barked, and then his happiness went away.

"What's the matter, Hannah?"

"Who is Michele?"

I put my paw on Ethan's leg to let him know I was ready to play with the football, if he wanted.

"Michele? Who do you mean?" Ethan laughed, but the

laughter stopped after a second, as if he had run out of air. "What's wrong?"

They walked me in circles around the big yard, talking, so intently involved in conversation they didn't notice when I ate a half of a hot dog, some popcorn, and bits of a tuna sandwich. Before long nearly everyone else had left, but they kept walking around and around.

"I don't know this girl," Ethan kept saying. "Who did you talk to?"

"I don't remember his name. He knew Bailey, though."

I froze at my name, wondering if I was going to get in trouble for the candy wrapper I was stealthily eating.

"Everybody knows Bailey; he comes to all the games."

I quickly swallowed, but apparently I wasn't in trouble. After another circuit around the big yard, made uninteresting by the fact that I'd pretty much found everything edible, the boy and the girl stopped and hugged. They did that a lot. "You're all sweaty," the girl laughed, pushing him away.

"Want to go for a car ride, Bailey?" the boy asked.

Of course I did! We went home, and there was some more quiet talking, and they fed me and I was content to fall asleep on the living room floor while the girl and the boy wrestled silently together on the couch.

We had a new dog door now, from the back door right out into the yard, and no one ever tried to suggest I should have to sleep in the garage anymore. I was glad I broke the family of *that* habit. I went outside to relieve myself and was astonished to find a piece of meat lying in the grass by the fence.

The funny thing was, it didn't smell right. There was a sharp tang to it, an odd, bitter odor. Even more strange, Todd's scent was all over it.

I picked up the piece of meat and carried it to the back patio, where I dropped it, the bitter taste causing foam in my mouth. Then I sat and looked at it. It was a pretty bad flavor, but then, it was a nice hunk of meat. If I chewed it fast enough, I could probably swallow it without tasting it.

I poked the meat with my nose. Why, I wondered, did it smell so strongly of Todd?

FOURTEEN

When Mom came outside the next morning and saw me, I hung my head and tapped the patio with just the tip of my tail. For some reason, though I had done nothing wrong, I felt really guilty.

"Good morning, Bailey," she said. Then she saw the meat. "What's that?"

When she bent over to look more closely at the meat, I dropped onto my back for a tummy rub. I'd been staring at that piece of meat all night, it seemed, and I was exhausted and needed reassurance I had done the right thing, even if I didn't understand why. There was just something wrong, here, and it had prevented me from taking advantage of the free meal.

"Where did this come from, Bailey?" Mom stroked my belly lightly, then reached over and picked up the meat. "Ugh," she said.

I sat up alertly. If she was going to feed it to me, it meant it was okay. Instead, she turned away to take it into the house. I rose up on my back legs a little—now that she was removing it, I'd changed my mind; I wanted to eat it!

"Yuck, Bailey, you don't want that, whatever it is," Mom said. She dropped the meat into the garbage.

Hannah sat in my seat for the car ride to the giant silver school buses, and I sat alone in the car for a long time while Ethan and Hannah stood and hugged. When the boy came back to the car, he felt sad and lonely, so I put my head in his lap instead of sticking my nose out the window.

The girl came back to visit again the day after the family sat around the indoor tree and tore up papers for Merry Christmas. I was in a bad mood because Ethan gave Mom a new black and white kitten, named Felix. He had no manners whatsoever and attacked my tail when I sat down and often lunged out at me from behind the couch, batting at me with his tiny paws. When I tried to play with him, he wrapped his legs around my nose and bit me with his sharp teeth. Hannah paid way too much attention to the kitty when she first arrived, though I had known the girl longer and was obviously the favorite pet. Dogs have important jobs, like barking when the doorbell rings, but cats have no function in a house whatsoever.

One thing the kitten couldn't do was go outside. The ground was coated with a thick layer of snow, and the one time Felix ventured to put a foot into the stuff he turned around and ran back into the house as if he'd been burned. So when Hannah and Ethan built a big pile of snow in the front yard and put a hat on it, I was right there with them. The boy liked to tackle me and drag me around in the white stuff, and I let him catch me for the sheer joy of having his arms around me, the way he'd played with me every day when he was younger.

When we went sledding, Hannah sat in the back and I ran alongside the sled, barking and trying to pull the mittens off of the boy's hands.

One afternoon the sun was out and the air was so cold and clean I could taste it all the way down my throat. All of the children from the neighborhood were there at the sledding hill, and Hannah and Ethan spent as much time pushing the younger ones as riding themselves. I soon grew tired of running up and down the slope, which was why I was at the bottom when Todd drove up.

He looked at me when he got out of the car, but he didn't say anything to me, or reach out his hand. I kept my distance.

"Linda! Come on, time to come home!" he shouted, his breath whipping out of his mouth in a steamy cloud.

Linda was on the slope with three of her little friends, coming down in a saucer-shaped sled at about one mile an hour. Ethan and Hannah flashed past them on their sled, laughing. "I don't want to!" Linda yelled back.

"Now! Mom says!"

Ethan and Hannah came to a halt at the bottom of the hill, tumbling out of their sled. They lay on top of each other, giggling. Todd stood and watched them.

Something in Todd came to the surface, then. Not anger, exactly, but something worse, something dark, an emotion I'd never felt from anyone before. I felt it in the way he stared at Ethan and Hannah, his face very still.

Ethan and the girl stood up, wiping snow off each other, and came over to see Todd, their arms still intertwined. They radiated such love and joy it blinded them to the hate-filled currents emanating from Todd.

"Hey, Todd."

"Hi."

"This is Hannah. Hannah, this is Todd; he lives down the street."

Hannah reached her hand out, smiling. "Nice to meet you," she said.

Todd stiffened a little. "Actually, we already met."

Hannah cocked her head, wiping hair out of her eyes. "We did?"

"When was that?" Ethan asked.

"At the football game," Todd said. Then he laughed, a short bark.

Ethan was shaking his head blankly, but Hannah blinked. "Oh. Oh, right," she said, suddenly subdued.

"What?" Ethan asked.

"I have to pick up my sister. Linda!" Todd yelled, cupping his hands. "Come home now!"

Linda detached herself from her pile of friends and trudged through the snow dejectedly.

"He's . . . he's the one I talked to," Hannah told Ethan. Some worry flickered through Hannah, and I glanced at her curiously, then jerked my head at Ethan when I felt a rising anger from him.

"Wait, what? You? Todd, you were the person who told Hannah I'd been with Michele? I don't even *know* Michele."

"I got to go," Todd mumbled. "Get in the car, Linda," he told his sister.

"No, wait," Ethan said. He reached his hand out and Todd jerked away from it.

"Ethan," Hannah murmured, putting a mitten on his arm.

"Why would you do that, Todd? Why would you lie? What's wrong with you, man?"

Though the conflicts and emotions boiling through Todd were hot enough to melt the snow we were standing on, he just stood there, staring back at Ethan, not saying a word.

"This is why you don't have any friends, Todd. Why can't you just be normal? You're always doing stupid things like this," Ethan said. "It's sick." The anger was leaving him, but I could feel how upset he still was.

"Ethan," Hannah said more sharply.

Todd wordlessly got in his car, slamming the door. His face, when he looked back at Hannah and Ethan, was absolutely blank.

"That was mean," Hannah said.

"Oh, you don't know him."

"I don't care," Hannah replied. "You shouldn't have said he doesn't have any friends."

"Well, he doesn't. He's always doing stuff, like when he said this one guy stole his transistor radio. The whole thing was a lie."

"He's not . . . there's something different about him, right? Like is he in special education?"

"Oh no, he's really smart. That's not it. He's just Todd, that's all. He's always been *twisted*, you know? We used to be friends, when we were kids. But he had all these weird ideas for what was fun, like throwing eggs at the preschoolers when they were waiting for the van to summer school. I told him I didn't want to do it—his own sister was one of the kids; I mean, come on—and so he just stomped on the carton of eggs he'd brought over. Made a mess in my driveway that I had to hose off before my dad got home. Bailey liked that part, though."

I wagged at my name, glad to think we might be talking about me, now.

"I'll bet he did," Hannah laughed, reaching down and petting me.

A few days after Hannah left, the snow came down and the wind blew so hard that we stayed inside all day, sitting in front of the heater. (At least, that is what I did.) That night I slept *under* the covers on Ethan's bed, and stayed there even when I got so hot I panted, just because it was so wonderful to be pressed up against him like when I was a puppy.

The next morning the snow finally stopped and Ethan and I went outside and dug for hours in the driveway. Running in that deep, heavy snow was tough going, and I would leap ahead for only a few feet before needing to stop and rest.

The moon came out right after dinner, so bright that I could see really well, and the air was thick with the fragrance of fireplace smoke. Ethan was tired and went to bed early, but I went out the dog door and stood in the yard, my nose to the faint breeze, galvanized by the exotic light and crisp night air.

When I discovered that the snow had drifted in a huge pile against the fence, I was delighted to climb right up to the top of the mound and drop over the other side. It was a perfect night for an adventure. I went over to Chelsea's house to see if Duchess was available, but there was no sign other than a fairly recent patch of urine-soaked snow. I thoughtfully lifted my leg on the area so she'd know I was thinking of her.

Normally when I went for a little nighttime exploration, I ventured along the creek. It reminded me of hunting with Sister and Fast when I was a wild puppy, and the smells were always exciting. Now, though, I was forced to stick to the plowed roads, turning up driveways that were clear to sniff at the cracks between garage doors and the pavement. Some people had already dragged their indoor trees outside, though at Ethan's house it still stood in the front window, with objects and lights hanging from it for Felix to attack. When I came across the indoor trees lying in the plowed driveways, I marked them with my scent, and it was this, the seemingly endless procession of trees to tag, that kept me out so late. If it hadn't been for the scent of yet another misplaced tree luring me onward, I would have returned back home and maybe would have arrived in time to prevent what happened.

Finally I was caught square in the headlights of a passing car, and it slowed for a minute, and the smell of it reminded me of Mom's car whenever she and Ethan came looking for me when I'd been out too long on an adventure, and I felt a quick stab of guilt. I lowered my head and trotted back home.

Turning up the shoveled sidewalk, I was struck by several things at once, all of them wrong.

The front door was open, and the aroma of home was wafting out in great gusts, propelled into the frosty night air by the force of the furnace. Riding on the currents of that air was a chemical smell both sharp and familiar—I smelled it whenever we went for a car ride and stopped at the place where Ethan liked to stand by the back of the car with a thick black hose. And backing out of the house was someone I initially thought was the boy. Not until he turned to shake some more chemical-laden liquid into the front bushes did I pick up his scent.

It was Todd. He took three steps back and pulled out some paper from his pocket and lit it, the fire flickering against his stony blank face. When he tossed the burning papers into the bushes, a blue flame popped up, making an audible noise.

Todd didn't see me; he was watching the fire. And I never

barked, I never growled, I just ran up that sidewalk in silent fury. I leaped for him as if I had been taking down men my whole life, and surging through me was a sense of power, as if I were leading a pack.

Any reluctance I might have felt to attack a human being was overridden by the sense that whatever Todd was doing, it was causing harm to the boy and to the family I was there to protect. There was no stronger purpose than that.

Todd yelled and fell and kicked at my face. I took the foot that the kicking offered, biting into it and holding on while Todd screamed. His pants ripped, his shoe came off, and I tasted blood. He struck at me with his fists, but I kept my grip on his ankle, shaking my head, feeling the flesh tear some more. I was in a fury, completely oblivious to the fact that my mouth was filled with the unique flavor of human skin and blood.

A sudden piercing noise distracted me, and Todd managed to work his foot loose as I turned to look at the house. The indoor tree was totally aflame, and thick, acrid smoke was pouring out the front door and up into the night. The electronic shriek was painfully high and loud, and I instinctively backed away from it.

Todd stood and limped away as fast as he could, and I registered his retreat out of the corner of my eye, no longer caring. I sounded my own alarm, barking, trying to draw attention to the flames, which were spreading quickly through the house and were curling upstairs toward the boy's room.

I ran around the back of the house but was frustrated to discover that the pile of snow that had assisted me on my escape was on the wrong side of the fence. While I stood there barking, the patio door slid open and Dad and Mom stumbled into view. Mom was coughing.

"Ethan!" she screamed.

Black smoke was coming out the patio door. Mom and Dad ran to the gate, and I met them there. They shoved past me, running through the snow to the front of the house. They stood looking up at the dark window to Ethan's room.

"Ethan!" they shouted. "Ethan!"

I broke from them and raced around to the now open back gate. I darted through it. Felix was outside on the patio, huddled under a picnic bench, and she yowled at me, but I didn't stop. I squeezed through the patio door, my eyes and nose filled with smoke. Unable to see, I staggered toward the stairs.

The sound of the flames was as loud as the wind when we went for a car ride with the windows down. The smoke was suffocating, but it was the heat that beat me back. The intensity of the fire burned my nose and ears, and in frustration I lowered my head and ran out the back door, the cold air instantly salving my pain.

Mom and Dad were still yelling. Lights had come on across the street and in the house next door, and I could see one of the neighbors looking out his window, talking on the phone.

There was still no sign of the boy.

"Ethan!" Mom and Dad yelled. "Ethan!"

FIFTEEN

I had never before felt such fear as what was pouring off of Mom and Dad as they shouted at the boy's window. Mom was sobbing and Dad's voice was tight, and when I began barking again, frantically, they made no move to tell me to be quiet.

My ears picked up the thin wail of a siren, but mostly I could only hear my barking, Mom and Dad calling Ethan's name, and, over all of it, the roar of the fire, so loud I could feel it as a vibration through my whole body. The bushes in front of us were still burning, clouds of steam rising as the snow melted with a sizzle.

"Ethan! Please!" Dad shouted, his voice cracking.

Just then, something burst through Ethan's window, showering glass into the snow. It was the flip!

Frantically I picked it up, to show Ethan that yes, I had it.

His head appeared in the hole the flip had made, black smoke framing his face.

"Mom!" he yelled, coughing.

"You've got to get out of there, Ethan!" Dad roared.

"I can't open the window, it's stuck!"

"Just jump!" Dad responded.

"You've got to jump, honey!" Mom shouted at him.

The boy's head disappeared back inside. "The smoke is going to kill him; what's he doing?" Dad said.

"Ethan!" Mom screamed.

The boy's desk chair came through the window, smashing it, and, a second later, the boy plunged out. He appeared to get hung up on the remaining bits of wood and glass, though, so that instead of sailing out over the flaming bushes he dropped directly into them.

"Ethan!" Mom shrieked.

I barked frantically, the flip forgotten. Dad reached into the fire and grabbed Ethan and pulled him out into the snow, rolling him over and over. "Oh God, oh God," Mom was sobbing.

Ethan lay on his back in the snow, his eyes closed. "Are you okay, son? Are you okay?" Dad asked.

"My leg," the boy said, coughing.

I could smell his burned flesh. His face was blackened and oozing. I pressed forward, the flip in my mouth, feeling the stabbing pain in him and wanting to help.

"Go away, Bailey," Dad said.

The boy opened his eyes, and he grinned weakly at me. "No, it's okay. Good dog, Bailey, you caught the flip. Good dog."

I wagged. He reached out with one hand and petted my head, and I spat out the flip, which to tell the truth didn't taste very good. His other hand was curled up against his chest, blood dribbling out of it.

Cars and trucks began arriving, lights flashing. Men ran up to the house and began spraying it with large hoses. Some people brought over a bed and put the boy on it and lifted it up and put it into the back of a truck. I tried to crawl in after him, but the man at the truck's back doors pushed me away. "No, sorry," he said.

"Stay, Bailey; it's okay," the boy said.

I knew all about Stay; it was my least favorite command. The boy was still hurting, and I wanted to be with him.

"May I go?" Mom asked.

"Of course; let me help you," the man replied.

Mom crawled into the back of the truck. "It's okay, Bailey." Chelsea's mother approached, and Mom looked up at her. "Laura? Could you watch Bailey?"

"Sure."

Chelsea's mother took hold of my collar. Her hands smelled like Duchess. Dad's hand, though, smelled of the fire, and I knew he was in pain. He climbed in to be with Mom and the boy.

Nearly everyone in the neighborhood was out in the street, but no dogs. The truck drove off and I gave it a single mournful bark. How did I know the boy would be safe now? He needed me with him!

Chelsea's mother stood off to the side, holding me. I could tell she was a little unsure what to do now; most of the neighbors were collected in the street, but she'd been close to the house and now everyone acted like they expected her to remain there instead of joining her friends.

"No question but that it is arson," one of the men said, talking to a woman who had a gun on her belt. I'd learned that people who dressed like this were called police. "The bushes, the tree, all of it went up at once. Multiple ignition points, lots of accelerant. Family is lucky to be alive."

"Lieutenant, look at this!" another man called. He had a gun, too—the men in rubber coats didn't carry guns and were still spraying hoses.

Chelsea's mother hesitantly eased up to see what they were all looking at. It was Todd's shoe. I turned my head away guiltily, hoping no one would notice me.

"I got this tennis shoe, looks like there's blood on it," the man noted, illuminating the snow with a flashlight.

"The boy got pretty cut up going out his window," someone else observed.

"Yeah, over there. But not here. All I got here are dog tracks and this shoe."

I cringed that the word "dog" had come up. The woman with the gun took out a flashlight and aimed it in the snow. "What do you know," she said.

"That's blood," someone else said.

"Okay, you two, see where the trail leads, okay? Let's tape this off. Sergeant?"

"Yes, ma'am," a man said, approaching the group.

"We've got a blood trail. I want eight feet on either side of it cordoned off. Keep the traffic off the street, and have those people move back."

The woman stood and Chelsea's mother bent down, suddenly paying attention to me. "You okay, Bailey?" she asked, petting me.

I wagged.

She abruptly stopped petting me and looked at her hand.

"Ma'am, do you live here?" the policewoman with the gun asked Chelsea's mother.

"No, but the dog does."

"Could I ask you to . . . well, wait, are you a neighbor?"

"I live two houses down."

"Did you see anyone tonight, anyone at all?"

"No, I was asleep."

"Okay. Could I ask you to join the others over there? Or if you're cold, please just give us your contact information and you can go home."

"Yes, but . . . ," Chelsea's mother said.

"Yes?"

"Could someone look at Bailey? He seems to be bleeding."

I wagged.

"Sure," the woman replied. "Is he friendly?"

"Oh yes."

The woman bent down. "Are you hurt, boy? How did you get hurt?" she asked softly. She took out a flashlight and probed carefully at my neck. I tentatively licked her face, and she laughed.

"Okay, yes, he's friendly. I don't think that's his blood, though. Ma'am, we'll need to hold on to the dog for a while; is that okay?"

"I can stay, if you need me to."

"No, that's all right," the woman said.

I was taken over to one of the cars, where a very gentle man took some scissors and snipped off some of my fur, putting it into a plastic bag.

"What do you want to bet it's the same blood type that's on the shoe? I'd say our four-legged friend here was on canine patrol tonight and got himself a good bite of arsonist. We get a suspect, the blood is going to help put him away," the woman told the man who was giving me the haircut.

"Lieutenant," a man said, approaching. "I can tell you where our perp lives."

"Oh, do tell," the woman replied.

"I got the dumb ass bleeding his way in a straight line to a home about four houses down. You can see the blood on the snow from the sidewalk; it goes right up to a side door."

"I'd say we have enough for a search warrant," the woman replied. "And I'm going to lay odds that somebody who lives there has a couple of teeth marks in his leg."

For the next several days I lived at Chelsea's house. Duchess seemed to think I was there to supply her with a twenty-four-hour-a-day playmate, but I couldn't dispel the nervous tension that kept me pacing back and forth, waiting for Ethan to come home.

Mom showed up the second day. She told me I was a good dog, and I could smell the boy on her clothes, so I cheered up a little and played Duchess's favorite game of tug-on-the-sock for an hour or so while Chelsea's mother served strong-smelling coffee.

"What in the world was that boy doing? Why would he set your house on fire? You could all have been killed."

"I don't know. Todd and Ethan used to be friends."

I turned at Ethan's name, and Duchess used the moment to yank the sock out of my mouth.

"Is it for sure Todd? I thought the police said the blood work would take longer."

"He confessed when they took him in for questioning," Mom said.

"Did he explain why he did it?"

Duchess was shoving the sock at me, daring me to take it. I pointedly looked away.

"He said he didn't know why he did it."

"Well, for heaven's sake. You know, I always did think that boy was strange. Remember when he pushed Chelsea into the bushes for no reason? My husband had a fit. He went down and talked to Todd's father and I thought the two of them were going to get into a fight."

"No, I never heard that. He pushed her?"

"And Sudy Hurst says she caught him trying to see in her bedroom window."

"I thought she wasn't sure who it was."

"Well, now she says it was Todd."

With a sudden lunge, I grabbed the sock. Duchess dug her feet in and growled. I pulled her around the room, but she didn't let go.

"Bailey's a hero, now. Todd's leg took eight stitches."

At the mention of my name, both Duchess and I froze. Dog biscuits, maybe? The sock went slack between us.

"They want his picture for the paper," Mom said.

"Good thing I gave Bailey a bath," Chelsea's mom replied.

What? Another bath? I'd just had a bath! I spat out the sock, Duchess shaking it joyously, prancing around the room in victory.

"How is Ethan?"

Mom put her coffee cup down. The boy's name and the flash of worry and grief coming off of her caused me to go over to her and put my head in her lap. She reached down and petted my head.

"They had to put a pin in his leg, and he'll have . . . scarring." Mom gestured toward her face and then pressed her hands to her eyes.

"I'm so, so sorry," Chelsea's mother said.

Mom was crying. I put a paw on her leg to comfort her.

"Good dog, Bailey," Mom said.

Duchess stuck her idiot face right in front of me, the sock loosely dangling from her jaws. I gave her a low growl and she backed away, looking bewildered.

"Be nice, please, guys," Chelsea's mother said.

A little while later Chelsea's mother gave pie to Mom but not to the dogs. Duchess lay on her back and held the sock with her paws above her mouth, just like I used to do with Coco in the Yard, what seemed like forever ago.

Some people came and I sat with Mom in the living room and blinked at the bright flashes, like lightning with no sound. Then we went over to the house, which was now covered in plastic sheeting that flapped in the wind, and some more flashes went off.

A week later, Mom gave me a car ride and we moved into the "apartment." This was a small house built into a big building full of houses, and there were lots of dogs everywhere. Most of them were pretty little, but in the afternoons Mom would take me over to see them in a big cement yard. She would sit on a bench and talk to people while I ran around, making friends and marking territory.

I didn't like the apartment, and neither did Dad. He yelled at Mom a lot more there than at the house. The place was small, and, even worse, we were there without the boy. Both Dad and Mom would often smell like Ethan, but he wasn't living with us anymore, and my heart ached. At night I would pace the house, compelled to wander around restlessly, until Dad would yell at me to lie down. Dinner, the high point of my day, was not as interesting when Mom served it to me—I just didn't feel hungry, and sometimes didn't finish it.

Where was my boy?

SIXTEEN

We were still living in the apartment the day the boy came home. I was curled up on the floor, with Felix the kitty sleeping up against me. I'd given up trying to shove him away; Felix apparently thought I was his mother, which was insulting, but he was a cat and therefore, in my opinion, completely brainless.

I'd learned to identify our cars by the sounds of their engines as they pulled into the parking lot, so when Mom's car arrived I jumped to my feet. Felix blinked at me in bewilderment while I trotted over to the window and jumped up, pressing my paws against the frame so I could watch Mom come up the steps.

What I saw down in the parking lot caused my heart to race: it was the boy, struggling to stand up out of the car. Mom was bending to help him, and it took several seconds for him to get upright.

I couldn't help myself; I was barking and spinning, racing from the window to the door to be let out and then back to the window so I could see. Felix panicked and dove under the couch and watched me from there.

When keys jangled in the lock, I was right there at the door, quivering. Mom opened the door a crack, and the boy's smell wafted in on the air currents.

"Now, Bailey, get back. Down, Bailey, stay down. Sit."

Well, I couldn't do *that*. I briefly touched my butt to the floor and then jumped up again. Mom put her hand in and snagged my collar, pushing me back as the door swung wide.

"Hey, Bailey. Hey, boy," Ethan said.

Mom held me away from the boy while he limped in, holding what I would soon learn were called crutches. He went over to the couch and sat down while I twisted and turned in my collar, whimpering. When Mom finally released me I soared across the room in one leap, landing on the boy's lap, kissing his face.

"Bailey!" Mom said sternly.

"No, it's okay. Bailey, you are such a doodle dog," the boy praised me. "How are you, huh? I missed you, too, Bailey."

Every time he spoke my name, a shiver of pleasure ran through me. I could not get enough of the feel of his hands running through my fur.

The boy was back.

Gradually, over the next couple of days, I came to understand that things were not right with the boy. He had pains that he'd never coped with before, and walking was awkward and difficult for him. A mournful sadness drifted off of him, coupled with a gloomy anger that flared sometimes when all he was doing was sitting there looking out the window.

That first week or two the boy would leave every day for a car ride with Mom, and when he came home he was tired and sweaty and usually wound up taking a nap. The weather turned warm and the leaves came out and Mom had to go to work, so the boy and I were left alone in the apartment with Felix, who spent all of his time plotting to escape out the front door. I have no idea what he thought he was going to accomplish out there, but the boy had a rule against the cat going outside, so that was that—except Felix didn't follow any rules, which I found to be maddening. He often scratched at a post in the living room, but the *one time* I decided to lift my leg on the thing everyone shouted. He never finished his dinner, though nobody ever thanked me when I cleaned up after him—in fact, this was something else I got yelled at about. Part of me wanted to see him get away with his plans to run off, just so I wouldn't have to put up with him anymore. On the other hand, he was always up for a little wrestling, as long as I didn't get too rough. He would even make a game of chasing a ball when Ethan rolled it down the hallway, usually veering off to let me grab it and take it back, which I thought was very sporting of Felix. He really didn't have much choice, though, since I was, after all, the dog in charge.

It was not as fun as the Farm, nor even as fun as the house, but I was happy in the apartment because the boy was there nearly all the time.

"I think it is time you should go back to school," Mom said at dinner one night. I knew the word "school" and looked at the boy, who crossed his arms. I felt the sad anger inside of him.

"I'm not ready," the boy said. His finger raised up and touched a deep purple scar on his cheek. "Not until I can walk better."

I sat up. Walk? Were we going for a walk?

"Ethan. There's no reason—"

"I don't want to talk about it, Mom!" Ethan shouted.

Ethan never shouted at Mom and I could immediately feel that he was sorry, but neither of them said anything after that.

A few days later, though, there was a knock on the door and, when Ethan answered, the apartment filled with boys. I recognized some of their smells as the boys who played football in the big yards, and most of them called me by name. I glanced over to see how Felix was taking my special status, but he was pretending it didn't make him jealous.

The boys laughed and shouted and stood around for about an hour, and I felt Ethan's heart lifting. His happiness made me happy, so I went and got a ball and carried it around in my mouth in the living room. One of the boys grabbed it and rolled it down the hallway, and we played for several minutes.

A few days after all the boys came to visit, Ethan got up early and left with Mom.

School.

The boy was walking with the help of a polished stick called a cane when we moved out of the apartment. The cane was very special: the boy never threw it, and I instinctively understood that I wasn't supposed to chew on it, not even a little.

I didn't know where we were going when we all loaded into the car, but I was excited just the same. Car rides were always exciting, no matter where we went.

I grew pretty excited when the familiar smells of the creek and the street came through the window, and I bounded in through the front door of the house as soon as they let me out of the car. Though I could still smell smoke, the air was also filled with the scent of new wood and carpet, and the windows in the living room were larger. Felix seemed very suspicious of his surroundings, but I was out the dog door and racing around in the relative freedom of the backyard within seconds of arriving. When I barked with joy, Duchess answered from down the street. Home!

We'd barely settled in when we took the big car ride to the Farm. Life was finally back on track, though the boy was much less inclined to run than to walk, leaning on the cane.

One of the first places we went was to Hannah's house. I knew the route pretty well and galloped way ahead, so I saw her first. "Bailey! Hi, Bailey!" she called. I ran up for some of her in-depth cuddling and scratching, and then the boy came up the driveway, panting a little. The girl went down the steps and stood there in the sun, waiting for him.

"Hi," the boy said. He seemed a little uncertain.

"Hi," the girl said.

I yawned and scratched at an itch on my jaw.

"Well, are you going to kiss me or what?" the girl asked. Ethan went to give her a long hug.

He dropped his cane.

Some things were different that summer. Ethan began waking up long before sunrise and driving Grandpa's truck up and down the county roads, shoving papers into people's boxes. They were the same papers that the boy had once placed all over the carpet in the house, but somehow I didn't think it would be appreciated very much if I urinated on them, even though there had been a time, when I was a puppy, when wetting down the papers would have gained me high praise.

Hannah and the boy spent many hours together, sitting quietly by themselves, sometimes not talking, just wrestling. Sometimes she even went on the early morning car rides, though normally it was just the boy and me, Bailey the front-seat dog.

"Got to earn some money, Bailey," he sometimes said. I would wag at my name. "No football scholarship now, that's for sure. I'll never be able to participate in sports again."

At the sadness in him I always pushed my nose under his hand.

"My whole life's dream. All gone now, because of Todd."

Ethan had brought the flip with him to the Farm, for some reason, and sometimes he would cut it up and resew it, generally making it even more embarrassing than it had been before. But my favorite time was when we'd swim together in the pond. It seemed the only time that the boy's leg didn't give him pain. We even played the sinking game, as we had been doing for years; now, though he was much heavier, harder to drag out of the water than ever before. When I dove after him I felt so happy, I never wanted it to end.

I knew it would, though. I felt the nights growing longer, and that meant we'd soon be going home.

I was lying under the table one evening while Mom and Grandma talked. Ethan had gone on a car ride with Hannah and had not taken me, so I assumed they had to do something that wasn't very fun.

"I want to talk to you about something," Grandma told Mom.

"Mother," Mom said.

"No, just listen. That boy has completely changed since coming here. He's happy, he's healthy, he's got a girl . . . why take him back to the city? He can finish high school right here."

"You make it sound like we live in the ghetto," Mom complained with a laugh.

"You're not answering me because . . . well, we both know why. I know your husband will be against it. But Gary is traveling almost one hundred percent, now, and you said your hours at the school are killing you. The boy needs a family around him while he rebuilds."

"Yes, Gary's traveling, but he still wants to see Ethan when he's home. And I can't just quit my job."

"I'm not telling you to. You know you are welcome to come up any time you want, and why can't Gary fly into our little airport here on a given weekend? Or, and please know that I only want the best for you, wouldn't it be good for the two of you to be alone right now? If you and Gary are going to fix the problems between you, you need to do it somewhere other than in front of Ethan."

I pricked up my ears a little at the boy's name. Was he home? I cocked my head but didn't hear his car.

When the nights turned cool and the baby ducks were all as big as their mother, Mom packed the car. I paced nervously, afraid I'd be left behind, and when the moment was right I jumped neatly into the backseat. For some reason, everyone laughed. I sat in the car and watched as Mom hugged Grandma and Grandpa and then, curiously, Ethan, who then came over and opened the car door. "Bailey? Do you want to go with Mom, or stay here with me?"

There was nothing in the question that I understood, so I just looked at him.

"Come on, doodle dog. Bailey! Come!"

I reluctantly jumped out into the driveway. No car ride?

Mom drove off in the car, with Ethan and Grandma and Grandpa waving. Though it made no sense, the boy and I were staying on the Farm!

That suited me just fine. Almost every day started with a long car ride in the dark, driving from house to house to drop off papers. By the time we got home, Grandma would be cooking breakfast, and Grandpa always slipped me something under the table—bacon, ham, a piece of toast. I learned to chew silently so that Grandma wouldn't say, "Are you feeding the dog again?" The tone in her voice when I picked up the word "dog" suggested to me that Grandpa and I needed to keep the whole operation quiet.

The word "school" was back in play, but there was no bus, just Ethan driving off—though sometimes the girl came over and they took a car ride in her car. I understood that there was no reason for alarm, that Ethan would be back by the end of the day and Hannah would eat dinner with us as often as not.

Mom came to visit a lot, and Mom and Dad were there during Merry Christmas. Mom's hands smelled like Felix the kitty when she reached down to pet me, but I didn't mind.

I thought the boy and I had decided to stay at the Farm forever, but toward the end of that summer I sensed we were headed for yet another change. The boy started putting things in boxes, a sure signal that we were soon going to be on our way home. Hannah was around nearly all the time, and she felt a little sad and fearful. When she hugged the boy, there was so much love between them I couldn't help but try to squirm in between their bodies, which always made them laugh.

One morning, I knew it was time. Grandpa loaded the boxes into the car, Grandma and Mom talked, and Ethan and Hannah hugged. I paced, looking for an opening, but Grandpa had gotten pretty good at blocking me and I hadn't yet managed to get inside the car.

The boy came over to me and knelt beside me. I could feel

some sadness coming from him. "You be a good dog, Bailey," he said.

I wagged to show him that I understood that I was a good dog and that it was time to go on the big car ride home.

"I'll be home at Thanksgiving break, okay? I'm going to miss you, doodle dog." He gave me a big, loving hug. I half-closed my eyes—there simply was no better feeling in the world than to be hugged by my boy.

"You'd better hold him; he's not going to understand," Ethan said. The girl stepped forward and grabbed my collar. The sadness was coming off of her in waves, and she was crying. I was torn between wanting to comfort her and needing to get in the car. Reluctantly I sat at her feet, waiting for this strange drama to end so I could sit in the seat with my nose out the car window.

"Write me every day!" Hannah said.

"I will!" Ethan called back.

I stared in disbelief as he and Mom got into the car and slammed the doors. I pulled away from Hannah, who didn't understand that I was supposed to go with them! She held tight. "No, Bailey, it's okay. You Stay."

Stay? *Stay?* The car honked and drove off down the driveway. Grandpa and Grandma were waving—couldn't anybody see that I was still here?

"He'll do just fine. Ferris is a good school," Grandpa said. "Big Rapids is a nice town."

They all turned from the driveway, Hannah loosening her grip just enough for me to break free.

"Bailey!" she shouted.

Though the car was out of sight, the dust trail was still in the air, easy to follow as I chased after my boy.

SEVENTEEN

Cars are fast.

I never really knew this. Back home, before Marsh-mallow went away, she used to run down into the street, barking at cars, and they usually stopped, or at least slowed down enough that she could catch them, though all she ever did at that point was veer off and pretend she never wanted to attack them in the first place.

As I ran after the boy's car, I had the sense that it was pulling farther and farther away from me. The scent of dust and exhaust grew thin and tenuous, but I picked up a clear sign of a right turn where the road became pavement, though after that I wasn't sure I could smell him at all. But I couldn't give up; I turned myself over to the mindless panic and continued my pursuit.

Ahead of me I heard the loud rumble of a train, clanking and shaking, and when I topped a rise and saw it I finally caught a whiff of the boy. His car, windows down, was parked on the road at the train crossing.

I was exhausted. I had never run so far or so fast in my life, but I ran harder still when the side door opened and the boy stood up.

"Oh, Bailey," he said.

While every part of me wanted to tackle him and be loved, I wasn't going to miss my chance, and I veered from him at the last second and bounded into the car.

"Bailey!" Mom laughed.

I licked them both, forgiving them for forgetting me. After the train passed, Mom started the car and turned it around, then stopped because Grandpa showed up in his truck—maybe he was coming home with us this time!

"Like a rocket," Grandpa said. "Hard to believe he got this far."

"How long would you have gone, huh, Bailey? You doodle dog," Ethan told me affectionately.

It was with great suspicion that I jumped into Grandpa's truck, though—suspicion that proved justified, because while Ethan and Mom drove on, Grandpa turned around and took me back to the Farm.

Mostly I liked Grandpa. From time to time he'd do "chores," which meant we'd go into the new barn, toward the back, where soft hay was piled, and take a nap. During cold days Grandpa had a couple of heavy blankets he'd wrap around us. But the first few days after the boy left, I sulked in Grandpa's presence, punishing him for bringing me back to the Farm. When that didn't work, all I could think to do was chew up a pair of Grandma's shoes, but that still didn't bring the boy back.

I just couldn't get past the utter betrayal of it all. I knew that out there somewhere, probably back home, the boy needed me, didn't understand where I was.

Everyone was infuriatingly calm, seemingly oblivious to the catastrophic change that had struck the household. I became so frantic I even dug into the boy's closet and brought out the flip, running down and tossing it into Grandma's lap.

"What in the world is this?" she exclaimed.

"It's Ethan's big invention," Grandpa said.

I barked. *Yes! Ethan!*

"You want to go outside and play, Bailey?" Grandma asked me. "Why don't you take him for a walk."

Walk? Walk to see the boy?

"I thought I'd watch a little of the game here," Grandpa replied.

"For heaven's sake," Grandma said. She went to the door and tossed the flip out in the yard, barely sending the thing five yards. I bounded over, grabbed it, and then stared in absolute noncomprehension when she shut the door, leaving me outside.

Well, okay then. I spat out the flip and trotted past Flare, heading down the driveway. I went over to the girl's house, which I had already done several times since Ethan left. I could smell her scent everywhere, but the boy's scent was gradually fading away. A car pulled into her driveway and Hannah jumped out. "Bye!" she said. She turned and looked at me. "Well, hi, Bailey!"

I ran up to her, wagging. I could smell several other people's scents in her clothes, but there was no sign of Ethan. Hannah did go for a walk with me back home, and when she knocked on the door Grandma let her in and fed some pie to her but not to me.

I often dreamed of the boy. I dreamed of him jumping into the pond, with me swimming down and down to play rescue.

I dreamed of him doing the go-kart, how happy and excited he was. And sometimes I dreamed of him jumping out of the window, the sharp crack of pain rising in a shout from his lips as he fell in the flaming bushes. I hated those dreams, and I was just awakening from one of them one night when I saw the boy standing above me.

"Hi, Bailey!" he whispered, his scent flowing off of him. He was back on the Farm! I jumped to my feet, putting my paws on his chest to lick his face. "Shhh," he told me. "It's late; I just got here. Everybody's sleeping."

It was Happy Thanksgiving time, and life was back to normal. Mom was there, but not Dad. Hannah came over every day.

The boy seemed happy, but I could also feel that he was distracted. He spent a lot of time looking at papers instead of playing with me, even when I brought him the stupid flip to try to shake him out of it.

I wasn't surprised when he left again. This was my new life, I realized. I lived on the Farm with Grandpa and Grandma, and Ethan only came home for visits. It wasn't what I wanted, but as long as the boy always returned, I had an easier time seeing him leave.

It was on one of his visits, when the air was warm and leaves were freshly out, that Ethan and I went to see Hannah running around in a big yard. I could smell her, as well as other boys and girls, because the wind flowed off the yard and their bodies were sweating as they ran. It looked like fun, but I stayed by Ethan's side, because it seemed that while we stood there the ache in his leg became more pronounced, spreading through his body. Odd, dark emotions swirled inside him as he watched her and the others run.

"Hey!" Hannah came over to see us. I licked her leg, which was salty with sweat. "What a nice surprise. Hi, Bailey!" she said.

"Hi."

"My times are really coming down in the four hundred," the girl said.

"Who was that guy?" Ethan asked.

"Oh. Who? What do you mean?"

"That guy you were talking to and hugging, you two seemed really friendly," Ethan said. His voice sounded strained. I glanced around but couldn't see any danger.

"He's just a friend, Ethan," the girl said sharply. The way she spoke his name, it sounded like the boy had been bad.

"Is it that guy, what's his name, Brett? He's certainly fast on his feet." Ethan stabbed at the ground with his cane, and I sniffed at the tuft of earth that he overturned.

"Well, what is that supposed to mean?" Hannah asked, her hands on her hips.

"Go on back; your track coach is looking over here," Ethan said.

Hannah looked over her shoulder, then back at Ethan. "I do, I do need to get back . . . ," she said uncertainly.

"Fine," Ethan said. He turned and limped away.

"Ethan!" Hannah called. I looked at her, but the boy just kept walking. The dark, confused mixture of sadness and anger was still there. Something about the place apparently made Ethan feel bad, because we never went back.

That summer brought some big changes. Mom came to the Farm, and this time a truck followed her up the driveway and men unloaded some boxes and carried them up to her bedroom. Grandma and Mom spent a lot of time talking quietly to each other, and sometimes Mom would cry, which made Grandpa uncomfortable, so he'd go out to do chores.

Ethan had to leave all the time to go to "work," which was just like school in that I couldn't go with him, but when he came home he smelled deliciously of meats and grease. It reminded me of the time, after Flare abandoned us in the woods, that Grandpa fed me food out of a bag in the front seat of the truck.

The biggest change in our lives, though, was that the girl no longer came around to see us. Sometimes the boy would take me for a car ride and as we passed her house I would smell Hannah, so I knew she was still around, but the boy never stopped or turned in her driveway. I found that I missed her; she loved me and smelled wonderful.

The boy missed her, too. When we drove past Hannah's house, he always stared out the side window, always slowed down a little, and I could feel his yearning. I didn't understand why we couldn't just drive up to her house and see if she had any biscuits, but we never did.

That summer Mom went down to the pond and sat on the dock and was very sad. I tried to make her feel better by barking at the ducks, but she could not be cheered up. Finally she pulled something off her finger, it wasn't food and was made of metal, a small round thing that she threw into the water, where it slipped beneath the surface with a tiny plop.

I wondered if she wanted me to go after it, and gazed up at her, ready to give it a shot even though I knew it was hopeless, but she just told me to come, and the two of us went back to the house.

After that summer, life settled into a comfortable pattern. Mom started doing work, too, and came home smelling of fragrant and sweet oils. Sometimes I would go with her past the goat ranch and over the rumbling bridge and we would spend the day in a big room full of clothes and stinky wax candles and uninteresting metal objects and people would come in to see me and sometimes they would leave with items in bags. The boy came and went for Happy Thanksgiving and Merry Christmas and Spring Break and Summer Vacation.

I pretty much had gotten over my resentment toward Flare, who didn't do anything anymore but stand and stare into the wind all day, when Grandpa showed up with a creature who moved like a baby horse and smelled unlike anything I'd ever encountered before. His name was Jasper the donkey. Grandpa liked to laugh as he watched Jasper skip around in the yard, and Grandma would say, "I don't know why you think we need a donkey," and go back inside.

Jasper was not at all afraid of me despite my position as top predator on the Farm. I played with him a little, but it seemed as if I was so easily tired all the time, it just wasn't worth investing myself in a creature who didn't know how to pick up a ball.

One day a man named Rick came to dinner. The feeling from Mom was happy and embarrassed, and from Grandpa it was suspicious, and from Grandma it was ecstatic. Rick and Mom sat on the porch just like Hannah and Ethan used to do, but they didn't wrestle. After that, though, I started seeing more and more of Rick, who was a big man with hands that smelled of wood. He would throw the ball for me more than anybody, so I liked him a lot, though not as much as the boy.

My favorite time of day was when Grandpa did chores. Sometimes when he didn't do chores I would go and take a nap in the barn just the same. I was taking a lot of naps and no longer had any interest in going out on long adventures. When Mom and Rick took me for a walk, I was always exhausted when we got back.

About the only thing that could make me excited was when the boy would come to the Farm for a visit. I'd still dance and wiggle and whimper, and I would play at the pond or walk in the woods or do anything else he wanted, even chase the flip, though the boy thankfully seemed to have forgotten where it was. Sometimes we went to town to the dog park, and while I was always glad to see the other dogs, I thought the younger ones were juvenile with their relentless playing and wrestling.

Then one evening the oddest thing happened: Grandpa set dinner down before me, and I didn't feel like eating. My mouth filled with drool, and I drank some water and went back to lie down. Soon a thick, heavy pain came through my body, leaving me panting for breath.

I lay there all night on the floor by my food bowl. The next morning, Grandma saw me and called to Grandpa. "There's something wrong with Bailey!" she said. I could hear the alarm in her voice when she said my name, and wagged my tail so she'd know I was okay.

Grandpa came and touched me. "You okay, Bailey? What's wrong?"

After some conversation, Mom and Grandpa carried me to the truck and we went to the clean, cool room with a nice man, the same nice man we'd been visiting more and more often in recent years. He felt me all over and I wagged a little, but I didn't feel very well, and didn't try to sit up.

Mom came in, and she was crying, and Grandma and Grandpa were there, and even Rick came. I tried to let them know I appreciated all of their attention, but the pain was worse, and it was all I could do to roll my eyes to look at them.

Then the nice man brought out a needle. I smelled a sharp

and familiar smell and felt a tiny jab. After a few minutes, my pain felt a lot better, but now I was so sleepy, I just wanted to lie there and do chores. My last thoughts, as I drifted off, were, as always, of the boy.

When I woke up, I knew I was dying. There was a sense within me of a rising darkness, and I had faced this before, when I was named Toby and was in a small, hot room with Spike and some other barking dogs.

I hadn't given it any thought at all, though I suppose deep down I knew that one day I would wind up like Smokey the cat. I remembered the boy crying the day they buried Smokey in the yard, and I hoped he wouldn't cry over my death. My purpose, my whole life, had been to love him and be with him, to make him happy. I didn't want to cause him any unhappiness now—in that way, I decided it was probably better than he wasn't here to see this, though I missed him so much at that moment the ache of it was as bad as the strange pains in my belly.

The nice man came into the room. "You awake, Bailey? You awake, fella? Poor fella."

My name, I wanted to say, *is not Fella.*

The nice man leaned over me. "You can let go, Bailey. You did a good job; you took care of the boy. That was your job, Bailey, and you did a good job; you are a good dog, a good dog."

I had the sense that the nice man was talking about death; there was a feeling of kind finality and peace emanating from him. Then Mom and Grandma and Grandpa and Rick all came in, and they hugged me and said they loved me and told me I was a good dog.

Yet from Mom I felt a tension, a sure sense of something— not danger, exactly, but something I needed to protect her from.

I gave her hand a feeble lick and, as the darkness came from within me, I pushed back against it. I had to stay alert; Mom needed me.

The tension seemed to rise after another hour went by, first Grandpa joining in Mom's mood, then Grandma, and then even Rick, so that just as I felt myself flagging, a new resolve to protect my family from this unknown threat would renew my strength.

And then I heard the boy. "Bailey!" he shouted. He burst into the room and the tension left everyone at once—this, I realized, was what they had been waiting for. Somehow, they'd known the boy was coming.

The boy buried his face in my neck and sobbed. It took everything I had to lift my head up and lick him, to let him know it was all right. I wasn't afraid.

My breathing turned raspy, and everyone remained with me, holding me. It felt wonderful to receive so much attention, but then a shudder of pain shot through my stomach so sharp I couldn't help but cry out loud. The nice man came in then, and he had another needle.

"We need to do this now; Bailey shouldn't have to suffer."

"Okay," the boy said, crying. I tried to wag my tail at the sound of my name, but I found I couldn't manage even a twitch. There was another jab in my neck.

"Bailey, Bailey, Bailey, I'm going to miss you, doodle dog," Ethan whispered in my ear. His breath was warm and delightful. I closed my eyes at the pleasure of it, the sheer pleasure of love from the boy, love by the boy.

And then, just like that, the pain was gone—in fact, I felt like a puppy again, full of life and joy. I remembered feeling like this the first time I ever saw the boy, coming out of his house and running to me with his arms open wide. That made me think of diving after the boy during rescue, the fading light as I dove deeper, the way the thick water pushed against my body, just like now. I could no longer feel the boy's hands touching me; I could just feel the water on all sides: warm and gentle and dark.

EIGHTEEN

Awareness came long after I'd come to recognize my mother's smell and learned how to fight my way to her teat for nourishment. My eyes were open and my vision was starting to sharpen well enough for me to see my mother's dark brown face the day I understood, with a jolt, that I was a puppy again.

No, that wasn't quite it. It was more that I was a puppy who suddenly remembered being *me* again. I had this sense of drifting in my sleep, aware of nothing but the long, long passage of time, not dreaming, not even thinking, and then, in a blink, I was looking at the world through the eyes of a very young dog. Yet somehow I remembered being this same puppy since birth, scrambling for my mother's milk without any awareness of my previous lives.

Now that I remembered everything that had come before, I was truly puzzled. I'd felt so complete, there just didn't seem to be any reason for me to go on—how could I possibly have a more important mission than loving the boy?

I missed Ethan so much I sometimes whimpered, which my new siblings always mistook for a weakness and jumped on me with the intent to dominate. There were seven of them, all dark brown with black markings, and I was impatient with the idea that they didn't recognize who was going to be in charge, here.

A woman took care of us most of the time, though there was a man who often came down into the basement to feed us and it was he who carried us in a box to the backyard when we were a few weeks old. A male dog in a cage sniffed at us when we all ran over to see him, and I understood instinctively that this was our father. I'd never met a father before, and was curious as to what he was doing there.

"He seems fine with them," the man said to the woman.

"You going to be okay, Bernie? You want to come out?" The woman opened Father's cage—his name was obviously Bernie—and the male dog bounded out, sniffed at us, and then went over to pee on the fence.

We all galloped after him, falling on our faces because our puppy legs could barely move. Bernie put his face down and one of my brothers jumped up and disrespectfully bit at his ears, but Bernie didn't seem to mind. He even played with us a little, knocking us around before trotting over to the back door to be let in.

A few weeks later I was in the yard, showing one of my brothers who was boss, when I stopped and squatted and all at once realized I was a female! I sniffed in amazement at my urine, snarling a warning when my brother took the opportunity to barrel into me. What would Ethan think?

How could I, Bailey, be a girl dog?

Except I wasn't Bailey. One day a man came and played with us in an unusual fashion. He clapped his hands, and the puppies who didn't cower from the noise (I was one of these) he put into a box. Then one at a time he took those of us in the box out into the yard—when it was my turn, he turned and walked away from me as if he had forgotten I was there, so I followed. He told me I was a good dog just for doing that—this guy was a pushover. He was about the age that Mom had been the day she broke the car window and gave me some water, the first day I ever saw the boy.

The man put me inside a T-shirt and then spoke to me, calling me. "Hey, girl, can you find your way out?" I figured he'd changed his mind about wanting me bagged up inside the shirt, so I jumped out and ran over to him again for more praise.

The woman had come out into the yard to watch.

"Most of them take a minute to figure it out, but this one's pretty bright," the man remarked. He flipped me over on my back, and I squirmed with it, playing, thinking to myself that it was unfair since he was so much bigger than I was.

"She doesn't like that, Jakob," the woman observed.

"None of them like it. The question is will she stop struggling and let me be the boss, or will she keep fighting? I got to have a dog that knows I'm the boss," the man said.

I heard the word "dog," and it didn't sound angry—I wasn't being punished, but I *was* being pinned down. I figured I didn't know what sort of game we were playing now, so I just relaxed without struggle.

"Good girl!" he said again.

Then he took a ball of paper and showed it to me, waving it around until I became absolutely tantalized. I felt stupid and uncoordinated, trying to get a bite of the thing with my little puppy mouth when it was right there in front of me, but I couldn't move my head fast enough. Then he tossed it a few feet away, so I ran over and pounced on it. Aha! Try to get it now!

Then I remembered Ethan and the stupid flip, how happy it made him when I brought the thing back to him. I turned around and trotted back to the man, dropping the ball at his feet and sitting for him to throw it again.

"This one," the man said to the woman. "I'll take this one."

I whimpered when I saw the kind of car ride I was going to be taking—in the back of a truck, locked in a cage very similar to the one that had taken me to the hot noisy room with Spike. I was a front-seat dog; anyone could tell that!

My new home reminded me of the apartment where we went to live after the fire. It was small, with a balcony over a parking lot, but it was down the street from a nice park where the man took me several times a day.

I knew I was far away from Ethan by the smell of the trees and bushes—this wasn't a wet place like the Farm, with frequent rain, though it was lush with flowers and shrubbery. The air was tinged with a strong smell of automobiles, which I could hear driving in the near and far distance every single hour of the day. Somedays a hot, dry wind blew in, reminding me of the Yard, but other days the air was thick with moisture, which never happened when I was Toby.

The man's name was Jakob, and he named me Elleya. "It's Swedish for 'moose.' You're not a German shepherd; you're a Swedish shepherd, now." I wagged in noncomprehension. "Elleya. Elleya. Come, Ellie, come."

His hands smelled of oil and his car and of papers and people.

Jakob wore dark clothes and wore metal objects on his belt, including a gun, so I figured he was a policeman. When he was gone during the day a nice woman named Georgia came over every few hours to play with me and take me for a walk—she reminded me of Chelsea, who had lived down the street from Ethan and me and had a dog named Marshmallow and then later Duchess. Georgia had all sorts of names for me, some of them really silly, like Ellie-wellie Cuddle-Coo. It was sort of like being called a doodle dog—it was my name, but different, delivered with an extra dose of affection.

I was doing my best to adjust to this new life as Ellie, so different from my life as Bailey. Jakob gave me a dog bed very similar to the one I'd been given in the garage, but this time I was expected to sleep in it—Jakob pushed me away when I tried to crawl under the covers with him, even though I could see he had plenty of room.

I understood that what was expected of me was to live with the new rules, the way I'd learned to live with Ethan going to do college. The sharp pain I felt when I thought about how much I missed the boy was just something to get used to: a dog's job was to do what people wanted.

There was, though, a difference between obeying commands and having a purpose, a reason for being. I thought my purpose was to be with Ethan and that I'd fulfilled that purpose, being by his side as he grew up. If that was the case, why was I now Ellie? Could a dog have more than one purpose?

Jakob treated me with a calm patience—when my little bladder suddenly signaled and let go all in the same rush, he never yelled and ran me out the door like the boy used to; he just gave me such praise for when I went outside that I resolved to get my body under control as soon as I could manage. But Jakob didn't gush affection the way the boy did. Jakob focused on me in the businesslike fashion Ethan focused on Flare, the horse, and to an extent I liked the sense of direction it gave me—though there were other times I pined for the feel of the boy's hands on my fur and couldn't wait for Georgia to come over and call me Ellie-wellie Cuddle-Coo.

There was, I came to feel, something broken inside Jakob. I didn't know what it was, but I could sense something drawing energy from his emotions, a dark bitterness that seemed to me very similar to what I felt inside Ethan when he first came home after the fire. Whatever it was, it kept Jakob's feelings toward me in check—whenever he and I did something together, I could feel him evaluating me with cool eyes.

"Let's go to work," Jakob would say, and he would load me in the truck and off we'd go to a park for games. I learned "Drop," which meant to lie down, and I learned that to Jakob "Stay" really meant "stay" and I was expected to remain in the same spot until he told me, "Come."

The training helped me keep my mind off Ethan. At night, though, I often fell asleep thinking of the boy. I thought of his hands in my fur, the smell of him as he slept, his laugh and his voice. Wherever he was, whatever he was doing, I hoped he was happy. I knew I would never see him again.

Georgia started coming over less often as I got older, but I found that I didn't miss her, as I became more and more immersed in our work. One day we went to some woods and met a man named Wally, who petted me and then ran away. "What's he doing, Ellie? Where's he going?" Jakob asked me. I watched Wally, who was looking over his shoulder at me, waving excitedly.

"Find him! Find!" Jakob told me.

Uncertainly I started trotting off after Wally. What was this? Wally saw me coming after him and dropped to his knees, clapping, and when I caught up to him he showed me a stick and we played with it for a few minutes. Then Wally stood up. "Look, Ellie! What's he doing? Find him!" Wally said.

Jakob was strolling off, and I ran after him. "Good dog!" Jakob praised.

As intelligent games go, I'd probably put it right up there with chasing the flip, but Wally and Jakob seemed to enjoy it, so I went along with it, especially since afterward we got to play Tug-On-a-Stick, which in my mind beat Find Wally hands down.

It was around the time I started learning Find that a strange sensation gripped me, a restless anxiousness accompanied by an embarrassing odor from my rear end. Mom and Grandma used to complain any time I released fragrant gasses from under my tail, so when I started discharging this smell I knew I was a bad dog. (Grandpa was so offended by bad odors that he'd say, "Oh, Bailey!" even when the smell came from him.)

Jakob didn't notice the odor, but he did register alarm at all the dogs lifting their legs on the bushes around the apartment, dogs I knew instinctively were milling around because of me.

Jakob's reaction was most curious: he put me into a pair of shorts like the ones he wore under his pants, my tail sticking out of a hole in the back. I'd always felt sorry for dogs who wore sweaters and other clothes, and here I was, playing dress up in front of all those male dogs. It was more than a little embarrassing, especially given that there was something compelling about the attention I was being shown by the motley pack of males who were so busy wetting the shrubbery outside my home.

Jakob said, "Time to see the vet," and took me for a car ride to a place that was very familiar, a cool room with bright lights and a metal table. I feel asleep and, predictably, was wearing a stupid cone-shaped collar when I awoke back home.

As soon as the cone came off, Jakob and I were back at the park almost every day for the next several months. The days grew shorter, though it never got cold or came close to snowing, and finding Wally became harder and harder because they kept changing the rules on me. Sometimes Wally wouldn't even be there when we arrived and I'd have to go find him where he'd wandered off to. He'd be lying around like Grandpa doing chores, and I learned another command, "Show Me!" which meant leading Jakob back to where I'd come across Wally's lazy body sprawled under a tree. Somehow, Jakob could tell when I had Found something, even when it was just one of Wally's socks left on the ground—the man was a disaster, always dropping his clothing for us to Find and pick up. Jakob would read my look when I came running back to him. "Show me!" he'd say, but only when I had something to Show.

We did other work, too. Jakob taught me how to climb up a slide and to ease myself down the ladder on the other side, making me do it a step at a time instead of just jumping from the top as I preferred. He taught me to crawl into tight tubes and to leap up on a stack of logs, and one day he had me sit while he removed the gun from his side and shot off some explosions that made me flinch the first couple of times.

"Good girl, Ellie. This is a gun. See? No reason to be afraid. It makes a loud noise, but you're not afraid, are you, girl?"

I sniffed at it when he held it out to me and was very glad when he didn't try to make me fetch it. The thing smelled bad and looked like it would fly worse than the flip.

Sometimes Jakob would sit at an outside table with other

people with guns and drink from bottles. It was at times like these that his internal turmoil was most evident to me: the people at the table would laugh, and sometimes Jakob would join in, and other times he'd turn inward, dark and sad and alone.

"Isn't that right, Jakob," one of the men said one time. I heard the name, but Jakob was staring off into space, not paying attention. I sat up and nuzzled his hand, but when he petted me I sensed he didn't really register that I was there.

"I said isn't that right, Jakob."

Jakob turned and looked at everyone watching him, and I sensed he felt embarrassed. "What?"

"If Y2K is as bad as they say it's going to be, we're going to need every K-9 unit we can get. Be like Rodney King all over again."

"Ellie's not that kind of dog," Jakob said coldly. I straightened at the sound of my name, conscious as I did so that all the men at the table were looking at me. I felt uneasy for some reason, just as some of the men seemed uncomfortable with Jakob's stare. When they started talking again, it was to each other, ignoring Jakob. I nuzzled his hand once more, and this time he responded by scratching my ears.

"Good dog, Ellie," he said.

Find Wally evolved into just Find. Jakob and I would go somewhere and sometimes I'd be given something to sniff, an old coat or a shoe or a glove, and I'd have to Find the person who belonged to the item. Other times there'd be nothing to sniff and I'd course back and forth over a huge area, alerting any time I picked up the scent of something interesting. I Found a lot of people who weren't Wally, and sometimes they were obviously not informed of the game and would call, "Here, boy!" or otherwise react to me when they saw me. I'd always Show Jakob these people, and he always praised me, even if the people I'd

Found weren't bright enough to know what was going on. The point, I realized, was to Find people and to take Jakob to them and let Jakob decide if they were the right people or not. That was my job.

I had been with Jakob for about a year when he started taking me to his work every day. A lot of people dressed like Jakob milled around and were mostly friendly to me, though they drew back respectfully when Jakob told me to heel. He took me to a kennel in back with two other dogs, Cammie and Gypsy. Cammie was jet-black, and Gypsy was brown.

Despite the fact that we were all caged together, my relationship with Cammie and Gypsy was different than I'd ever had with other canines. We were working dogs and didn't feel free to play much because we always needed to be ready to serve our masters—most of the time we just alertly sat at the fence.

Gypsy worked with a policeman named Paul and was gone a lot, and sometimes I watched Paul and Gypsy work in the yard. They did it all wrong: Gypsy would just smell in between boxes and piles of clothing and would alert for no reason, though Paul always praised her anyway, pulling out a package from the items and telling Gypsy she was a good dog.

Cammie was older and didn't bother to watch Gypsy, probably feeling embarrassed for the poor dog. Cammie worked with a policewoman named Amy and didn't go out much. When he did, though, he went out fast—Amy would come get him and they'd leave at a run. I never knew what Cammie's work was, but I suspected it wasn't as important as Find.

"Where you working this week?" Amy asked Paul once.

"Back out at the airport until Garcia comes off sick leave," Paul told her. "How's life on the bomb squad?"

"Quiet. I'm worried about Cammie, though. His scores have been a little off; I'm wondering if his nose is going."

At the sound of his name Cammie raised his head, and I looked over at him.

"He's what, ten years old, now?" Paul asked.

"About that," Amy said.

I stood up and shook myself off because I could sense Jakob coming, and a few seconds later he walked around the corner. He and his friends stood and talked while we dogs watched them, wondering why they didn't let us out in the yard to be with them.

Suddenly I felt some excitement off Jakob. He spoke to his shoulder. "10-4, unit Eight-Kilo-Six responding," he said while Amy ran over to the gate. Cammie jumped up. "Ellie!" Amy commanded. "Come!"

We were out of the yard and I was up in the truck in just moments. I found myself panting, picking up on Jakob's excitement.

Something told me that whatever was happening, it was far more important than Find Wally.

NINETEEN

Jakob drove us to a large flat building, where several people were gathered in a circle. I could feel the tension in them as we pulled up. Jakob came around and petted me but left me in the truck. "Good dog, Ellie," he said absently.

I sat and watched him anxiously as he approached the group of people. Several of them spoke at once.

"We didn't notice her missing until lunch, but we don't have any idea how long she's been gone."

"Marilyn's an Alzheimer's patient."

"I don't understand how she got away with no one seeing."

While I sat there, a squirrel climbed down the trunk of a tree and busied itself foraging for food in the grass. I stared at it, astounded at its audacious disregard for the fact that I, a vicious predator, was a mere ten feet away!

Jakob came to the cage and opened the door. "Heel!" he com-manded, giving me no chance to catch the squirrel. I snapped to it: time to work. Jakob led me away from the people, to a corner of the front yard of the building. He held out two shirts that smelled reminiscent of Grandma, a little. I stuck my nose into the soft cloth, inhaling deeply. "Ellie. Find!"

I took off, running past the knot of people. "She wouldn't have gone that way," someone said.

"Let Ellie work," Jakob replied.

Work. I carried the sense memory of the clothing in my mind as I held my nose up to the air, coursing back and forth as I'd been trained. There were a lot of people smells, dog smells, car smells, but I couldn't Find. Frustrated, I turned back to Jakob.

He read my disappointment. "That's okay, Ellie. Find." He began walking down the street, and I leaped ahead, cruising up and down the yards. I turned the corner and slowed down: there it was, tantalizing, coming to me. . . . I zeroed in on it and raced ahead. Forty feet in front of me, lying at the base of some bushes, her scent was clear. I turned and ran back to Jakob, who had been joined by several police officers.

"Show me, Ellie!"

I took him back to the bushes. He bent, poking at something with a stick.

"What is it?" one of the officers asked, coming up behind Jakob.

"A tissue. Good dog, Ellie, good dog!" He grabbed me and wrestled with me briefly, but I sensed there was more work.

"How do we know that's hers? It could have been dropped by anybody," one of the policemen objected.

Jakob bent down, ignoring the men behind him. "Okay, Ellie. Find!"

I could follow her scent, now, faint but traceable. It went ahead two blocks, then turned right, getting stronger. At a driveway it made an abrupt right, and I tracked her through an open gate, to where she was sitting on a swing set, moving gently. There was a real sense of happiness flowing from her, and she seemed glad to see me.

"Hello, doggy," she said.

I ran back to Jakob, and I could tell from his excitement that he knew I'd found her before I got up to him, though he waited for me to reach him before he reacted. "Okay, Show me!" he urged.

I took him to the lady on the swing set. I felt Jakob's relief when he saw the woman. "Are you Marilyn?" he asked gently.

She cocked her head at him. "Are you Warner?" she replied.

Jakob spoke into the microphone on his shoulder, and soon we were joined by the other policemen. Jakob took me aside. "Good dog, Ellie!" He pulled out a rubber ring and sent it bouncing across the lawn, and I jumped on it and brought it back, holding it out for him to grip and tug on. We played for about five minutes, my tail whipping the air.

As Jakob shut me in the cage on the back of the truck, I could feel the pride coming off of him. "Good dog, Ellie. You are such a good dog."

It was, I reflected, as close as Jakob could come to the unrestrained adoration I once felt from Ethan, and from it I realized that today I truly understood my purpose as Ellie: not just to Find people but to save them. The worry that poured off the knot of people in front of the building could not have been more clear, just as their relief when we returned was clear. The lady had been in some sort of danger, and by Finding her Jakob and I saved her from the danger. That is what we did together, that was our work, and that's what he cared most about. It was like the game I played with Ethan: Rescue.

The next day Jakob took me to a store and purchased some fragrant flowers, which he left in the truck while we did some work. (Wally was hiding on top of a strong-smelling trash Dumpster, but he couldn't fool me.) Then Jakob and I went for a long car ride—so long that I became tired of holding my nose up to the side of the cage and lay down on the floor.

When Jakob came to let me out, there was a heaviness in him—whatever was always hurting him inside seemed stronger than ever. We were in a big yard filled with stones. Subdued, not sure what we were doing, I stayed next to Jakob as he walked a few dozen yards, carrying his flowers. He knelt and put the flowers down next to one of the stones, the pain twisting in him so deeply that tears fell silently down his cheeks. I nuzzled his hand, concerned.

"It's okay, Ellie. Good dog. Sit."

I sat, grieving with Jakob.

He cleared his throat. "I miss you so much, honey. I just . . . sometimes I don't think I can get through the day, knowing you're not going to be there when I get home," he whispered hoarsely.

I lifted my ears at the word "home." *Yes,* I thought, *let's go home, let's leave this sad place.*

"I'm on K-9 patrol right now, search and rescue. They don't want me on regular patrol because I'm still taking antidepressants. I've got a dog, her name is Ellie, a one-year-old German shepherd."

I wagged my tail.

"We just got certified, so we'll be going out, now. I'll be glad to get off the desk; I've gained about ten pounds from all the sitting." Jakob laughed and the sound of it was so peculiar, such a sad, tortured laugh, with no happiness in it at all.

We remained there, nearly motionless, for about ten minutes, and gradually the feeling from Jakob shifted, became less raw pain and more like what I felt when Ethan and Hannah would say good-bye at the end of the summer—something similar to fear. "I love you," Jakob whispered. Then he turned and walked away.

From that day forward, we spent a lot more time away from the kennel. Sometimes we would ride on airplanes or helicopters, both of which vibrated so much they made me sleepy despite the noise. "You're a chopper dog, Ellie!" Jakob told me whenever we rode on the helicopters. One day we even went to the biggest pond I'd ever seen, a huge expanse of water full of exotic smells, and I tracked a little girl down the sand to a playground full of children who all called to me when I approached.

"Want to play in the ocean, Ellie?" Jakob asked me after I Showed him the little girl, and a mother and father took her away for a car ride. We went to the pond and I splashed and ran in the water, which was very salty when the spray came up into my nose. "This is the ocean, Ellie, the ocean!" Jakob laughed. Playing in the ocean, I felt the thing that had such a tight clench on his heart loosen just a little.

Running through the shallow water reminded me of chasing Ethan on his sled—I had to lunge upward to make any progress, exactly the same gait I'd used in the snow. It made me realize that though the sun's cycles suggested a couple of years had passed, there was never any snow here. It didn't bother the children, though—they had sleds they rode on the waves. I stood and watched them play, knowing Jakob would not want me to chase them. One boy looked something like Ethan when he was younger, and I marveled that I could remember my boy when he was little and also when he was a man. An ache overtook me then, a sharp stab of sadness that didn't go away until Jakob whistled me back to his side.

When I did go to the kennel, Cammie was often there, but Gypsy almost never was. On one such day I was trying to interest Cammie in a glorious game of I've Got the Ball when Jakob came out to get me. "Ellie!" he called.

I'd never heard such urgency in his voice.

We drove very fast, the tires making screeches as we turned corners that I could hear above the wail of the siren. I lay down on the floor of my cage to keep from sliding around.

As usual, when we arrived at the place to work, there were a lot of people standing around. One of them, a woman, was so afraid she couldn't stand up, and two people were holding her. The anxiety rippling off Jakob as he ran past me to talk to these people was so strong it made the fur on my back stand up.

It was a parking lot, big glass doors on a building swinging open for people carrying small bags. The woman who had collapsed reached into her bag and pulled out a toy.

"We've got the mall locked down," someone said.

Jakob came to my door and opened it. He handed me a toy to sniff. "Ellie, okay? Got it? I need you to Find, Ellie!"

I leaped out of the truck and tried to sort through all the smells, to Find one that matched the toy. I was concentrating so hard I didn't notice that I'd trotted out in front of a moving car, which rocked when the driver hit the brakes.

Okay, I had it. There was a scent, a scent that was oddly married to another, a strong male smell. I tracked them both, sure of myself.

The smell vanished at a car—rather, next to the car, telling me that the people we were working had driven away in a different vehicle and this one had pulled in to take its place. I alerted Jakob, cringing at his sense of frustration and disappointment.

"Okay, good girl, Ellie. Good girl." His play was perfunctory, though, and I felt like a bad dog.

"We've tracked her to here—it looks like she got into a vehicle and left. Do we have surveillance on the parking lot?"

"We're checking now. If it is who we think it is, though, the car's stolen," a man wearing a suit told Jakob.

"Where would he take her? If it's him, where would he go?" Jakob asked.

The man in the suit turned his head, squinting at the green hills behind us. "The last two bodies we found were up in Topanga Canyon. The first one was in Will Rogers State Park."

"We'll head up that way," Jakob said. "See if we can pick up anything."

I was startled when Jakob put me in the front seat of the truck. He'd never let me be a front-seat dog before! His mood was still tense, though, so I stayed focused and didn't bark when we passed some dogs who yipped at me with unrestrained jealousy. Jakob and I drove out of the parking lot, and he held the same toy out to me, which I dutifully sniffed. "Okay, girl, I know this is going to sound strange, but I want you to Find."

At the command, I turned and stared at him in bewilderment. Find? In the truck?

The smells coming in the window lured my nose in that direction. "Good girl!" Jakob praised. "Find! Find the girl!"

My nose was still filled with the scent from the toy, which was why I alerted when a stray breeze brought me her smell, still entwined with the man's. "Good girl!" Jakob said. He stopped the car, watching me intently. Behind us, cars honked. "Got it, girl?"

I couldn't smell her anymore. "That's okay; that's okay, Ellie. Good girl," he said.

I understood, now—we were working from inside the truck. He drove and I kept my nose out the window, straining, rejecting everything except the smell from the toy.

I felt the tilt of the truck as we headed uphill, and with it a rising sense of disappointment from Jakob.

"I think we've lost her," he muttered. "Nothing, Ellie?"

At my name, I turned, then went back to my work.

"Unit Eight-Kilo-Six, what's your twenty?" the radio squawked.

"Eight-Kilo-Six, we are proceeding up Amalfi."

"Any luck?"

"We had something on Sunset. Nothing since."

"Roger that."

I barked.

I normally didn't bark when I caught a scent, but when this hit it was strong and steady, carried on a current of air that filled the cab of the truck. "Eight-Kilo-Six, we've got something, corner of Amalfi and Umeo." The truck slowed, and I stayed on point. I could still smell her, and the man's scent was strong as ever. Jakob eased to a stop. "Okay, which way here, Ellie?" Jakob asked.

I climbed across the seat, shoving my face out his window. "Left on Capri!" Jakob shouted excitedly. A few minutes later the truck started to bump. "We're on the fire road!"

"10-4, we're on our way," the radio said.

I was on alert, focused dead ahead, while Jakob wrestled with the truck to keep it on the narrow road. Suddenly we banged to a stop, facing a yellow gate. "Be advised, we need the fire department up here; there's a gate."

"10-4."

We jumped out of the car. A red car was parked off to the side, and I ran right to it, on alert. Jakob was holding his gun out. "We've got a red Toyota Camry, empty; Ellie says it belongs to our man." Jakob led me around to the back of the vehicle, watching me intently. "No indication anyone is in the trunk of the car," Jakob stated.

"Roger that."

The scent from the car wasn't as strong as what was coming from the air currents rising up from the canyon below. A steep road held the man's scent as it descended, while the girl's was more delicate. He'd carried her.

"Be advised, suspect took the road down to the camp. He's on foot."

"Eight-Kilo-Six, hold and wait for backup."

"Ellie," Jakob said to me, putting his gun back on his belt. "Let's go find the girl."

TWENTY

I felt strong fear from Jakob as we descended down into the canyon, so strong I kept returning to him for reassurance. Then the girl's scent pulled me forward and I galloped ahead, racing toward a collection of small buildings.

I spotted the little girl sitting quietly on some steps that led up to a big porch while a man pulled at the front door to the building with some sort of tool. She seemed sad and scared, but she perked up when she saw me approach, holding out a tiny little hand.

The man suddenly whirled, staring at me. My hackles rose when our eyes met—I felt the same dark sickness from him that I'd felt in Todd, only stronger, more vicious. He jerked his head up, looking over toward the road I'd come from.

I ran back to Jakob, the little girl calling, "Doggy!" as I peeled away.

"You got her," Jakob said. "Good girl, Ellie. Show me!"

I took him back to the building. The little girl was still sitting on the porch, but the man was nowhere to be seen.

"Eight-Kilo-Six, victim is secured and unharmed. Suspect fled on foot," Jakob said.

"Stick with the victim, Eight-Kilo-Six."

"Roger that."

I could hear in the distance the *wap-wap-wap* of a helicopter blade beating the air, and the sound of footsteps running down the road behind us. Two policemen came around the bend, sweating.

"How are you, Emily? Are you hurt?" one of them asked.

"No," said the little girl. She picked at a flower on her dress.

"My God, is she all right? Are you okay, little girl?" a third policeman asked breathlessly as he ran up, putting his hands on his knees. He was larger than the other men, both taller and built more heavily. I smelled ice cream on his breath.

"Her name is Emily."

"Can I pet the doggy?" the little girl asked shyly.

"Yes, sure. Then we've got to go back to work," Jakob said kindly.

I perked up my ears at the word "work."

"Okay, I'll . . . go with you," the large policeman said. "Johnson, you guys remain here with the girl. Watch that he doesn't circle back around."

"If he were close, Ellie would tell us," Jakob said. I looked at him. Were we ready to go to work?

"Find!" Jakob said.

The brush was thick in places, the soil underneath sandy and loose. I could easily track the man, though—he was headed steadily downhill. I found an iron rod coated with his scent and ran back to Jakob. "Show!" Jakob commanded.

When we returned to the tool, we had to wait more than a minute for the bigger policeman to catch us. "I fell . . . couple times," he gasped. I could sense his embarrassment.

"Ellie says he was carrying this crowbar. Looks like he dropped his weapon," Jakob observed.

"Okay, now what?" the policeman wheezed.

"Find!" Jakob commanded.

The man's scent was painted on bushes and hanging in the air, and it wasn't long before I could hear him ahead, scuffling along. I closed in on him in a place where the breeze was moist from a tiny stream and the trees lifted their limbs high overhead, providing shade. He saw me and ducked behind one of these trees, just like Wally might do. I ran back to Jakob.

"Show me!" Jakob said.

I stayed close to Jakob as we entered the woods. I knew the man was hiding, I could smell his fear and his hate and his fetid odor. I led Jakob straight to the tree, and when the man stepped out from behind it I heard Jakob shout, "Police! Freeze!"

The man raised his hand and a shot rang out. Just a gun. I'd been assured guns were okay, except that I sensed a flash of pain from Jakob and he fell to the ground, his warm blood spraying the air. Jakob's gun clattered away.

I got it, then, connecting separate pieces of information in a flash: Grandpa's guns, and the way Ethan's cans leaped off the fence. Todd's firecrackers, and the snap of pain when he threw one too close to me. The man by the tree was using his gun to hurt Jakob.

He was still standing there, his gun pointed at us. His fear and fury had turned to elation.

What came over me then was exactly the same primal impulse that had seized me when I attacked Todd on the night of the fire. I didn't growl; I just lowered my head and charged. Two loud shots rang out, and then I had the man's wrist in my mouth, his gun falling to the dust. He screamed at me and I held on, shaking my head violently, feeling my teeth tear into his arm. His foot smacked into my ribs.

"Let go!" he shouted.

"Police! Freeze!" the big policeman yelled, coming forward.

"Get the dog off me!"

"Ellie, it's okay. Down, Ellie, Down!" the policeman commanded. I let go of the man's arm and he fell to his knees. I smelled his blood. His eyes met mine and I growled. I could feel his pain but also his cunning, his sense that he was going to get away with something.

"Ellie, come," the policeman said.

"Dog ripped off my arm!" the man shouted. He waved at something behind and to the left of the policeman. "I'm over here!" he yelled.

When the policeman quickly turned to see who the man was shouting at, the man lunged forward, scooping up his gun. I barked. He fired and then the policeman fired, several shots punching deep pain into the man. The man lay down in the dirt. I felt the life go out of him in a whoosh, the black, angry sickness unclenching its hold on him and letting him slide away peacefully.

"Cannot believe I fell for that one," the policeman muttered. He still pointed his gun at the now dead man, cautiously advancing and kicking the other man's gun away.

"Ellie, you okay?" Jakob asked faintly.

"She's okay, Jakob. Where you hit?"

"Gut."

I anxiously lay down by Jakob's side, nuzzling his unresponsive hand. I could feel the pain working its way through his body, and the blood smell was alarming for how much of it there was.

"Officer down, suspect down. We're . . ." The man looked up at the sky. "We're under some trees down the canyon. Need medivac for the officer. Suspect is 10-91."

"Confirm suspect 10-91."

The policeman walked over and gave the man a kick. "Oh, he's dead all right."

"Who is the officer?"

"Eight-Kilo-Six. We need help down here *now*."

I didn't know what to do. Jakob seemed unafraid, but I was so filled with fear I was panting and trembling. I was reminded of the night when Ethan was caught inside the fire and I couldn't get to him, the same feeling of helplessness. The policeman came back and knelt next to Jakob. "They're on their way, bro. You just got to hang on, now."

I felt the concern in the policeman's voice, and when he gingerly opened Jakob's shirt to get a look inside the shock of fear shooting through him made me whimper.

Soon I could hear crashing and stumbling as several people ran toward us. They knelt by Jakob, shouldering me aside, and began pouring chemicals on him and wrapping him in bandages.

"How's Emily?" Jakob asked them faintly.

"Who?"

"The little girl," the policeman explained. "She's fine, Jakob; nothing happened. You got to her before he was able to do anything."

More people arrived and eventually they carried Jakob out on a bed. When we got to where the cars had been parked, a helicopter waited.

The policeman held me as they loaded Jakob on the helicopter, his limp arm hanging off of the bed. As the loud machine rose into the air I twisted free and ran beneath it, barking. I was a chopper dog; why didn't they let me go? I needed to be with Jakob!

People watched as I circled helplessly, my front legs in the air.

Eventually Amy came and put me in a cage on a different truck, one filled with Cammie's scent. She took me on a car ride back to the kennel and exchanged me for Cammie, who trotted past me and leaped up into the truck as if offended I'd been in it. Gypsy was nowhere to be seen.

"Someone will check on you, and we'll figure out where you're going to live, Ellie. You be a good dog; you are a good dog," Amy said.

I lay down on my bed in the kennel, my head swimming. I did not feel like a good dog. Biting the man with the gun was not part of Find, I knew. And where was Jakob? I remembered the scent of his blood, and it made me whine in anguish.

I'd fulfilled my purpose and found the girl and she was safe. But now Jakob was hurt and was gone and I was sleeping at the kennel for the first night ever. I couldn't help but feel that somehow I was being punished.

The next several days were confusing and distressing for everyone. I lived in the kennel and was only let out into the yard a couple times a day, always by a policeman who radiated awkwardness with the unexpected new duty of dog care. Amy talked to me and played with me a little, but she and Cammie were gone a lot of the time.

There was no sign of Jakob, and gradually his scent faded from the surroundings, so that even when I concentrated, I couldn't locate him anymore.

One day Cammie and I were in the yard together. All Cammie wanted to do was nap, even when I showed him a rubber bone one of the policemen had given me. I didn't understand what Cammie's purpose was, why anyone would want to have a nap dog.

Amy brought her lunch out to a table in the yard, and Cammie was willing to wake up for *that*. He walked over to where Amy sat and lay down heavily at her feet, as if burdened with many cares that could only be cured with a bite of her ham sandwich. A woman came out and joined Amy.

"Hi, Maya," Amy said.

Maya had dark hair and dark eyes and was tall for a woman, with strong-looking arms. Her pants smelled faintly of cats. She sat down and opened a little box and began chomping on something spicy. "Hi, Amy. Hello, Ellie."

The woman didn't greet Cammie, I noted smugly. I moved closer to her, and she petted me with a fragrant hand. I caught a whiff of soap and tangy tomatoes.

"Did you put in your paperwork?" Amy asked.

"Fingers crossed," Maya replied.

I lay down and gnawed on the rubber bone so that Maya would conclude I was having so much fun I could only be enticed into paying attention to her with a little lunch.

"Poor Ellie. She's got to be so confused," Amy said.

I looked up. Lunch?

"You sure you really want to do this?" Amy asked.

Maya sighed. "I know it's hard work, but what isn't, you know? I'm just getting to that point, it's the same old thing every day.

I'd like to try something new, do something different for a few years. Hey, you want a taco? My mom made them; they're really good."

"No thanks."

I sat up. Taco? I wanted a taco!

Maya wrapped up her lunch as if I weren't even there. "You people in K-9 are all in such good shape. Losing weight is so hard for me . . . do you think I can hack it?"

"What? No, you're fine! Didn't you pass the physical?"

"Sure," Maya said.

"Well, there you go," Amy said. "I mean, if you want to run with me, I usually go to the track after work. But I'm sure you'll be great."

I felt a tinge of anxiety come off Maya. "I sure hope so," she said. "I'd hate to let Ellie down."

I decided that no matter how many times they said my name, this conversation wasn't going to result in anything edible. I sprawled out in the sunshine with a sigh, wondering how much longer it would be before Jakob came back.

TWENTY-ONE

Maya was happy and excited the day she took me for a car ride.

"We're going to work together; isn't that great, Ellie? You won't have to sleep in the kennel anymore. I bought a bed for you; you can sleep in my room."

I sifted through her statement: "Ellie," "kennel," "bed," "room." There was nothing there that made any sense to me whatsoever, but I was glad to stick my nose out the window and breathe the scent of something besides Cammie and Gypsy.

Maya parked in the driveway of a small house that I knew, as soon as we crossed the threshold, was where she lived—painted everywhere was her smell, plus the distinctly disappointing odor of cats. I inspected the dwelling, which was tinier than Jakob's apartment, and immediately encountered an orange feline, sitting on a chair at the table. She regarded me with cold eyes, and when I approached her, wagging, she opened her mouth and gave an almost silent hiss.

"Stella, be nice. That's Stella. Stella, this is Ellie; she lives here now."

Stella yawned, unimpressed. A flash of gray and white motion out of the corner of my eye drew my attention.

"Tinker? That's Tinkerbell; she's shy."

Another cat? I followed her into the bedroom, where a third feline, a heavy black and brown male, sauntered out and sniffed at me with fish breath. "And that's Emmet."

Stella, Tinkerbell, and Emmet. Why on earth would a woman want three cats?

Tinkerbell was hiding under the bed, thinking I couldn't smell her there. Emmet followed me into the kitchen and looked curiously into the bowl Maya filled with food, then lifted his head and walked away as if he didn't care that I was eating and he was not. Stella watched me unwinkingly from her perch on the chair.

After eating, Maya let me out into her tiny yard, which was unmarked by dogs. I did my business with dignity, aware that at least some of the cat population were observing me. "Good girl, Ellie," Maya enthused. Apparently she was of the "excited to see you peeing in the yard" persuasion.

Maya made her own dinner, which smelled pretty good and drew the attention of Stella, who jumped right up on the table and waltzed around like a bad cat! Maya didn't say anything to her, apparently feeling that cats were worthless, untrainable animals.

We went for a walk on the leash after dinner. There were a lot of people out in the yards, many of them children, which made me feel restless. I had not done any work in several weeks and there was a tension in my muscles; I wanted to run, to Find, to save people.

As if picking up on my mood, Maya began to trot. "Want to run a little, girl?" she asked. I increased my pace, sticking right to her side as Jakob had taught me. Before long she was huffing, and I could smell her sweat break out from her pores. The heat was coming off the pavement and into my paws, and as we passed houses dogs barked enviously.

And then Maya abruptly stopped. "Whew!" she panted. "Okay, we're going to need to spend more time on the treadmill, that's for sure."

I didn't really get what was happening until that night. I was lying on the rug while Maya took a bath and dressed in different clothing, and then she called me into her bedroom. "Okay, lie down here, Ellie. Good girl," she said, patting a dog bed. I obediently curled up in it, but I was mystified. Apparently I would be staying here for a while. Was this where I lived, now? What about Jakob? What about my work?

The next morning Maya and I did do work, though it was a little strange. Wally was there and greeted me like an old friend, along with a woman who sometimes came along to play Find with us. Her name was Belinda, and Wally's smell was always all over her, so I suspected that when we weren't there Belinda and Wally played Find with each other.

Wally stayed with Maya while Belinda went off into the woods. He talked with Maya, teaching her the hand signals and commands we used during work. Then Maya said, "Ellie, Find!" and I raced off while Wally and Maya followed. Belinda was sitting inside a car, which fooled me not at all, and I returned to Maya.

"See now; see how she looks?" Wally said. "She Found Belinda; you can tell by her expression."

I waited impatiently for Maya to tell me to Show, but she and Wally were too busy talking.

"I'm not sure; she doesn't look much different than the other times she came back," Maya said.

"Look at her eyes, the way her mouth is tightened. Her tongue's not out. See? She's on alert; she has something to show us."

At the word "show" I trembled, caught in half lunge. It hadn't really been a command.

"So now I tell her to Show?" Maya asked.

Quit teasing me! Were we working, or not?

"Show!" Maya finally called.

Belinda came out of the car laughing when we Found her. "Such a good dog, Ellie," she told me.

"Now you play with Ellie. It's important; it's her reward for such hard work."

When Maya played with me, it was different from Jakob's play. Maya seemed to actually enjoy it; it wasn't just something she did at the end of Show. She had the rubber bone from the kennel, and I dug in my feet and clenched it in my jaws while she tried to take it away.

Maya had a life different from anyone else I had ever encountered. Not only was she burdened with too many cats, but most nights she went to a larger home with lots of people and a wonderful-smelling woman named Mama. Mama was like Grandma, always cooking, and there were little children running around playing with each other every time we went for a visit. The children climbed on me until Maya asked them to stop, and the boys played ball with me, which I loved, and the girls put hats on me, which I tolerated.

Maya had a neighbor named Al who liked to come over and ask Maya about "help." "Do you need help carrying those boxes, Maya?" he would ask. "No, no," she would say. "Do you need help fixing your door?" "No, no," Maya would say. Maya always seemed anxious, her skin warming and her palms sweating, when Al came over, but she wasn't frightened of him. When Al walked away, Maya's feelings changed to sadness.

"Did you get a new dog?" Al asked. He reached down and scratched me behind the ears in a way that made me instantly love him. He smelled of papers and inks and coffee.

"Yes, she's the department search-and-rescue dog."

I knew they were talking about me, and wagged my tail in friendship.

"Do you need help training your new dog?" Al asked.

"No, no," Maya said. "Ellie has already been trained. We need to learn to work together as a team."

I wagged over the words "Ellie" and "work."

Al stood up from his scratching. "Maya, you . . . ," he started to say. He felt nervous.

"I probably should go," Maya said.

"Your hair is very pretty today," Al blurted.

The two of them stared at each other, both so anxious it felt as if we were under danger of imminent attack. I glanced around but could see nothing more threatening than Emmet, watching us through the window.

"Thank you, Al," Maya said. "Would you like . . ."

"I'll let you go," Al said.

"Oh," Maya said.

"Unless . . . ," Al stammered.

"Unless . . . ?" Maya repeated.

"You . . . do you need help with anything?"

"No, no," Maya said.

Maya and I worked almost every day. Maya would tell me to Find and we would plunge off into the woods, sometimes chasing Wally or Belinda and sometimes chasing one of the older boys from Mama's house.

Maya was much slower than Jakob, panting and sweating from the moment we started. Often real pain would come off of her, and I learned not to be impatient when I returned to her and all she could do was put her hands on her knees for a few minutes. Sometimes a burst of helplessness and frustration would overtake her and she would cry, but she always cleaned up her face before we came to Wally.

One afternoon she and Wally sat at a picnic table and drank cool beverages while I lay in the shade of a tree. Maya's worry was clear to me, but I had learned to live with it and not to let it interfere with the work.

"We're not good enough to get certified, are we?" Maya said.

"Ellie's about the best dog I've ever seen," Wally replied. I sensed some alarm and caution in his voice and looked at him curiously.

"No, I know it's me. I've always been heavy."

"What? No, I mean . . . ," Wally said, his alarm increasing. I sat up, wondering what the danger was.

"It's okay. I've actually lost some weight, like four pounds."

"Really? That's great! I mean, but you weren't fat or anything," Wally stammered. I smelled the sweat pop on his forehead. "You, I don't know, maybe go to the track, that would help, or something?"

"I do go to the track!"

"Right! Yes!" Wally radiated pure fear, and I yawned anxiously. "Well, okay, I should go now."

"I don't know, I didn't realize there would be so much *running*. It's a lot harder than I thought it would be. Maybe I should resign, let somebody take over who is in better shape."

"Hey, why don't you talk to Belinda about this?" Wally said desperately.

Maya sighed and Wally, full of relief, got up and left. I lay back down. Whatever horrible danger had been lurking was now apparently no longer a threat.

The next day, Maya and I didn't work. She put on some soft new shoes, grabbed my leash, and took me to a long road that ran along the sand next to the big pond, the ocean. Dogs were everywhere, but though we weren't doing work I sensed a grim determination in Maya and ignored them as we ran and ran down that road, the sun rising steadily in the sky. It was the longest run we'd ever taken together, it went on and on, and it wasn't until I could feel her body fill with pain and exhaustion that Maya turned around to head back. She stopped a few times for me to drink water out of faucets set into the concrete next to very smelly buildings, but for the most part the return trip was as determined, just slower. By the time we got to the truck, she was limping. "Oh my," Maya said.

We were both panting pretty hard. She drank water and hung her head between her legs, and I watched in sadness as she vomited in the parking lot.

"You okay?" a young woman asked sympathetically. Maya waved a hand without even looking up.

The next day we did Find Belinda for work. Maya's gait was so stiff and painful I deliberately did Find at half speed, slowing down as soon as I was out of sight. I returned for direction far more than was necessary, just to check on her, and when I finally found Belinda sitting under a tree she had fallen asleep.

"Good dog, you are such a good dog, Ellie," Maya whispered to me. We woke up Belinda, who checked her wrist and emanated a quick shock of surprise.

"Just . . . had an off day," Maya said. Belinda didn't reply.

That night Maya called me while she was in the bathtub. I sniffed curiously at the bubbles in the tub and lapped up a little of the water, wondering why anyone would want to swim in such a small enclosure. Certainly the cats weren't interested. Tinkerbell was, as usual, hiding from the world, Stella was conducting an unauthorized examination of my bed (I could tell by the smell of it that she'd even tried sleeping there!), and Emmet was in the bathroom with me, licking himself and waiting for something to happen that he could ignore.

Maya was sad. She reached a wet hand out and stroked my head. "I'm sorry, Ellie; I'm just not good enough. I just can't keep up with you in the field. You're such a good dog, you need someone who can handle you."

I wondered if she would be happier if I got into the tub with her. I put my paws up on the edge of the tub, testing the theory a little. Emmet stopped licking himself and looked at me without any of the proper respect, then lifted his tail and waltzed out of there as if daring me to chase him down and reduce the cat population in the house.

"Tomorrow, I have a surprise for you, Ellie," Maya said, still sad.

Well, okay, I'd gone this far . . . I climbed into the tub, sinking through the insubstantial bubbles.

"Ellie!" Maya laughed, her delight blowing out the sadness like a candle.

TWENTY-TWO

The next morning I was excited to go for a car ride because, well, it was a car ride! I also picked up some happy anticipation from Maya, so I knew we weren't going to work, because lately there hadn't been much happiness associated with that. But it wasn't until she stopped and opened the door that I realized where I was.

Jakob's apartment.

I ran ahead of Maya, bounding up the stairs and barking at the door, which I would never have done when I lived with him. I could smell Jakob inside and hear him moving to the door. He opened it and I barreled into him, leaping and twisting joyously.

"Ellie! How are you, girl? Sit," he commanded.

I dropped my bottom onto the floor, but it didn't want to stay there.

"Hi, Jakob," Maya said from the doorway.

"Come on in, Maya," Jakob said.

I was so thrilled to see Jakob I sat by his side as he eased into a chair. I wanted to climb into his lap and it if had been Ethan I probably would have, but with Jakob there was never any nonsense like that.

I sniffed around the apartment while the two of them talked. My bed was gone, I noticed, but my scent was still in the bedroom and I would have no problem sleeping on the carpet or in Jakob's bed if he wanted.

Then I trotted back out to be with Jakob, passing by Maya, who reached a friendly hand out to stroke my back, and that's when it hit me: going back to Jakob would mean leaving Maya.

Dogs are not allowed to choose where they live; my fate would be decided by people. But I nonetheless felt torn inside, conflicted.

Jakob was far better at work than Maya. But Maya didn't carry that inner core of sadness with her all the time; she felt genuine joy at Mama's house, where there were all the children to play with. Yet Jakob didn't have any cats.

I had a clear purpose—to Find, Show, and save people. I was a good dog. Both Maya and Jakob were focused on work, and that meant neither one of them could ever love me with the utter abandon of Ethan. But Maya embraced me with an unguarded affection that Jakob never allowed himself to feel.

I began to pace anxiously.

"Do you need to go out?" Maya asked me. I heard "out," but she didn't say it with any enthusiasm, so I didn't react.

"No, when she needs to do that, she sits by the door," Jakob said.

"Oh. Right, I've seen her do that," Maya said. "I just leave my back door open a lot of the time, so, you know. She can come and go."

They were silent for a bit. I eased into the kitchen, but as usual the floor was antiseptically clean, free of anything edible.

"I heard you're taking disability," Maya said.

"Yeah, well, I've been shot twice in five years; that'd be enough for anybody," Jakob replied with a gruff laugh.

"You'll be missed," Maya observed.

"I'm not leaving town, I'm enrolled at UCLA. Full-time, I only have a year and a half left for my law degree."

There was another silence. A tiny signal of distress came off of Maya, something I'd noticed before when others tried to talk to Jakob and instead wound up sitting there without saying anything. Something about him made people uncomfortable.

"So when are you up for certification?" Jakob asked.

I picked a neutral spot on the floor between the two of them and lay down with a sigh, unable to figure out what was going to happen.

"Two weeks, but . . ." Maya trailed off.

"But?" Jakob prompted.

"I'm thinking of resigning from the program," Maya confessed in a rush. "I just can't keep up. I didn't realize . . . well, someone else would probably be better."

"You can't do that," Jakob said. I raised my head and looked at him curiously, wondering why he was feeling angry. "You can't keep switching handlers on a dog. Ellie is the best dog anyone has ever seen. You dump her like that, you could ruin her. Wally says the two of you have a rapport."

I thumped my tail a little at my name and Wally's being mentioned by Jakob, but his tone was still very stern.

"I'm just not cut out for it physically, Jakob," Maya said. I could feel anger stirring in her, too. "I'm not an ex-Marine; I'm just a beat cop who can barely pass the physical every year. I've been trying, but it is just too hard."

"Too hard." Jakob glared at her until Maya shrugged and looked away. Her anger turned to shame, and I went over to her to nuzzle her hand. "What about how hard it would be on Ellie? Doesn't that matter?"

"Of course it matters."

"You're saying you're not willing to work."

"I'm saying I'm not cut out for this, Jakob! I don't have what it takes inside."

"What it takes. Inside."

I could sense that Maya was grappling with the rising tide of emotion that sometimes led to a flood of tears. I wanted to comfort her and shoved my nose under her hand again. When Jakob spoke again, he wasn't looking at Maya and his voice was quieter.

"When I was shot the first time, my shoulder was so messed up, I had to learn to use it all over again. I went to physical therapy every day, and there was this little two-pound weight on a pulley and that thing *hurt* . . . and my wife was in her final round of chemo. More than once, I wanted to give up. It was too *hard*." Jakob turned his head and blinked at Maya. "But Susan was dying. And she never gave up, not until the very end. And if she could keep going, I knew I had to. Because it's important. Because failure isn't an option if success is just a matter of more effort. I know it's difficult, Maya. Try harder."

The same old dark pain swirled around inside Jakob like a storm, and the anger left him as if blown away by a gust of wind. He sagged in his chair, suddenly exhausted.

Somehow I knew then that I wouldn't be staying with Jakob. He just wasn't interested in Find anymore.

Sadness was flowing through Maya, but through it I felt a rising resolve, a strength like what came over her the day she took me running along the ocean.

"Okay. You're right," she told Jakob.

Jakob petted my head when we left, saying good-bye without regret. The last glimpse I had of him was as he shut the door, and he wasn't looking at me. He and Maya had decided my fate, and it was up to me to do what they wanted.

Later Maya and I drove up into the hills. She ran until she was so tired she stumbled, and the next day, after work, we ran some more. It was gloriously fun, except that Maya often felt full of despair and pain by the end of the course.

A few evenings later, we pulled into the driveway and Maya was literally too tired to get out of the car. We sat there, sweat running from her face, with the windows open. "I'm going to fail, Ellie. I'm so sorry," Maya said mournfully.

I could see Emmet and Stella both watching from the window—they probably didn't even know what a car was. Tinkerbell, I assumed, had become alarmed at the sound of our approach and was cowering under something.

"Are you okay, Maya?" Al asked softly. The wind was working against me, so I hadn't smelled his approach. I put my head out the window for him to pet.

"Oh, hi, Al." She stood up out of the car. "Yes, I was just . . . thinking."

"Oh. I saw you pull up in your car."

"Yes."

"So I came over to see if you needed any help."

"No, no. I was just running with the dog."

I slid out of the front seat and squatted in the yard, staring pointedly at Emmet and Stella, who looked away in disgust.

"Okay." Al drew in a deep breath. "You've lost weight, Maya."

"What?" Maya stared at him.

Al recoiled in horror. "Not that you were fat, I just noticed, in your shorts, your legs look so thin." A gust of misery flowed off of him, and he was backing away. "I should go."

"Thank you, Al; that was sweet," Maya said.

He arrested his retreat and stood up straight. "In my opinion, you don't need to exercise anymore; you are perfect the way you are."

Maya laughed at this, and then Al laughed. I wagged my tail to show the cats at the window that I understood the joke and they didn't.

A week or so later Maya and I did one of my favorite things, which was to go to the park with a lot of other dogs and work on the toys. At her command I crawled into the tight tube and up and down the tippy board. I climbed slowly down a ladder and demonstrated that I could sit patiently on a narrow beam two feet off the ground, all the while ignoring the other dogs.

Our Find consisted of locating a man who had dropped some old socks as he blundered off into the woods. Maya was bursting with eagerness, so I went at it full speed, even when she began to huff and sweat. I knew he was high in a tree even before I found him, because Wally had tried that on me a few times and it always affected the way the human scent drifted on the wind. Maya was a little mystified, though, that I was alerting at the base of the tree when clearly the man wasn't standing there. I sat, patiently staring up at the grinning man, until she got it.

That night there was a big party at Mama's house. Everyone was petting me and saying my name.

"Now that you are certified, you need to eat," Mama told Maya.

The doorbell rang, which hardly ever happened at that house; people usually just burst in. I followed Mama to the door, and when she opened it Mama's heart soared. It was Al, and he gave some flowers to Mama. I remembered Ethan giving Hannah flowers, and I was confused because I thought Al liked Maya, not Mama, but I'll never really understand people when it comes to stuff like this.

The whole family grew quiet when Al stepped out into the backyard where the picnic tables were set up. Maya went over to Al and they both felt nervous as he briefly pressed his mouth to her face. Then Maya said everyone's name and Al shook hands with the men and everyone started talking and laughing again.

Over the next several days we found and saved two children who had wandered away from their houses, plus backtracked a horse's path to find a woman who had fallen off and hurt her leg. I remembered Flare dumping Ethan in the woods, and wondered why people even bothered to own horses, since they were obviously unreliable. If people had a dog or two and were still not satisfied, they should probably consider getting a donkey like Jasper the donkey, who at least made Grandpa laugh.

Maya and I also found an old man in the woods who was dead. I was depressed to sniff out his cold body lying in the dirt, because that wasn't saving people, and though Maya praised me, neither one of us was much interested in playing with the stick afterward.

We went to Al's house and he served Maya a chicken dinner and they both laughed and then ate a pizza a boy brought over. I sniffed at the chicken pieces Al put on the floor for me and ate them more out of politeness than anything, since they were so encrusted with what tasted like soot.

Later that evening I could tell she was telling him about the dead man, because her feeling of sadness was the same. Jakob and I had found a few dead people, too, but it never made him sad, the same way that finding people and saving them never really seemed to make him glad. He just did the work, not feeling much one way or the other.

When I thought about Jakob, I realized that his cold dedication to Find helped me get over my separation from Ethan— there was no time for grieving; I had too much work to do. Maya, though, was more complex, and the way she loved me made me miss my boy. Not with the same sharp, painful ache in my chest but with a wistful sadness that often came to me as I was lying down for the night and rode with me into my dreams.

One day Maya and I took a plane ride and then a chopper ride straight south. I thought about the day Jakob was taken away, and was glad I was back to being a chopper dog. She was both excited and uneasy on the flight, which wasn't, frankly, nearly as much fun as a car ride, because the noise hurt my ears.

We landed in a place unlike any I'd ever been to before. There were lots of dogs and policemen, and the air was filled with the sound of sirens and the smell of smoke. Buildings everywhere were in a state of collapse, their roofs sometimes all the way on the ground.

Maya seemed stunned, and I pressed up against her, yawning anxiously. A man approached us; he was dirty and wore a plastic helmet. His hands, when he held them to me, smelled of ashes, blood, and clay. He shook hands with Maya.

"I'm coordinating the U.S. response in this sector; thanks for coming down."

"I had no idea it was going to be this bad," Maya said.

"Oh, this is just the tip of the iceberg. The El Salvadoran

government is completely overwhelmed. We've got more than four thousand people injured, hundreds dead—and we're still finding folks trapped. There've been more than a half dozen aftershocks since January 13, some of them pretty bad. Be careful going in these places."

Maya put me on a leash and led me through the maze of rubble. We'd come to a house and some men who were following us would check it, and then sometimes Maya would let me off the leash and I'd go in and sometimes she'd keep me on the leash and we would just Find along the outside of the house.

"This one's not safe, Ellie. I have to keep you on a leash so you don't go in there," Maya told me.

One of the men was named Vernon, and he smelled like goats, reminding me of trips to town with Ethan and Grandpa. It was one of the rare times I thought of Ethan while working—doing Find meant putting all of that away and concentrating on the job.

Over the next several hours, Maya and I Found four people. They were all dead. My excitement over Find soured after the second one; by the time I came across the fourth person, a young woman lying beneath a jumble of bricks, I almost didn't alert Maya. She sensed my mood and tried to reassure me, petting me and waving the rubber bone at me, in which I had very little interest.

"Vernon, would you do me a favor and go hide somewhere?" she asked. I lay down tiredly at her feet.

"Hide?" he asked uncertainly.

"She needs to find someone alive. Would you go hide? Like over in that house we just searched. And when she locates you, act all excited."

"Um, yeah, okay."

I registered Vernon's departure without interest. "Okay, Ellie, ready? Ready to Find?"

I wearily rose to my feet. "Let's go, Ellie!" Maya said. Her excitement seemed fake, but I trotted over to a house we'd already searched. "Find!" Ellie commanded.

I went into the house and stopped, puzzled. Though we'd all been in here already, I thought Vernon's smell was somehow more intense. Curious, I padded to the back of the house. Yes! There was a pile of blankets in the corner, from which came a strong Vernon scent, full of sweat and heat and goats. I raced back to Maya. "Show!" she urged.

She followed me at a run, and when she peeled back the blankets Vernon leaped up, laughing.

"You found me! Good dog, Ellie!" he shouted, rolling on the blankets with me. I jumped on him and licked his face, and we played with the rubber bone for a while.

Maya and I worked all night and we Found more people, including Vernon, who became better and better at hiding—but I'd worked with Wally, so no one could fool me for very long. Everyone else Maya and I found was dead.

The sun was coming up when we came to a building from which sharp, acrid smoke still rose. I was back on the leash, my eyes watering at an intense chemical smell coming out from the collapsed concrete.

I Found a dead man lying crushed beneath a flat section of wall and alerted Maya.

"We know about him," someone told Maya. "We can't get him out just yet; whatever is in those barrels is toxic. Going to need a cleanup crew."

Some metal barrels leaked a steady stream of liquid that

filled my nose with a scalding odor. I concentrated on pushing the scent away, trying to Find.

"Okay, good dog. Let's go somewhere else, Ellie."

There! I smelled another person and alerted, going rigid. It was a woman, and her scent was faint, riding out just behind the chemicals clogging the air.

"It's okay, Ellie. We're going to leave this one here. Come on," Maya said. She tugged gently on my leash. "Come, Ellie."

I alerted again, agitated. We couldn't leave!

This one was alive.

W e see the victim, Ellie. We're going to have to leave him here. Come on," Maya said.

I understood that she wanted to leave and wondered if perhaps she thought that I was alerting because of the dead person.

"Does she want to Find me again?" Vernon asked.

I stared up at Maya, willing her to understand.

Maya glanced around. "Here? Everything's collapsed; it's too dangerous. Tell you what, though, it would be fun for her to chase you a little. Go up the street a little bit and call her, and I'll let her off the leash."

I didn't pay attention to Vernon as he trotted away. My focus was on the person hidden in the rubble. I could smell fear, though the biting odor from the chemicals was clawing at my nose the way I'd once felt the spray from a skunk. Maya unsnapped my leash. "Ellie? What's Vernon doing? Where's he going?"

"Hey, Ellie! Look!" Vernon shouted. He started to run slowly up the street. I stared after him: I wanted to chase him and play, but I had work to do. I turned back to the collapsed building.

"Ellie! No!" Maya called.

Had it been Jakob, the word "no" would have stopped me dead, but Maya didn't command me with the same hard tones. I dove headfirst into a narrow space next to the dead person, digging my way forward. My feet encountered a wet spill and started to sting, and the smell from the chemicals was so intense it blotted out everything else. I was reminded of playing rescue with Ethan, how I could find him in the depths by the merest whisper of his scent in the water.

Choking, I tunneled ahead. Cooler air touched my face, and I squirmed though a hole and dropped into a narrow shaft. An updraft brought cleaner air into this area, though my nostrils were still aflame with the burning wet acid that had splashed on my snout.

After a moment, I saw a woman huddled in the corner of the shaft, pressing a cloth to her face. Her eyes were big as they regarded me.

I barked, unable to return to Maya to Show.

"Ellie!" Maya called, coughing.

"Get back, Maya," Vernon warned.

I kept barking. "Ellie!" Maya shouted again, sounding closer. This time the woman heard her and started screaming back, the terror tumbling out of her.

"There's someone in there, someone alive!" Maya yelled.

I sat patiently with the woman, feeling her fear turn to hope when a man wearing a helmet and a mask poked a flashlight into the shaft and waved the light over both of us. My eyes were watering and my nose was running, my whole face still stinging from whatever it was I'd gotten on myself. Soon the sounds of digging and hammering reverberated through the space, and then a square of daylight broke into the shaft from above and a man lowered himself down on a rope.

The woman had obviously never practiced being lifted with a rope harness and was very afraid when the fireman tied her up and they hoisted her out, but I'd been through the maneuver several times and stepped unhesitatingly into the loops of rope when it was my turn. Maya was there at the top when they hauled me through the hole they'd dug in the wall, but her relief turned to alarm when she saw me.

"Oh my God, Ellie, your nose!"

We ran together to a fire truck, where Maya, much to my disgust, talked one of the firefighters into giving me a bath! Well, it was more of a rinsing, cold water flowing down my face and bringing some relief to the burn on my nose.

Maya and I took another chopper ride that day, and then a plane ride, and then we went to the man in the cool room, the vet, who carefully looked at my nose and put some cream on it that smelled awful but felt wonderful.

"What was it, some kind of acid?" the vet asked Maya.

"I don't know. Is she going to be okay?" I felt Maya's love and concern, and closed my eyes when she stroked my neck. I wished there were some way I could let her know that the pain wasn't all that bad.

"We'll want to watch for any signs of infection, but I don't see any reason why she shouldn't heal up just fine," he told Maya.

For the next two weeks or so, Maya would gently rub the cream into my nose. Emmet and Stella seemed to find this pretty amusing, and would sit on the counter and watch. Tinkerbell, though, *loved* it. She came out of wherever she'd been hiding and sniffed at the cream and then rubbed her head against mine, purring. When I'd lie down, Tinkerbell would sit and smell me, her tiny little nose bobbing up and down, and she even started curling up against me to sleep.

It was almost more than I could stand.

I was relieved to get away from the cats and go back to work. When Maya and I got to the park, I bounded up to Wally and Belinda, who were excited to see me.

"I hear you are the hero dog, Ellie! Good dog!"

I wagged, excited to be a good dog. Wally then ran off while Belinda and Maya sat at a picnic table.

"So how are you and Wally doing?" Maya said. I sat impatiently—if we went after him now, we could Find Wally right away!

"He's taking me to meet his parents over the Fourth, so . . . ," Belinda replied.

"That's good."

I groaned at all this conversation. Humans were capable of so many amazing things, but too often they just sat making words, not doing anything. "Down, Ellie," Maya said. I reluctantly lay down, pointedly looking off in the direction Wally had taken.

After what seemed ages, Maya and I were finally allowed to Find. I joyously took off, not having to slow down, because she was able to keep pace with me.

Wally had done an excellent job of disguising his scent! I lifted my nose, searching for any trace of him. There were few odors on the air today to distract me, but I couldn't Find Wally. I coursed back and forth, returning to Maya for direction. Carefully she worked the area, and when I didn't pick up a scent she moved me to a new place and I tried there.

"What's the matter, girl? You okay, Ellie?"

Oddly, though the wind was coming from behind him, I actually heard Wally before I smelled him. He was walking straight toward us. I rocketed forward until my nose told me it was him, and then returned to Maya, who had already started talking to Wally, her voice a shout.

"We're having sort of an off day!" she said.

"I guess so. I've never seen her fail before. Hey, Ellie, how are you doing?" Wally said to me. We played a little with a stick.

"Tell you what, Maya. You focus her attention away from me. I'm going to go over that ridge, there, and double back a little. Give me about ten minutes," Wally said.

"You sure?"

"She's been out of action for a couple of weeks; let's allow her to have an easy one."

I was conscious of Wally leaving, even though Maya had handed me the rubber bone and was now trying to get it away from me. I could hear him and knew he was hiding again, which made me happy. When Maya finally shouted, "Find!" I took off eagerly, heading in the direction I'd heard him go.

I ran up a small hill and stopped, uncertain. I didn't know how he was doing it, but somehow Wally was keeping his scent out of the air. I ran back to Maya for direction, and she sent me off to my right. I snaked back and forth, searching.

No Wally.

Then she directed me to the left. Again, no sign of Wally. This time, she had me return left and walked with me, leading me around the base of the hill. I was virtually upon Wally when I found him—he moved, and I alerted. There was no need to run back, because Maya was standing there.

"This isn't good, is it?" Maya asked. "The vet said she should be fully recovered by now."

"Well . . . let's give it another week, see if she gets any better," Wally said. He felt sad, for some reason, so I nuzzled his hand.

Maya and I didn't work very much over the next couple of weeks, and when we did, Wally continued to fool me, disguising his scent so that I could only pick it up when he was right there in front of me.

"What does it mean that Ellie is decertified? Does it mean you will lose your job?" Al asked one night. I'm not a big fan of feet, but I allowed Al to take off his shoes and rub my tummy with his toes because they didn't smell as bad as usual.

"No, but I'll be reassigned. I've been on a desk for the past several weeks, but I'm not really cut out for that. I'll probably request a transfer to go back out on patrol," Maya replied.

Stealthily Al dropped a tiny piece of meat on the carpet in front of me. It was the main reason why I liked to lie in front of him at dinner. I silently licked it up while Stella gave me dirty looks from the couch.

"I don't like to think about you being on patrol. It is so dangerous."

"Albert," Maya sighed.

"What about Ellie?"

I looked up at my name, but Al didn't hand down any more meat.

"I don't know. She can't work anymore; her sense of smell is too damaged. So she'll be retired. She'll live with me. Right, Ellie?"

I wagged, pleased with the way she said my name, full of affection.

After dinner we took a car ride to the ocean! The sun was setting, and Maya and Al set a blanket out between two trees and talked while the waves came in.

"It's so beautiful," Maya said.

I figured they probably wanted to play with a stick or a ball or something, but I was on a leash and couldn't go find one for them. I felt bad that they had nothing to do.

Al got my attention by becoming afraid. His heart started to pound audibly, and I could feel his nervous energy as he wiped his hands on his pants over and over.

"Maya, when you moved here . . . so many months I wanted to talk to you. You are so beautiful."

Maya laughed. "Oh, Al, I'm not beautiful; come on."

Some boys down by the water ran by, tossing a saucer at each other. I watched it alertly, thinking of Ethan and the stupid flip. I wondered if Ethan had ever been to the ocean and, if he had, if he brought the flip and threw it out into the waves, where I hope it sank and was never found again.

Ethan. I could remember how he never did anything without taking me with him, except school. I loved the sense of purpose I got from work, but there were certainly days, like this one, when I thought of Ethan and missed being a doodle dog more than anything.

Al was still afraid, and I glanced at him curiously, pulled away from the sight of the boys by his continued alarm. Was there some sort of danger? I couldn't see any; we were all alone in this part of the park.

"You are the most wonderful woman in the world," he said. "I . . . I love you, Maya."

Maya started to feel afraid, too. What was going on? I sat up.

"I love you, too, Al."

"I know I'm not rich, I know I'm not handsome . . . ," Al said.

"Oh my God," Maya breathed. Her heart was beating now, too.

"But I will love you all my life if you will let me." Al turned on the blanket, rising to his knees.

"Oh my God, oh my God," Maya said.

"Will you marry me, Maya?" Al asked.

TWENTY-FOUR

One day Maya and Mama and all of the brothers and sisters and other family members came together in a big building and sat quietly while I demonstrated a new trick I'd been taught, which was to walk very slowly down a narrow path between wooden benches, mount some carpeted stairs, and stand patiently while Al removed something from a small pack I carried on my back. Then everyone sat and admired me while Maya and Al had a conversation. Maya was wearing a big fluffy outfit, so I knew we weren't going to the park to play afterward, but that was okay because everyone seemed so glad at how well I'd done the trick. Mama even cried, she was so happy.

Then we went to Mama's house and children ran around and fed me cake.

A few months later, we all moved into a different house with a much better backyard. It had a garage, too, but thankfully no one suggested I sleep out there. Al and Maya slept together and, though they didn't mind when I jumped up to be with them, there was frankly no room to get a good night's sleep and anyway the cats kept climbing up there, too, so I eventually learned to lie on the floor next to Maya's side, where I could get up and follow her if she awoke during the middle of the night and went anywhere.

Gradually, I came to understand that we wouldn't be doing work anymore. I could only conclude that we'd Found everybody who needed to be Found and that Wally and Belinda had lost interest in the whole process. Maya still went running, though, and Al sometimes went with us, though he had trouble keeping up.

I was therefore surprised when Maya excitedly loaded me into the truck and took me for a car ride. It felt like we were going to do work, except that Maya's mood was different, less urgent.

She took me to a big building and told me it was a school. This was confusing to me, as I had learned that school was something where Ethan went away—it wasn't a *place*; it was a state of being without the boy. I stuck to Maya's side, though, as we entered a big noisy room filled with children, who were all excited and laughing. I sat with Maya and watched the children who were doing their best to sit still. I was reminded of Ethan and Chelsea and the children in our neighborhood, always full of energy.

A bright light was in my eyes. A woman spoke, and then all the girls and boys clapped, startling me. I wagged my tail, feeling a collective joy washing off the children.

Maya walked me forward, and when she spoke her voice was

very loud and seemed to come from both next to me and at the back of the room.

"This is Ellie; she is a retired search-and-rescue dog. As part of our outreach program, I wanted to come to talk to you about how Ellie has helped find lost children, and what you can do if you ever become lost," Maya said. I yawned, wondering what this was all about.

After we stood around doing nothing for about half an hour, Maya led me down off the stage and the children lined up and then came up in small groups to pet me. Some of them hugged with unabashed affection, and some of them held back, a little afraid. I wagged my tail in reassurance, and one girl put a timid hand out, which I licked. She snatched her hand back, squealing, no longer frightened.

Though Maya and I no longer did work, we very often did school. Sometimes the children were little, and sometimes they weren't children at all but people as old as Grandma and Grandpa. Sometimes Maya and I went to places full of chemical smells and people who were in pain or feeling sad and sick as they lay in bed, and we would linger with these people until some of their sadness lifted.

I could always tell when we were doing school, because Maya would take extra time getting dressed in the morning. The days we didn't do school, she dressed hurriedly and sometimes ran out the door, with Al chuckling. Then Al would leave, too, and I'd be stuck at home with the stupid cats.

Though I no longer wore nose cream, Tinkerbell persisted in hanging near me and cuddling up against me when I'd take a nap. I was glad that Al wasn't there to see it. Al had a lot of affection for me, but for the cats, not so much. Tinkerbell hid from Al, while Stella only approached him when Al had food, and Emmet would occasionally strut over to Al and loftily rub against him as if putting cat fur on his pants was doing him some kind of favor.

We'd been doing school for several years when Maya broke the pattern. We were in a place called class, which was smaller than some of the rooms in which I'd been and which was filled with children who all seemed about the same age. These particular children were very little and sat on the floor on blankets. I was a little envious—most of my time at home was spent napping and I didn't seem to have the energy that I'd once had, so I decided that if the children wanted me to lie on a blanket with them, I'd be willing to do so.

Maya called forward one of the children, who approached shyly. Her name was Alyssa, and she gave me a hug. When I licked her face, the children laughed—but Maya and I had never done this before, had a single child come forward, and I wasn't sure what it was about.

The woman who sat at the big desk, the teacher, said, "Alyssa has never actually met Ellie before, but if it weren't for Ellie, Alyssa would never have been born."

Soon all the children were touching me, which was much more typical of how school went. Sometimes the children were a little rough and at this school a boy pulled sharply on my ears, but I just let him do it.

At the end of school, the children raced out the door, but the little girl Alyssa stayed behind, as did the teacher. Maya seemed excited about something, so I waited expectantly, and then a man and a woman came into the classroom and Alyssa ran to them.

The man was Jakob.

I bounded over to him. He stooped down, scratching my ears. "How are you, Ellie! Look how gray you're getting."

The woman picked up Alyssa. "Daddy used to work with Ellie; did you know that?"

"Yes," said Alyssa.

Maya hugged Jakob and the woman, who set Alyssa back down so she could pet me some more.

I sat and regarded Jakob. He was so different than when I last saw him—the coldness in him seemed to have gone away. This little girl Alyssa, I realized, was his child, and the woman was the girl's mother. Jakob had a family now, and he was happy.

That's what was different. In all the time I'd known him, Jakob had never once been happy.

"I'm glad you're doing this community outreach program," Jakob told Maya. "A dog like Ellie needs to work."

I registered my name and the word "work," but there was no sense in the room that we had an urgent need to Find. Jakob just always talked about work; that was his way.

It was very pleasant to be there with Jakob and feel the love pour out of him when he looked at his family. I eased down onto the floor, so happy I thought I might nap.

"We've got to get you home," the woman said to Alyssa.

"Can Ellie come?" Alyssa asked. Everyone laughed.

"Ellie," Jakob said. I sat up. He bent down again, holding my face in his hands. "You are a good dog, Ellie. A good dog."

The feel of his rough hands on my fur took me back to when I was a puppy, first learning my work. I wagged my tail, full of love for this man. Yet there was no question that I was happy with Maya, so when we all left each other in the hallway I un-questioningly followed her, my nails clicking.

"Good dog, Ellie," Maya murmured. "Wasn't it fun to see Jakob?"

"Bye, Ellie!" little Alyssa called, her tiny voice echoing in the quiet hall. Maya stopped and turned, so I did, too, and my last sight of Jakob was of him picking up his daughter, grinning at me.

That year Emmet and Stella both died. Maya cried and was very sad and Al was a little sad, too. The house seemed empty without them, and Tinkerbell needed constant assurance from me now that she was the only cat—several times a day I'd awaken from a nap to find her pressed up against me or, even more disconcerting, standing and staring at me. I didn't understand her attachment to me and knew it was not my purpose in life to be the substitute mother for a feline, but I didn't mind it much and even let her lick me sometimes because it seemed to make her happy.

The best days were when it rained, which it did infrequently— the smells seemed to leap off the ground, the way they did when I was a puppy. I could usually sense when the thickening clouds meant moisture, and remembered how much more often it rained back on the Farm.

I found myself thinking of the Farm much more often, now, the Farm and Ethan. Though my life with Fast and Sister, and the Yard with Coco, had faded to a distant memory, it seemed that sometimes I awoke with a start and lifted my head, thinking I'd just heard Ethan's car door slam and that he would soon walk in, calling my name.

One day when rain seemed imminent Maya and I were doing school, in a class with children who sat in chairs instead of on blankets. There was a sudden crack of lightning, and all the children jumped and laughed and then turned to look as a huge storm made the sky black and pounded the building with a roar of rain. I inhaled, wishing they'd open the windows to let in the fragrances.

"Settle down, class," said the teacher.

The door to the classroom suddenly opened and a man and a woman came inside, both of them wet. "We've lost Geoffrey Hicks," the man said. I picked up the tension in his voice and regarded the two of them alertly. The alarm coming off the two people was familiar, an emotion I'd encountered several times when I was doing work. "He's a first grader," the man told Maya.

The children all started talking. "Quiet!" the teacher snapped.

"They were playing hide-and-seek when the rain started," the woman said. "The storm just came up out of nowhere; one minute it was fine, the next . . ." She put her hands to her eyes, which were suddenly full of tears. "When I had everyone come in, Geoffrey wasn't with them. It was his turn to hide."

"Could the dog . . . ," the man asked.

Maya looked at me, and I sat up straighter. "You'd better call 911," she said. "Ellie hasn't worked search and rescue in seven or eight years."

"Won't the rain wash away the scent? It's really coming down out there," the woman asked. "I'm worried that by the time another dog got here—"

Maya bit her lip. "We will certainly help look. You need to call the police, though. Where do you think he might have gone?"

"There are some woods behind the playground. There's a fence, but the kids can lift it up," the man said.

"This is his backpack; will that help?" the woman asked, holding out a canvas bag.

I felt Maya's nervous excitement as we ran down the hallway. We stopped at the door, and a sense of defeat came over her. "Look at it rain," she muttered. "Okay. Ellie?" She lowered her face down to mine. "Ellie, you ready, girl? Here, smell this."

I took a deep whiff of the canvas bag. I could smell peanut butter, chocolate, crayons, and a person. "Geoffrey, Geoffrey," Maya said. "Okay?" She opened the door and the rain whipped into the hallway. "Find!"

I leaped out into the rain. In front of me was a wide expanse of wet pavement, and I coursed back and forth, my nails clicking. I could faintly smell many children, though the rain was beating the scents down. Maya was out, running away from the school. "Here, Ellie, Find here!"

We tracked all the way back to the fence: nothing. Maya felt frustrated and frightened as she sloshed through the wet ground. We found a section of fence that was bent back, but I could find nothing to alert on. "Okay, if he's in there, you'd smell him, girl, right? Geoffrey!" she shouted. "Geoffrey, come on out; it's all right!"

We hugged the fence heading back to the school, sticking to the other side of the yard. A police car pulled up, lights flashing, and Maya jogged over to speak to the man driving.

I continued to Find Geoffrey. Though I wasn't picking up much of anything, I knew if I just concentrated, as I had been trained, if I just focused, I could separate the smell from the backpack from all the others, if I didn't quit . . .

There. I had something, and whipped my head around. There was a small gap in the fence, two poles between which no adult person could climb, but I could smell Geoffrey—he'd squeezed through here. He had left the playground.

I ran back to Maya and alerted. She was speaking to the policeman and didn't notice at first, but then she turned to me, shocked. "Ellie? Show me!"

We ran back through the rain to the two poles. Maya peered through the small gap. "Come on!" she shouted, running along the fence toward the front of the school. "He left the school grounds! He's on the other side of the fence!" she yelled at the policeman. He ran after us.

From the other side of the fence I could smell Geoffrey at the two poles, and from there I could track which direction he'd headed. Yes, he had gone this way!

Abruptly the scent faded. Just two steps on the route he'd taken and I'd lost all sign of him, though it had been so strong there for a second.

"What is it?" the policeman asked.

"He might have gotten into a car," Maya said. The policeman groaned.

I dropped my nose, and that's when I picked it up again. I reversed direction, and the scent got stronger. In the street, water rushed down in a steady stream by the curb, gurgling into a storm drain. I shoved my snout into the gap, ignoring the smells carried into the drain by the rushing water, and concentrated on my nose. If I wanted to, I could wriggle through that gap and into the loud, wet drain, but there was no need to—I could smell Geoffrey now; he was right in front of me even though I couldn't see him in the darkness.

I looked up at Maya.

"My God, he's in there; he's in the sewer!" Maya shouted.

The policeman popped on a flashlight and beamed it into the storm drain. We all saw it at the same time: the pale face of a frightened little boy.

TWENTY-FIVE

G eoffrey! It's okay; we're going to get you out of there!"
Maya yelled at him. Heedless of the water, she knelt in
the street, straining to reach the boy. The water had pressed him
back away from the small opening, and he was clinging to the
far wall, the terror coming off him so strong it was blinding.
Right behind Geoffrey, a black tunnel sucked in the rainwater
with a loud roar. Grunting, Maya pushed in as far as she could,
but she couldn't reach the boy.

"How did he get in there?" the policeman shouted.

"It's a tight fit; he must have squeezed in before it started
raining. God, it's really coming down!" Maya's voice was full of
frustration.

A circular iron plate was set into the concrete right above
Geoffrey's head. The policeman pried at it with his fingers,

muttering. "I need to get a tire iron!" he bellowed. He handed the flashlight to Maya and ran off, his feet sloshing in the water.

Geoffrey was shivering with cold, and his eyes were dull when they looked into the beam from Maya's flashlight. He had the hood of his thin yellow rain slicker pulled up over his head, offering him scant protection from the chill. "Hold on, okay, Geoffrey? You hang on; we're going to get you out of there, okay?"

Geoffrey didn't respond.

The patrol car's siren came on and within less than a minute it was whipping around the corner, sliding a little as it came to a stop next to us. The policeman jumped out and ran to his trunk.

"Fire and rescue are on the way!" he hollered.

"There's no time!" Maya shouted back. "He's slipping into the water!"

The policeman came around the trunk with a bent piece of iron. "Geoffrey, hang on; don't let go!" Maya yelled. The policeman went to work on the circular plate with his tool. When Maya jumped up to watch I went with her, which was how I saw the spatter of mud fall on Geoffrey's face when the iron plate was knocked aside. He lifted his hand to wipe it away, and as he did so he lost his grip on the wall and fell into the water. For a brief second he was looking up at us, and then he was swept into the tunnel.

"Geoffrey!" Maya screamed.

I was still on Find, so I didn't hesitate, plunging headfirst after him. The second I hit the water, the brute force of it carried me into the tunnel, and I swam in that direction.

It was dark in the tunnel, and as I bobbed up and down in the current my head struck the cement above me. I ignored all of it, concentrating on Geoffrey, who was ahead of me in the darkness, soundlessly fighting for his life. His scent was faint but there, vanishing and reappearing in the deadly waters.

Without warning the floor fell away beneath me, and in complete darkness I rolled and bounced—the smaller tunnel had joined a much larger one, the water deeper, the sounds louder. I zeroed in on Geoffrey's scent, swimming strongly. Though I couldn't see him, he was just a few yards in front of me.

A second before he went under I knew what was going to happen—how many times had Ethan pulled this same stunt on me, waiting until I was close before dropping down into the pond? And, just as I always knew where to find the boy in the dark depths, I now had a clear sense of Geoffrey, tumbling just below me. I dove, straining, my mouth open, blinded and battered by the rushing waters, and then I had his hood in my mouth. Together, we burst through to the surface.

There was no way to go in any direction except the way the water was taking us. I concentrated on holding Geoffrey's head out of the water, pulling back on the hood. He was alive, but he had stopped kicking.

Some weak light from up ahead flickered on the wet cement walls—the tunnel we were in was square and six feet across, with no way out. How was I going to save Geoffrey?

The light grew stronger, and as it did my ears filled with a loud roar, echoing back toward us. The current seemed to be accelerating. I kept my grip on Geoffrey's hood, sensing that something was about to happen.

We burst into daylight, tumbling down a cement chute and landing with a splash in a swift-flowing river. I struggled to keep us both on the churning surface, battered by the waves. The banks of the river were lined with cement, but as I tugged Geoffrey toward the nearest one, the current fought me, trying to suck us back. Exhaustedly, my jaw and neck aching from the effort, I dragged Geoffrey toward the bank, swimming as hard as I could.

Flashing lights caught my eye, and I saw men in raincoats downstream from me, running toward the bank. I would be swept past them before I could get Geoffrey to safety.

Two of the men plunged into the water. They were tied together, and the rope went back to all the other men, who braced themselves. The two men stood hip high, straining their hands out to catch us, and I put everything I had into aiming for their arms.

"Gotcha!" one of the men shouted as Geoffrey and I slammed into them. He grabbed my collar as the other man hoisted Geoffrey into the air. The rope went taut and we all thrashed our way through the water to safety.

Once I was on land, the man released me and knelt down over Geoffrey. They squeezed his little body and he vomited up a gush of brown water, coughing and crying. I limped over to Geoffrey, and as his fear drained out of him it took mine with it. He was going to be okay.

The men ripped Geoffrey's clothing off him and wrapped him in blankets. "You'll be okay, boy; you'll be okay. Is this your doggy? She saved your life." Geoffrey didn't answer, but he looked briefly into my eyes.

"Let's go!" one of the men shouted, and they ran Geoffrey up the hill and into a truck, which took off with its siren screaming.

I lay down in the mud. My limbs were shaking violently, and I, too, vomited, a clean pain slicing through me. I was so weak I couldn't really even see. The cold rain pelted me and I just lay there.

A police car pulled up, cutting its sirens as it did so. I heard doors slam. "Ellie!" Maya screamed from the road. I raised my head, too tired to even wag my tail. She frantically ran down the bank, wiping at her tears. She was soaking wet, but I could feel her warmth and love as she hugged me to her chest. "You are a good dog, Ellie. You saved Geoffrey. You are such a good dog. Oh God, I thought I'd lost you, Ellie."

I spent the night at the vet's, and for the next several days I was so stiff I could barely move. Then Maya and I did school, only this one was all adults her age. We sat with lights in our eyes while a man talked in a loud voice, and then he came over and put a silly collar around my neck while even brighter lights, the ones like silent lightning, popped on and off all around us, the way they did when I was with Mom, after the fire that hurt Ethan's leg. The man also pinned something on Maya's uniform, and everybody clapped. I felt pride and love coming off of Maya, and when she whispered to me that I was a good dog I felt proud, too.

Not long after that, a new mood swept through the house. Maya and Al were excited and nervous and spent a lot of time having conversations at the table.

"If it is a boy, why can't it be Albert?" Al asked. "That's a good name."

"It's a great name, honey, but then what do we call him? You are my Albert, my Al."

"We could call him Bert."

"Oh, honey."

"Well, what are we going to call him, then? Your family has so many people in it, you've used up every name there is. We can't call him Carlos, Diego, Francisco, Ricardo—"

"What about Angel?"

"Angel? You want my son to be named Angel? I think maybe we shouldn't trust the naming of this child to a woman who named her cat Tinkerbell."

The cat, who was sleeping against me, didn't even raise her head at the sound of her name. Cats are like that; you can't get their attention unless they want to give it to you.

Maya was laughing. "How about Charles?"

"Charley? No, my first boss was named Charley," Al objected.

"Anthony?"

"Don't you have a cousin named Anthony?"

"His name is Antonio," Maya corrected.

"Well, I don't like him. His mustache looks silly."

Maya collapsed into giggles at this. I thumped my tail once in recognition of all the hilarity. "George?"

"No."

"Raul?"

"No."

"Jeremy?"

"Of course not."

"Ethan?"

I jumped up, and Al and Maya stared at me in surprise. "I guess Ellie likes it," Al said.

I cocked my head at them, uncertain. Tinkerbell was giving me a surly look. I trotted over to the door, lifting my nose.

"What is it, Ellie?" Maya asked.

There was no sign of the boy, and I was no longer sure I had heard right. Outside, some children rode past on bicycles, but none of them were Ethan. What was I thinking, that Ethan, like Jakob, would suddenly reappear in my life? I knew instinctively something like that would never happen to a dog. Still, Maya had said the boy's name, hadn't she? Why would she do that?

I went to Maya for reassurance, then eased down with a sigh. Tinkerbell trotted over and pressed up against me, and I glanced away from Al's knowing look, a little embarrassed.

Before long we had a new person in the house: little Gabriella, who smelled like sour milk and seemed even less useful than the cat. When she first brought the child home, Maya carefully held Gabriella for me to sniff, but I wasn't too impressed. From that moment on, Maya would get up frequently during the night and I would go with her and she would clutch Gabriella to her chest while I lay at her feet. The unrestrained love flowing from Maya during those moments always nudged me into a deep, peaceful sleep.

The aches in my bones were familiar to me; I'd felt the same way when I was Bailey and spent most of my time helping Grandpa do chores. Sights and sounds became dim, and this, too, was familiar.

I wondered if Maya knew that the day was soon coming when I would no longer be with them. It only stood to reason that I would die, the way Emmet and Stella died, because that was what happened. When I was Toby, when I was Bailey, it was the same thing.

As I lay in a patch of sun, pondering this, I realized that I had spent my life as a good dog. What I had learned from my first mother had led me to Ethan, and what I had learned from Ethan had enabled me to dive into those black waters and find Geoffrey. Along the way, Jakob had taught me to Find and Show and I had helped save many people.

This had to be why, when I left Ethan, I was reborn as Ellie—everything that I had done, everything that I had ever learned, had been leading up to being a good dog who saved people. It wasn't as much fun as being a doodle dog, but I now

knew why these creatures, these human beings, had so fascinated me from the moment I saw them. It was because my fate
was inextricably linked with theirs. Especially Ethan—that was
the bond of a lifetime.

Now that I had fulfilled my purpose, I felt sure I was at the
end, that there would be no rebirth after this, and I was at peace
with that. As wonderful as being a puppy could be, I wouldn't
want to share it with anyone but the boy. Maya and Al had little
Gabriella to distract them, making me sort of an afterthought
in the family, except, of course, for Tinkerbell, who thought I
was the family.

I wondered briefly if cats also came back after death, then
dismissed the thought because as far as I had ever been able to
tell, cats do not have a purpose.

Embarrassingly, I had started to have trouble containing
myself in time to make it outside and was more and more frequently leaving messes in the house. Even worse, Gabriella had
the same problem, so that the trash can often contained both of
our bowel movements.

Al took me on several front-seat dog car rides to see the vet,
who petted me all over while I groaned with pleasure. "You're
a good dog; you're just getting old," Al said. I wagged at being a
good dog. Maya was very busy with Gabriella, so more and
more it was just me and Al, which was okay by me. I could feel
his tender affection every time he helped me up so we could
take a car ride together.

One day Al had to carry me out into the yard to do my business and I felt the sadness in him break sharply as he came to
terms with what this meant. I licked his face in reassurance and
put my head in his lap when he sat on the ground to cry.

When Maya came home she brought the baby outside and

we all sat together. "You've been such a good dog, Ellie," Maya said over and over. "You're a hero dog. You saved lives. You saved that little boy Geoffrey."

A neighbor lady came over and picked up Gabriella. Maya bent over her child, loving her, whispering something in her ear. "Bye-bye, Ellie," Gabriella said. She held out her hand and the lady stooped so I could lick it.

"Say 'bye-bye,' " the woman said.

"Bye-bye," Gabriella said again. The lady took Gabriella into the house.

"This is so hard, Al." Maya sighed.

"I know. If you want, I will do it for you, Maya," Al said.

"No, no. I need to be there for Ellie."

Al gingerly picked me up and carried me to the car. Maya got in the backseat with me.

I knew where we were going on this car ride. Groaning with all my aches, I collapsed on the seat, my head in Maya's lap. I knew where we were going and was looking forward to the peace it would bring me. Maya stroked my head, and I closed my eyes. I wondered if there were anything I would have wanted to do one more time—Find? Swim in the ocean? Stick my head out the car window? These were all wonderful things—I had done them all, though, and that was enough.

I wagged my tail when they laid me on the familiar steel table. Maya was crying, whispering, "You're a good dog," over and over, and it was her words, and the sense of her love, that I took with me when I felt the tiny prick by my neck and then was washed away by the wonderfully warm ocean waters.

TWENTY-SIX

My new mother had a big, black face and a warm pink tongue. I stared up at her numbly the first time I realized it was all happening again—it didn't seem possible, not after being Ellie.

I had eight other brothers and sisters, all of them black, all of them healthy and full of play. For the most part, though, I preferred to wander off by myself and ponder what it meant that I was a puppy once more.

It made no sense. I understood how I would never have been with Ethan if, as Toby, I hadn't learned how to open a gate, and from my days in the culvert learned that there was nothing to fear on the other side of the fence. With Ethan I learned about love and companionship, and felt I was truly accomplishing my purpose, just by accompanying him on his daily adventures. But

Ethan also taught me how to rescue from the pond, and so when I was Ellie and learned how to Find and Show I was able to save the little boy from the tunnel of water. I would not have been so good at work if I hadn't had the experience of being Ethan's dog—Jakob's cold distance would have been incomprehensible and painful to me.

But now what? What could possibly happen now that would justify my rebirth as a puppy?

We were in a well-kept kennel with a cement floor, and twice a day a man came in and cleaned it out and took us out into a yard to romp in the grass. Other men and women spent time with us, lifting us and looking at our paws, and while I felt joy coming from them, none radiated that special love that I'd had with Ethan and with Maya and Al.

"Congratulations, you've got a fine litter here, Colonel," one of them said, holding me up in the air as he spoke. "Fetch top dollar."

"I'm worried about that one you've got in your hands, there," another man replied. He smelled like smoke, and the way my new mother responded to him when he came into the kennel let me know he was her owner. "Doesn't seem to have much energy."

"You have the vet look at him?" The man holding me flipped me over, running his thumbs under my lips to expose my teeth. I passively allowed this; I just wanted to be left alone.

"There doesn't seem to be anything wrong. He just goes off by himself and sleeps," the one called Colonel replied.

"Well, they can't all be champions," the first man said, setting me down.

I felt unhappiness from Colonel as he watched me trot away. I didn't know what I could have done wrong, but I imagined I wouldn't be here long anyway. If previous experience had taught me anything, it was that people who had a litter of puppies liked them, but not enough to keep them.

I was wrong, though. A few weeks later, most of my brothers and sisters were taken away by people, leaving just three of us left. I felt a sad resignation from my new mother, who had stopped nursing us but who still lowered her nose affectionately when any of us approached her to lick her face. She had apparently been through this before.

Over the next several days, people came to visit us and play games, like putting us in pillowcases, jangling keys in front of us, and tossing a ball past our noses to see what we would do. None of this struck me as a very rational way to behave around puppies, but everyone seemed very serious about the whole thing.

"Lot of money for one so small," a man remarked to Colonel.

"Sire's a two-time national field champion; mother's placed in state six years in a row, won twice. I think you'll get your money's worth," Colonel said.

They shook hands and then it was just my mother and a sister I'd named Pounce because she always leaped on me as if I couldn't see it coming. With her other brother gone, Pounce was on me relentlessly, and I found myself wrestling with her in self-defense. Colonel took note of my more active relationship, and I felt something like relief coming off him.

Then Pounce was taken away by a woman who smelled like horses and I was all alone, which I have to admit was how I preferred it.

"Have to lower the price, I guess," Colonel remarked a few days later. "Shame, that." I didn't even raise my head or run over to him to try to convince him not to be disappointed in me, which he apparently was.

In truth, I was feeling heartsick. I just couldn't understand what was happening to me, why I was a puppy again. The idea of going through training, of learning Find with someone other than Maya or Jakob, of living another life, simply defeated me. I felt like a bad dog.

I didn't race over to the fence to see people when they visited, not even when they had children—I didn't want to do that again, either. Ethan was the only child I would ever be interested in.

"What's wrong with him? Is he ill?" I heard a man ask one day.

"No. He just prefers to be off by himself," Colonel answered.

The man came into the kennel and picked me up. He had light blue eyes and regarded me kindly. "You're just a mellow fellow, is that it?" he asked me. I sensed an eagerness inside him, and somehow knew I would be leaving the kennel with him that day. I wandered over to my new mother and gave her a farewell lick on the face. She seemed to know it, too, and nuzzled me in return.

"Give you two fifty," the man with the blue eyes said. I felt a sharp surprise in Colonel.

"What? Sir, this dog's paternity—"

"Yeah, I read the ad. Look, it's for my girlfriend. She's not going to take him hunting; she just wants a dog. You said you'd make a deal. Now, I have to figure, if you've got a three-month-old puppy and breeding dogs is what you do, there's some reason people don't want this one. I don't think *you* want this one, either. So I can go on-line and adopt a Lab for nothing. I figure, this one has all the papers and the pedigree, I'll go two hundred and fifty bucks. Anybody else lining up to buy this dog? I don't think so."

A little while later, the man was loading me into the backseat of his car. He shook hands with Colonel, who was letting me leave without so much as a farewell pat on the head. The man handed Colonel a small piece of paper. "If you are ever looking for a good deal on a luxury automobile, give me a call," the man said cheerfully.

I sized up my new owner. I liked that he was letting me be a front-seat dog, but when he gazed over at me I felt nothing like affection coming from him but rather a complete indifference.

I soon found out why: I would not be living with the man, whose name turned out to be Derek. My new home was with a woman named Wendi, who screamed and jumped up and down when Derek brought me into the house. Wendi and Derek immediately started wrestling together, so I found myself exploring the apartment in which I now lived. There were shoes and clothes scattered everywhere, and boxes with dried food stuck to the insides sitting out on a low table in front of the couch. I licked these clean.

Derek didn't radiate any particular affection toward Wendi, either, even though he hugged her as he was walking out the door. Whenever Al used to leave the house, the quick rush of love he felt toward Maya always made me wag my tail, but this man wasn't like that at all.

Wendi's love for me was instant but confusing, a jumble of emotions that I didn't understand. Over the next several days she named me Pooh-Bear, Google, Snoopdog, Leno, and Pistachio. Then I was Pooh-Bear again, though she soon just stuck with Bear and its variations: Barry-Boo, Bear-Bear, Honeywoney Bear, Cuddle Bear, and Wonder Bear. She would hold me down and kiss me all over and squeeze me as if she couldn't get enough of me, and then the phone would ring and she'd drop me to the floor to answer it.

Every morning Wendi rummaged through her belongings,

her feelings wrapped up in a roiling panic, saying, "I'm late! I'm late!" She would bang out the door and then I'd be alone all day, bored silly.

She put newspapers on the floor, but I couldn't remember if I was supposed to pee on them or avoid them, so I did a little of both. My teeth were so sore my mouth was watering, so I wound up chewing on a couple of shoes, which sent Wendi into a screaming fit when she saw it. Sometimes she forgot to feed me and then I had no choice but to dive into the trash can for something, and this, too, caused screaming.

As far as I could see, life with Wendi had no purpose whatso-ever. We didn't train together; we didn't even walk together much—she would open the door and let me run around in the yard at night, but hardly ever during the day, and only then with an odd, furtive fear, as if we were doing something wrong. I be-came so frustrated, so full of pent-up energy, that I wound up barking, sometimes for hours straight, my voice ringing off the walls and back at me.

One day there was a loud knock on the door. "Bear! Come here!" Wendi hissed at me. She locked me in her bedroom, but I could easily hear a man speaking to her. He sounded mad.

"Not allowed to have a dog! It's in your lease!" I cocked my head at the word "dog," wondering if I might be the source of the man's anger. I hadn't, as far as I knew, done anything wrong, but all the rules were different at this crazy place, so who could say?

The next time Wendi left for work she broke the pattern, calling me over and sitting me down. She seemed completely unimpressed that I knew how to sit on command without being taught. "Look, Bear-Bear, you can't bark while I'm gone, okay? I'll get in trouble with the neighbors. No barking, okay?"

I could feel sadness at the edges of her feelings and wondered what it was all about. Perhaps she was bored all day, too. Why didn't she just take me with her? I loved car rides! I barked out my pent-up energy all afternoon, but I didn't chew any shoes.

A day or so later, Wendi opened the door with one hand and pulled a piece of paper off the outside of the door with another. I raced over to her, my bladder bursting, but she didn't let me out. Instead she looked at the paper and then started shouting angrily. I had no choice but to squat on the kitchen floor, and she smacked me on the bottom with an open palm and then opened the door.

"Here, you might as well go out; everybody knows you're here anyway," she muttered. I finished my business in the yard. I was sorry I had made the mess in the kitchen, but I simply hadn't had an option.

The next day, Wendi slept in late and then we got in the car and went for a long, long car ride. I was a backseat dog because of all the things piled on the front seat, but she did lower the window so I could poke my nose out it. We pulled up in the driveway of a small house with several vehicles in the yard—I could tell by the smell of them that they hadn't moved in a long time. I lifted my leg on one of them.

An older woman opened the door.

"Hi, Mom," Wendi said.

"Is that it? It's huge. You said it was a puppy."

"Well, I named him Bear; what did you think?"

"This isn't going to work."

"Mom! I have no choice! I got an eviction notice!" Wendi yelled angrily.

"Well, what in the world were you thinking, anyway?"

"He was a gift from Derek! What was I supposed to do, take him back?"

"Why would he get you a dog when you can't have dogs in the apartment?"

"Because I said I wanted him, too, okay, Mom? Are you happy? I said I wanted a dog. God."

The feelings the two women had toward each other were so complex, there was no way I could sort them out. Wendi and I spent the night in the tiny home, both of us a little afraid: there was a man named Victor who came home when it was dark, and he was so full of rage it made everything feel dangerous and crazy. While Wendi and I slept in a narrow bed in a cramped back room, Victor yelled in another part of the house.

"I don't want a dog here!"

"Well, it's my place and I'll do what I want!"

"What are we supposed to do with a dog?"

"That's a stupid question; what does anyone do with a dog?"

"Shut up, Lisa; just shut up."

"It will be okay, Barry-Boo. I wouldn't let anything happen to you," Wendi whispered to me. She was so sad I licked her hand in reassurance, but that just made her cry.

The next morning, the two women stood outside and talked next to the car. I sniffed along the door's edge, waiting to be let inside. The sooner Wendi and I left this place, the better.

"God, Mom, how can you put up with him?" Wendi said.

"He's not so bad. He's better than your father."

"Oh, don't start."

They stood silently for a minute. I gave the air a sniff—it carried with it the sour fragrance of the garbage stacked up next to the house, which, frankly, smelled delightful. I wouldn't mind digging around in there, someday.

"Well, call me when you get home," the older woman finally said.

"I will, Mom. Take good care of Bear."

"Yeah." The woman put a cigarette in her mouth and lit it, blowing smoke out sharply.

Wendi knelt beside me, and her sadness was so strong and familiar I knew what was coming. She stroked my face and told me I was a good dog, and then opened the door and slid inside without letting me in. I watched the car drive away without surprise, though I wasn't at all sure what I had done. If I was such a good dog, why was I being abandoned by my owner?

"Now what?" the woman standing next to me muttered, puffing her cigarette.

TWENTY-SEVEN

O ver the next several weeks, I learned to stay away from Victor. Most of the time this was easy, as I was chained to a post in the backyard and Victor never approached me. Often I could see him, though, sitting by a window in the kitchen, smoking and drinking. Sometimes at night he would come out into the backyard to urinate, and that was about the only time he talked to me. "Whatcha looking at, dog?" he'd shout at me. There was never any happiness in his laughter.

The days grew warmer, so for shade I dug out a scoop of earth between the sagging back fence and a machine that sat in the sun.

"Dog got dirt all over my snowmobile!" Victor yelled when he saw what I had done.

"Thing hasn't run in two years!" the woman, Lisa, screamed

back. They yelled at each other a lot. It reminded me a little of when Mom and Dad would get angry and shout, except that at this house I'd sometimes hear a thud and a cry of pain, usually accompanied by the sound of bottles knocking together and falling to the floor.

A nice old lady lived in a place behind the rotten wooden fence, and she started coming over to talk to me through the gaps and holes in the boards. "Such a nice doggy, do you have water today?" she whispered the first really hot morning. She left and soon reappeared with a pitcher, from which she poured a cool stream of water into my dirty bowl. I lapped it up gratefully and licked the thin, shaking hand she extended through the fence hole.

The flies buzzing around my stools landed on my lips and eyes, driving me a little crazy, but mostly I didn't mind lying in the backyard as long as I could be away from Victor. He scared me; the malevolence flowing from him communicated a real sense of danger. I was reminded of Todd, and the man with the gun who hurt Jakob. I'd bitten both men; did that mean I would someday be biting Victor?

I simply could not believe that my purpose in this life was to attack humans. It was beyond unacceptable. The mere thought made me sick.

When Victor was not home I would bark and Lisa would come out and feed me and let me off the chain a little bit, but I never once barked when he was in the house.

The lady on the other side of the fence brought me little pieces of meat, which she poked through the hole. When I caught the meat as it fell through the air, she laughed with real delight, as if I had performed an amazing trick. It seemed the only purpose I really had, bringing a little bit of joy to a mysterious woman whose face I couldn't quite see.

"This is a shame, a real shame. They can't do this to an animal. I'm going to call somebody," she'd say. I could feel how much she cared about me, though it was strange, because she never came into the yard to play.

One day a truck pulled into the driveway and a woman got out dressed just the way Maya used to dress, so I knew she was a police officer. For a moment it felt as if she had come to fetch me to Find, because she stood at the gate to the backyard and stared at me, writing something down. That didn't really make sense, though, and when Lisa came outside, her hands on her hips, I lay down. The police officer handed Lisa a piece of paper.

"The dog's just fine!" Lisa shouted at her, really angry. I sensed the old lady standing behind me, just on the other side of the fence. She was breathing quietly while Lisa raged.

That night Victor yelled about me even more than usual, the word "dog" popping up every few seconds.

"Why don't we just shoot the damn dog?" he yelled. "Fifty dollars? For what? We're not doing anything wrong!" Something crashed in the house, a violent noise that made me cower.

"We have to get a longer chain, and clean up all the crap in the yard. Read the ticket!" Lisa shouted back.

"I don't have to read the ticket! They can't make us do a damn thing! It's our property!"

That night, when Victor came out into the yard to urinate, he put his hand out to steady himself against the house and missed, tumbling to the ground. "What are you starin' at, stupid mutt," he mumbled at me. "Take care of you tomorrow. Not payin' any fifty bucks."

I slunk down low against the fence, not even daring to look back at him.

The next day my focus was distracted by a butterfly who was flittering around in front of my face, so I was startled when Victor suddenly appeared before me.

"You want to go for a car ride?" Victor crooned at me. I didn't wag at the words; somehow, he made it sound like a threat instead of a treat. *No,* I thought, *I do not want to go for a car ride with you.*

"It'll be fun. See the world," he said, his laugh turning into a cough that caused him to turn and spit on the ground. He unclipped my chain from the post and led me to his car, yanking me around to the back of it when I stopped at the door. He inserted his key and the trunk popped open. "In ya go," he said. I sensed his anticipation and waited for a command I understood. "Hokay," he said. He reached down and gripped me in the loose skin at the back of my neck and above my tail. There was a quick flash of pain as he hoisted me up and then I was in the trunk, sliding on some greasy papers. He unsnapped my leash and let it pool on the floor in front of me. The lid slammed down, and I was in near-total darkness.

I was lying on some smelly, oily rags that reminded me of the night of the fire, when Ethan hurt his legs, and some cold metal tools, so it was hard to get comfortable. One of the tools was easily identifiable as a gun; the acrid fragrance was unmistakable. I turned away from it, trying to ignore the sharp smells.

I lay in a half crouch, my nails extended in a hopeless attempt to keep from slipping from one side to the other in the narrow trunk as the car bounced and swayed.

It was the strangest car ride I'd ever had, and the only one I could remember that wasn't any fun. Still, car rides always resulted in a new place, and new places were always fun to explore. Maybe there would be other dogs, or maybe I was going back to live with Wendi.

The cramped, dark space soon became quite warm, and I found myself thinking of the room I'd been placed in with Spike, back when my name was Toby and I was taken from the senora. I hadn't thought about that scary moment in a long time. So much had happened since then. I was a completely different dog now, a good dog who had saved people.

After I spent a long, miserable time in that trunk, the car began to vibrate and ping and dust rose up in the air, a thick, choking cloud. I sneezed, shaking my head. Then the car braked to a sudden halt, sending me crashing against the inside of the trunk. The motor didn't shut off, though, and we sat for a minute.

Oddly, as soon as we stopped, I could sense Victor inside the car on the other side of the trunk, feel his presence. I had the distinct sense that he was trying to make up his mind about something—there was a feeling of indecisiveness. Then he said something sharply, a word that was muffled, and I heard the front door open. Victor's feet crunched on gravel as he came around to where I lay cringing, and I smelled him before the trunk popped open and cool air whooshed in around me.

He stared down at me. Blinking, I raised my eyes to his, then looked away so he wouldn't think I was challenging him.

"All right." He reached down and twisted at my collar. I expected him to attach my leash, so I was surprised when the collar itself fell away, leaving behind it an odd sensation, as if I were still wearing a collar, only one light as air. "Get on out of there, now."

My legs were cramped as I stood up. I recognized his hand gestures and jumped out of the car, landing awkwardly. We were on a dirt road, long green grass waving in the sun from both shoulders. Grit from the road painted the insides of my nose and settled on my tongue. I lifted my leg, looking over at him. What now?

Victor got back in his car and the engine made a loud noise. I stared at him in confusion as his tires bit at the road, spitting rocks. He turned the car around, pointing it in the opposite direction. Then he rolled down his window.

"I'm doing you a favor. You're free, now. Go catch some rabbits or somethin'." He grinned at me and took off, the car kicking up a huge cloud of dirt behind it.

Baffled, I watched it go. What sort of game was this? Hesitantly, I followed, easily tracking the dust as it drifted through the air.

I knew from my many years of Find that I was quickly losing the scent—Victor must be driving very fast. I gamely picked up the pace, no longer following the dust cloud but focusing instead on the signature smells from the back of his car, where I'd just spent so much time.

I was able to track him when he turned onto a paved road, but when another turn took me to a highway, with cars flashing past at amazing speeds, I knew I'd lost him. So many cars were whizzing by, each one with smells similar to (though not exactly like) Victor's. Picking out the one scent on which I was doing Find was impossible.

The highway was intimidating; I turned from it and headed back the direction I'd come. With nothing else to do I back-tracked along the same scent trail, now faint in the late afternoon breezes. When I came to the dirt road, though, I passed it and kept heading aimlessly up the pavement.

I remembered when I used the trick my very first mother had

taught me and escaped from the kennel when I was a puppy the second time, how it seemed like such an adventure to run out in the open, free and full of life. Then the man found me and named me Fella, and then Mom came and took me to Ethan.

This was nothing like that. I didn't feel free; I didn't feel full of life. I felt guilty and sad. I had no purpose, no direction. I would not be able to make my way home from here. It was like when Colonel turned away from me, the day Derek took me to live with Wendi—though no feelings came from Colonel, it was nonetheless good-bye. Victor had just done the same thing, except he had handed me to nobody.

The dust and heat made me pant, my thirst itching at my mouth. When I picked up the faint scent of water, it was the most natural thing in the world to turn in that direction, leaving the road and walking through high grasses that tossed themselves back and forth in the breeze.

The smell of water grew stronger, more tantalizing, drawing me through a stand of trees and down a steep bank to a river. I waded in to my chest, biting at the water, lapping it up. It felt glorious.

With my urgent thirst no longer my only concern, I allowed myself to open my senses to my surroundings. The river filled my nose with its wonderful damp smell, and along with the gurgle of the waters I could hear, very faintly, a duck squawking over some imagined outrage. I padded along the bank, my feet sinking into the soft soil.

And then it came to me with such a jolt I lifted my head in surprise, my eyes wide open.

I knew where I was.

TWENTY-EIGHT

A long, long time ago I had stood on the banks of this very river, perhaps on this very spot, when Ethan and I had gone for our long walk after Flare, the dumb horse, abandoned us. The scent was unmistakable—doing Find all those years had taught me how to separate out odors, categorize and store them in memory, so that now I could instantly remember this place. It helped that it was summer, the same time of year, and that I was young and my nose so sharp.

I couldn't possibly fathom how Victor might have known this, or what it meant that he had released me so that I would find the place. I had no sense as to what he wanted me to do. Lacking any better idea, I turned downstream and started trotting, retracing the very same steps Ethan and I had taken, those many years ago.

By the end of the day I was hungrier than I could remember ever being, so hungry my stomach cramped. Wistfully I thought of the old woman's pale hand poking through the fence and dropping little pieces of meat for me to snatch out of midair; the memory made me drool. The riverbank was choked with vegetation and made for slow going, and it seemed that the hungrier I became, the less certain I was of my course of action. Was this really what I should do, follow this stream? Why?

I was a dog who had learned to live among and serve humans as my sole purpose in life. Now, cut off from them, I was adrift. I had no purpose, no destiny, no hope. Anyone spotting me slinking along the shores at that moment might mistake me for my timid, furtive first mother—that's how far back Victor's abandonment had thrown me.

A giant tree that had snapped during the winter and fallen by the water formed a natural hollow on the bank, and as the sun faded from the sky I climbed into this dark place, sore and exhausted and completely puzzled by the changes in my life.

My hunger woke me the next morning, but lifting my nose into the air brought me nothing but the smells of the river and the surrounding forest. I followed the flow of water downstream because I had nothing better to do, but I was moving more slowly than the day before, hobbled by the empty ache in my belly. I thought of the dead fish that sometimes washed up at the pond—why had I merely rolled in them? Why hadn't I eaten them when I had the chance? A dead fish now would be heavenly, but the river yielded nothing edible.

So miserable was I that when the rough bank gave way to a footpath redolent with the scent of humans I hardly noticed. I ambled lethargically along, only halting when the path rose steeply and joined a road.

The road led to a bridge over the river. I raised my head, the fog lifting from my mind. Sniffing excitedly, I realized I had been here before. Ethan and I had been picked up by a policeman on this very spot and taken for a car ride back to the Farm!

Many years had obviously passed—some small trees I remembered marking at one end of the bridge had grown to be towering giants, so I marked them again. And the rotting planks on the bridge had been replaced. But otherwise, the smells were exactly the same as I remembered.

An automobile rattled by as I stood on the bridge. It honked at me and I flinched back from it. After a minute, though, I hesitantly followed it, abandoning the river for the road ahead.

I had no idea where to go now, but something told me that if I went in this direction, I would eventually arrive in town. Where there was a town there were people, and where there were people there was food.

When the road joined another, the same inner sense told me to turn right, and I did so, though I shrank guiltily away when I sensed a car coming, sliding into the high grasses. I felt like a bad dog, and my hunger only enforced this belief.

I passed many houses, most of them set far back from the road, and often dogs would bark at me, upset by my trespass. Around nightfall, I was slinking past a place with a dog smell when the side door opened and a man stepped out. "Dinner, Leo? Want dinner?" he asked, his voice carrying that deliberate excitement people use when they want to make sure a dog knows something good is happening. A metal bowl was dropped with a loud clang on the top step of a short set of stairs.

The word "dinner" arrested me in my tracks. I stood riveted as a squat dog with enormous jaws and a thick body eased down the steps and did his business a few feet into the yard. The way he moved suggested he was an old dog, and he didn't smell me. He went back and nosed around in his bowl a little, then reached up and scratched the door. After a minute, it opened back up.

"Are you sure, Leo? Are you sure you can't eat anything?" the man asked. There was a sadness in his voice that reminded me of the way Al cried in the yard, that last day I spent with him and Maya. "Okay, then. Come on in, Leo."

The dog groaned but couldn't seem to pull his back legs up the last step, so with tender gentleness the man bent and picked the dog up, carrying him inside.

I felt myself powerfully drawn to the man and was struck with the sudden thought that this could be a home for me. The man loved his dog, Leo, and would love me. He would feed me, and when I was old and weak he would carry me back inside his home. Even if I didn't do Find or school or any other work at all, if all I did was devote myself to the man in the house, I would have a place to live. This crazy, purposeless life I had led as Bear would be over.

I approached the house and did the sensible thing: I ate Leo's dinner. After the weeks of tasteless, gritty dog food at Lisa and Victor's home, the succulent, meaty meal in Leo's bowl was the best thing I'd ever tasted. When it was gone I licked the metal, and the clang of the bowl against the side of the house alerted the dog inside, who woofed warningly. I heard him approach his side of the door, wheezing, a low growl mounting in volume as Leo became more sure I was there.

It didn't sound as if Leo would be very receptive to the idea of me living in his house.

I bolted off the steps, so that by the time the light flicked on to illuminate the yard I was already back in the trees. The message in Leo's hostile growl was clear; I would have to find my own home. And that was okay—with my hunger sated, my longing to live here had gone away.

I slept in some tall grasses, tired but much more content, my stomach full.

I was hungry again by the time I found town, but I knew it was the right place. The approach fooled me; I passed so many houses, their streets bustling with cars and children, where my memory told me there should have been only fields. But then I came upon the place where Grandpa used to sit with his friends and spit vile juices out of his mouth, and it smelled the same, though there were sheets of old wood over the windows and the building next to it was gone, replaced by a raw, muddy hole. At the bottom of the hole was a machine that pushed great piles of dirt in front of it as it moved.

Humans can do that, take down old buildings and put up new ones, the way Grandpa built a new barn. They alter their environment to suit themselves, and all dogs can do is accompany them and, if they're lucky, go for car rides. The volume of noise and all the new smells told me that humans here had been very busy changing their town.

Several people stared at me as I trotted down the street, and each time I felt like a bad dog. I had no real purpose, now that I was here. A bag of trash had fallen out of a big metal bin, and it was with a huge sense of guilt that I tore the bag open and pulled out a piece of meat covered in a sticky, sweet sauce of some kind. Rather than eat the meal right there, I ran behind the metal bin, hiding from people just as my first mother had taught me.

My wanderings eventually brought me to the dog park. I sat at the edge, under some trees, and watched enviously as people threw soaring disks for their dogs to catch in the air. I felt naked without a collar and realized I should hang back, but the way the dogs were wrestling in the middle of the big yard drew me like a magnet, and before I could stop myself I was out there with them, rolling and running and forgetting myself in the sheer joy of being a dog at play.

Some dogs didn't come out to wrestle; they stayed with their people or sniffed along the perimeter of the park, pretending that they didn't care how much fun we were having. Some dogs were drawn to tossed balls or flying disks, and all of them eventually were called away by their people and given car rides. All except me, but none of the people seemed to notice or care that I didn't have anyone there with me.

Toward the end of the day, a woman brought a big female yellow dog to the park and let her off the leash. By this time I was exhausted from all the play and was just lying in the yard, panting, watching two other dogs wrestle. The yellow dog excitedly joined them, interrupting the play for sniffing and tail wagging. I lurched to my feet and went to greet this new arrival and was shocked by what I smelled along her fur.

It was Hannah. The girl.

The yellow dog grew impatient with my feverish examination of her scent and spun away, eager to play, but I ignored her inviting bow. I excitedly dashed across the park to the dog's owner.

The woman on the bench was not Hannah, though she, too, carried Hannah's smell. "Hello, doggy, how are you?" she greeted me as I approached, my tail wagging. The way she sat reminded me of Maya, shortly before Gabriella the baby arrived. There was a sense of tiredness, excitement, impatience, and discomfort, all mixed together and focused on the belly just below her hands. I thrust my nose at her, drinking in Hannah's scent, separating it from the woman, from the happy yellow dog, from the dozens of odors that clung to a person and were a jumble to a dog not trained in Find. This was a woman who had spent time with the girl very recently; I was sure of it.

The yellow dog came over, friendly but a bit jealous, and I finally allowed myself to be drawn into a tussle.

That night I folded my black body into the shadows, watching alertly as the last cars pulled out of the parking lot, leaving the dog park in silence. My stealth came to me so easily it was as if I'd never been taken from the culvert, as if I were still there with Sister and Fast and Hungry, learning from our first mother. Hunting was easy; trash cans were brimming with containers full of delicious scraps, and I avoided headlights and pedestrians with equal caution, hidden, dark, feral once more.

But there was a purpose to my life, now, a sense of direction even more powerful than the one that had brought me to town in the first place.

If, despite all the time and changes, the girl Hannah was here, then maybe the boy was here, too.

And if Ethan was still here, I would track him. I would Find Ethan.

TWENTY-NINE

After more than a week, I was still living in the dog park.
    Most days the woman with Hannah's scent would bring
her happy yellow canine—Carly was the dog's name—to the park.
The smell of the girl reassured me, somehow, made me feel that
Ethan was nearby, though Carly never had the boy's smell on her
fur, not once. Seeing the woman and Carly always brought me
racing joyously out from the bushes; it was the high point of my day.

Otherwise, I was a bad dog. Regulars to the park were starting
to act suspicious toward me, staring at me and radiating caution
as they pointed at me and spoke to each other. I no longer approached their dogs for play.

"Hey there, fella. Where's your collar? Who are you here
with?" a man asked me, reaching out with gentle hands. I danced
back from him, sensing his intention to grab me and not trusting

the name Fella. That's when I felt the deep suspicion in him and realized my first mother had been right all along—to remain free, one had to steer clear of people.

My thought was to find the Farm the way I'd found the town, but that proved more difficult than I would have supposed. Whenever I'd gone for a car ride to town with Ethan or Grandpa, I'd always used the smell of the goat ranch as my point of reference, a beacon for my nose. But all traces of the goats had mysteriously vanished from the air. Also vanished was the bridge whose rattle signaled the divide between car ride and car ride in town—I couldn't find the place at all, not by smell, nor by any other sense. Padding along quiet streets after dark, I'd be confident of my direction, and then a large building would block both my path and my nose with the smells of hundreds of people and dozens of cars. A fountain of water in front of the place added even more confusion to the air, the mist carrying with it a faint chemical smell, like when Maya washed clothes. I lifted my leg against the thing, but that provided only momentary comfort.

At night, my black fur felt like protection from discovery. I melted into shadows, hiding from cars, emerging when there was no one around, always on Find, always concentrating on what I could remember about the Farm and its scent when I breathed in the night air. Frustratingly, I couldn't pick up a trace of anything.

Meals came from trash cans and the occasional dead animal by the side of the road—rabbits were best, crows the worst. I had competition: an animal the size of a small dog, with a very heavy scent, thick, bushy tail, and dark black eyes, prowled the bins, adroitly climbing up their sides. Whenever I encountered one of these things it snarled at me and I gave it a wide berth, seeing nothing in those teeth and claws but an invitation to pain. Whatever they were, they were obviously too stupid to realize I was much bigger and that they should be afraid of me.

Also stupid were the squirrels in the park, who descended from their trees and bounced around in the grass as if the entire area weren't protected by dogs! I had come very close to catching one, except they always darted up trees and then sat up there complaining. Carly the yellow dog often joined me in the hunt, but even together we were thus far unsuccessful. I knew if we kept trying, one day we'd capture one, though I wasn't sure exactly what we would do then.

"What's the matter, honey? Why are you so skinny? Don't you have a home?" Carly's owner asked me. I picked up the concern in her voice and wagged my tail, wishing she would just take me for a car ride and drop me off at the Farm. When she stood up off the bench, struggling to get to her feet, I sensed a hesitation in her, as if she was going to invite me to walk with them. I knew it would be okay with Carly, who always ran out into the dog park looking specifically for me, but I pulled away from the woman's magnetic concern, acting as if I had someone nearby who loved me and was calling me. I trotted a dozen yards away before I stopped and glanced behind me—she was still watching me, one hand on her hip, the other hand resting on her stomach.

That afternoon a truck pulled into the parking lot with such a strong dog smell I instantly picked it up from where I lay in the grass at the edge of the park. A policeman got out and chatted with a few dog owners, who pointed at various places in the park. The policeman pulled out a long pole with a noose on the end, and I felt a chill go through me. I knew exactly who that pole was for.

The policeman walked around the edges of the park, gingerly peering into the bushes, but by the time he approached my hiding place I was gone, deep in the woods that lay beyond the park.

My panic kept me running; when the woods petered out into a neighborhood filled with dogs and children, I avoided human contact and did my best to stay in the foliage. I was far from town when I finally doubled back, taking comfort in the fact that my ally, darkness, was descending from the sky.

When the smell of dozens of dogs drifted toward me, I turned in that direction, curious. A volley of barking was coming from the back of a large building, a couple of dogs in cages howling at each other. A shift in the wind and they were barking at *me*, the timbre in their voices changing.

I had been here before: this was where the nice man the vet took care of me when I was Bailey. It was, in fact, the very last place I had ever been with Ethan. I decided to give the place a wide berth. I scooted around to the front of the building, and as I crossed the driveway I stopped dead, quivering.

When I was Bailey, a new baby donkey named Jasper had joined old, unreliable Flare in the yard one day. Jasper grew up to be much smaller than a horse but was built along similar lines, and he made Grandpa laugh and Grandma shake her head. I'd been nose-to-nose with Jasper; I'd sniffed him carefully when Grandpa brushed him; I'd played with him as best as I could. I knew Jasper's smell like I knew the Farm, and there was no mistaking that scent now, right here in the driveway. Tracking back toward the building, I could find a concentrated area in the parking lot where the scent was overwhelming and fresh—there was even a dusting of straw and dirt with Jasper painted all over it, lying thick in the gravel.

The dogs were still baying at me, outraged that I was free while they were penned, but I ignored the racket. Drinking in the rich mixture of smells in the dirt, I trailed down the driveway and out onto the road.

The first time a car rushed up behind me, honking as its lights played out into the night, I was startled, so focused was I on following Jasper's scent. I veered into the ditch by the side of the road, cringing from the accusatory wail of the car as it sailed past.

After that, I was more careful. While I was focused on Jasper, my ears were aware of the sounds of automobiles, and I slunk away from them long before their lights picked me up.

Though the track was long, it was easier than Find Wally—for more than an hour I traced in a straight line, finally making a left turn, and then another. Jasper's scent was weaker the farther I went, which meant I was trailing him backward and that there was a danger I might lose him altogether. But after a right turn I no longer needed the scent; I knew where I was. Right here was where the train crossed the road, the train that had stopped Ethan's car the first day he left to do college. I picked up the pace, Jasper's scent validating the instinctive turn I took to the right. Soon I was passing Hannah's house, which curiously emitted no scent of the girl herself, though the trees and the moss-covered brick wall by the road were still the same.

Turning up the driveway to the Farm was such a natural move it felt as if I had just been there yesterday.

Jasper's smell tracked right up to a large white trailer, a pile of grit and hay beneath it. His odors were painted everywhere and there was a new horse watching me with drowsy suspicion as I sniffed along the fence, but I was no longer interested in horses. Ethan, I could smell Ethan; he was everywhere. The boy must still live on the Farm!

Never before in my entire existence had I felt the joyous excitement that coursed through me then: I was dizzy with it.

The lights were on in the house, and as I circled around to the side, staying on the small grassy hill, I could see through the window into the living room. A man Grandpa's age sat in a chair, watching television, but he didn't look like Grandpa. Ethan was not in the room, nor was anyone else.

The dog door was still there in the outer metal door, but the big wooden door on the inside was firmly shut. Frustrated, I scratched at the metal door, then barked.

I heard vibrations within the house as someone approached. My tail was wagging so hard I couldn't sit down; it pulled my whole body back and forth. The light blinked on overhead, and the wooden door made a familiar scratching sound before it eased open. The man I'd seen sitting in the chair stood on the threshold, frowning down at me through the glass.

I scratched again at the metal; I wanted him to let me in so I could run in and be with the boy.

"Hey," he said, his voice muffled by the closed door. "Stop that."

I heard the rebuke and tried to sit obediently, but my butt bounced right back up.

"What do you want?" he asked finally. I heard the question in his voice, wondered what he was asking me.

Then I realized I didn't have to wait for him to make up his mind—with the inner door open, the dog door was free. I lowered my head and pushed through the plastic curtain, bursting into the house.

"Hey!" the old man shouted, surprised.

I was surprised, too. The second I was in the house, I clearly smelled the person blocking my way. I knew who he was: I would recognize that scent anywhere.

Unmistakably Ethan.

I'd found the boy.

THIRTY

T hough Ethan was standing, I tried to leap into his lap. I lunged up, straining to lick him, nuzzle him, climb on him. I couldn't stop the sobs coming from my throat; I couldn't keep my tail from flying.

"Hey!" he said, backing away and blinking. He tried to steady himself on his cane, and then he sat down heavily on the floor. I jumped on him, licking his face. He pushed my mouth away. "Okay, okay," he grumbled. "Stop it. Okay."

The feel of his hands on my face was the most wonderful sensation I'd ever encountered in my life. I half-closed my eyes with the pleasure of it. "Get back now; get back," he said.

The boy laboriously climbed back to his feet. I pressed my face into his hand, and he briefly stroked me. "Okay. Goodness. Who are you?" He snapped on another light, peering at me.

"Whoa, you're a skinny one. Doesn't anybody feed you? Huh? Are you lost or something?"

I could sit there all night and just listen to his voice and feel his gaze on me, but it wasn't to be. "Well, look, you can't come inside." He opened the outer door and held it. "Out now, go on outside."

It was a command I recognized, so, reluctantly, I went. He stood and looked at me through the glass. I sat expectantly. "You're going to have to go home, dog," he said. I wagged. I knew I was "go home," I was finally, finally "go home," on the Farm where I belonged, with Ethan, where I belonged.

He shut the door.

I waited obediently until the strain was just too much and then yipped a bark full of impatience and frustration. When there was no response, I yipped again, giving the metal door a good pawing as well.

I'd lost count of how many times I'd barked when the door opened again. Ethan was carrying a metal pan, succulent odors wafting off of it. "Here," he muttered. "You hungry, buddy?"

As soon as he set the pan down I dove into the dinner, bolting the food.

"It's mostly lasagna. I don't have much in the way of dog food around here. You look like you're not fussy, though."

I wagged.

"You can't live here, though. I can't have a dog; I don't have time for it. You're going to have to go home."

I wagged.

"Good lord, when was the last time you ate? Don't eat so fast; you'll make yourself sick."

I wagged.

When I was done, Ethan bent slowly down to pick up the pan. I licked his face. "Yuck, you have really bad breath, you know that?" He wiped his sleeve on his face and stood back up. I watched him, ready to do anything he wanted. Go for a walk? Go for a car ride? Play with the stupid flip? "Okay then. You go on home; dog like you obviously isn't a mutt. Somebody must be looking for you. Okay? Good night."

Ethan shut the door.

I sat there for a few minutes. When I barked, the light over my head went off with a click.

I went around to the small grassy hill by the side of the house and looked into the living room. Ethan was moving slowly across the floor, leaning on his cane, turning off one light after another.

My boy was so old, I never would have recognized him. But now that I knew it was him, the gait was familiar, if more stiff, and the way he turned his head and peered out into the night before snapping off the final lamp, ears cocked as if listening for something, was pure Ethan.

I was confused over being an outside dog, but the food in my belly and the exhaustion in my limbs soon overtook me and I curled up on the spot, tucking my nose near my tail even though the night was warm. I was home.

When Ethan came outside the next morning I shook myself off and ran over to him, trying to restrain myself from showering so much affection on him. He stared at me. "Why are you still here, huh, boy? What are you doing here?"

I followed him into the barn, where he let a horse I'd never seen before out into the yard. Naturally, the dumb animal didn't react when he saw me—just gazed at me the way Flare used to, no comprehension registering. *I'm a dog, you idiot!* I marked the yard while Ethan gave the horse some oats. "How are you doing today, Troy? You miss Jasper, don't you? You miss your pal Jasper."

Ethan was talking to the horse, which I could have told him was a complete waste of time. He stroked the horse's nose, calling him Troy and mentioning the name Jasper more than once, though when I went into the barn the donkey wasn't there, just his smell. Jasper's scent was particularly strong in the trailer.

"That was a sad day, the day I had to take Jasper in. He lived a good long time, though. Forty-four is pretty old for a little donkey."

I felt sorrow in Ethan and nuzzled his hand. He regarded me absently, his mind somewhere else. He gave Troy a final pat and went back into his house.

A few hours later I was sniffing around the yard, waiting for Ethan to come out to play, when a truck swung up into the driveway. As soon as it stopped I recognized it as the one I'd seen in the parking lot of the dog park, and the man who eased himself out of the front seat was the same policeman I'd smelled who'd been probing the bushes with the pole and noose, which he now grabbed from the back of the truck.

"You won't need that!" Ethan called, stepping outside. I turned from the man and went wagging over to my boy. "He's really cooperative."

"Just wandered up last night?" the policeman replied.

"That's right. Look at the ribs on the poor animal. You can tell he's a purebred, but someone sure hasn't been treating him right."

"We've heard reports of a nice-looking Labrador running loose down at the city park. Wonder if this is the same one," the policeman said.

"Don't know about that. Pretty far," Ethan replied dubiously.

The man opened a cage on the back of his truck. "You think he'll just go in? I'm not in a mood to chase him down."

"Hey, dog. Up here. Okay? Up here." Ethan patted the inside

of the open cage. I regarded him curiously for a moment and then gave a little leap, landing lightly inside. If that's what the boy wanted me to do, that's what I'd do. I would do anything for my boy.

"Appreciate it," the policeman said. He swung the cage door shut.

"So what happens now?" Ethan asked.

"Oh, dog like that will be adopted out pretty easy, I imagine."

"Well . . . would they call me, let me know? He's a really nice animal; I'd like to know he's okay."

"I don't know about that. You'll have to call the shelter, ask them to notify you. My job is just to pick them up."

"That's what I'll do, then."

The policeman and the boy shook hands. Ethan came over to my cage as the policeman slid into the front of the truck. I put my nose up against the bars, trying to make contact, breathing in Ethan's scent. "You take care of yourself, okay, buddy?" Ethan said softly. "You need a nice home with kids to play with. I'm just an old man."

I was astounded when we drove off, Ethan still standing there, watching us go. I couldn't help myself, I started barking, and I barked and barked all the way down the driveway and down the road past Hannah's and beyond.

This new development left me bewildered and heartbroken. Why was I being taken from Ethan? Was he sending me away? When would I see him again? I wanted to be with my boy!

I was taken to a building full of dogs, many of whom barked with fear all day long. I was put in a cage by myself, and within a day I was wearing a stupid plastic collar and had a familiar pain in my groin—was this why I was here? When was Ethan coming to take me for the car ride home?

Every time someone passed my cage I leaped to my feet, expecting it to be the boy. As the days wore on, I sometimes gave voice to my frustration, joining the nonstop chorus of barking that rang off the walls. Where was Ethan? Where was my boy?

The people who fed me and took care of me were gentle and kind, and I have to admit that I so craved human contact I went to them whenever one of them opened my cage, offering my head for stroking. When a family with three young girls came to visit me in a small room, I climbed into their laps and rolled on my back, so desperate was I to feel human hands on my body.

"Can we keep him, Daddy?" one of the girls asked. The affection pouring off the three children made me squirm.

"He is as black as coal," the mother of the family said.

"Coaly," the father said. He held my head, looking at my teeth, and then lifted my front paws one by one. I knew what this meant; I'd been through this type of examination before. A cold fear grew in my stomach. *No.* I couldn't go home with these people. I belonged to the boy.

"Coaly! Coaly!" the girls chanted. I regarded them numbly, their adoration no longer welcome.

"Let's go to lunch," the man said.

"Dad-eee!"

"But then when we're done, we'll come back and take Coaly for a car ride," he finished.

"Yay!"

I heard the words "car ride" clearly but was relieved when, after a lot more hugging from the girls, the family left. I was put back in my cage, and curled up for a nap, a little mystified. I remembered when Maya and I did school, how it was my job to sit and let children pet me. Maybe this was the same thing, only now the children would be coming to me.

I didn't mind; what was important was that I'd been wrong, the family had not been here to take me away with them. I would wait for my boy. Human motivation is unfathomable to dogs, so I wasn't sure why the two of us were separated, but I knew that when the time came, Ethan would Find me.

"Good news, boy, you've got a new home," the woman who fed me said as she passed in a bowl of fresh water. "They'll be back soon, and we'll get you out of this place for good. I knew it wouldn't take long." I wagged and let her scratch my ears, licking her hand, sharing her happy spirits. *Yes*, I thought in reply to her good mood, *I am still here.*

"I'm going to call that man who brought you in. He'll be happy to hear we found you a good family."

When she left I circled around a few times and settled down for a nap, back to waiting patiently for the boy.

Half an hour later I sat bolt upright out of my sleep. A man's voice had just come to me, an angry voice.

Ethan.

I barked.

"My dog . . . my property . . . I've changed my mind!" he was shouting. I stopped barking and held perfectly still—I could sense him on the other side of the wall, and I stared at the door, willing it to open so I could smell him. And a minute later it did, the woman who had given me water leading the boy down the hallway. I put my paws up on the cage, wagging.

The woman was furious; I could sense it. "Those children are going to be so disappointed," she said. She opened my cage and I lunged out, crushing myself against the boy, wagging and licking and whimpering. The woman's anger left her as she watched. "Well then," she said. "My goodness."

Ethan stood at the counter for a few minutes, writing something down while I sat patiently at his feet and tried not to paw him. Then we were outside the door and in the front seat of the car for a car ride!

Though it had been a long time since I'd had the wonderful thrill of a car ride with my nose out the window, what I wanted most was to put my head in Ethan's lap and feel his hand stroke me, so that's what I did. "You really do forgive me, don't you, buddy?"

I gave him an alert look.

"I put you in jail, and you don't care at all." We drove a bit in comfortable silence. I wondered if we were headed to the Farm. "You are a good dog," the boy finally said. I wagged with pleasure. "Okay, well, let's stop and get you some dog food."

Eventually we did go back to the Farm, and this time when Ethan opened the front door to the house he held it open for me so I could trot right in.

That night, after dinner, I lay at his feet, more content than I could ever remember being.

"Sam," he said to me. I raised my head expectantly. "Max. No. Winston? Murphy?"

I wanted so much to please him, but I had no idea what he was asking of me. I found myself wishing he would command me to Find; I loved the idea of demonstrating the kind of work I could do.

"Bandit? Tucker?"

Oh, I knew what this was about. I gazed at him expectantly, waiting for him to make up his mind.

"Trooper? Lad? Buddy?"

There! I knew that word. I barked and he started in surprise. "Whoa, is that your name? Did they used to call you Buddy?"

I wagged.

"Well, okay, Buddy. Buddy, your name is Buddy."

By the next day I was fully comfortable responding to "Buddy." It was my new name. "Here, Buddy," he would call. "Sit, Buddy! Well, hey, somebody trained you pretty well, looks like. Wonder how you came to find yourself here; were you abandoned?"

For the most part, I was afraid to leave Ethan's side, that first day. I was surprised when he went to Grandpa and Grandma's room to sleep, but didn't hesitate when he patted the mattress, jumping up on the soft bed and stretching out in a groan of pure luxury.

Ethan got out of bed several times that night to use the bathroom, and I loyally went with him on each occurrence, standing in the doorway while he did his business. "You don't have to follow me every time, you know," he told me. He also didn't sleep in as late as he used to but was up with the sunrise, fixing both of us a breakfast.

"Well, Buddy, I'm semi-retired now," Ethan said. "I still have a few clients I consult with, and I've got a phone call scheduled with one of them this morning, but after that we've got the day free. I was thinking the two of us should work in the garden today. That sound good to you?"

I wagged. I liked the name Buddy, I decided.

After breakfast (I had toast!) the boy talked on the phone, so I explored the house. Upstairs felt little used—the rooms held a musty odor, with barely any evidence of Ethan's presence. His room was still the same, but Mom's room had no furniture and was full of boxes.

A downstairs closet was firmly shut, but as I sniffed along the bottom crack a familiar scent wafted out.

The flip.

{ THIRTY-ONE }

There was a sadness in the boy, a deep hurt that was new to him and far more substantial than the pain that had settled in his leg.

"It's just me living here; I don't know who you're looking for," Ethan told me as I examined every corner of the house. "I always meant to get married—came close to it a couple of times, in fact—but it never seemed to work out. Lived with a woman in Chicago for a few years, even." The boy stood and stared sightlessly out the window, and the sadness in him increased. "John Lennon said that life's what happens when you're making other plans. I guess that sums it up, pretty much." I went over to him and sat, lifting a paw to press against his thigh. He dropped his gaze down to me, and I wagged. "Well, hey, Buddy, let's get you a collar."

We went upstairs to his bedroom, and he pulled a box down off a shelf. "Let's see. Okay, here it is."

A jangle sounded from the box as Ethan lifted a collar out of the box and shook it. The noise was so familiar I shivered. As Bailey, I had made that same jangling sound whenever I had moved. "This used to belong to my other dog, a long, long time ago. Bailey."

I wagged at the name. He showed it to me and I sniffed it, picking up the ever so faint scent of another dog. *Me*, I realized. I was smelling me—it was a very odd sensation.

He shook the collar a few times. "Now that was a good dog, that Bailey," he said. He sat for a moment, lost in thought, and then looked at me. When he spoke, his voice was rough, and I felt a surge of strong emotions come from him—sadness and love and regret and mourning. "I guess maybe we'd better get you your own collar, Buddy. It wouldn't be right to make you try to live up to this one. Bailey . . . Bailey was a pretty special dog."

I was tense when the car ride the next day led us into town— I did *not* want to go back to the cage, in the place with all the barking dogs. But it turned out we were just picking up bags of food and a stiff collar for my neck, to which Ethan affixed some jingling tags when we got home.

"It says: 'My name is Buddy. I belong to Ethan Montgomery,'" he told me, holding one of the tags in his hand. I wagged my tail.

After several such trips to town, I learned to relax my guard— it no longer felt as though Ethan were going to abandon me. I stopped haunting his side and took to wandering around on my own, stretching my territory out to include all of the Farm, paying special attention to the mailbox and additional places by the road where other male dogs had been.

The pond was still there, and there was still a flock of stupid ducks living on its banks. For all I knew, they were the very same ducks—it hardly mattered; they acted the same when they saw me, jumping into the water in alarm and then swimming back to look at me. I knew there was no point in chasing them, but I did so anyway, just for the sheer joy of it.

Ethan spent most of his day on his knees in a big, moist plot of ground behind the house, and I learned that he did not want me lifting my leg in that area. He talked to me while he played with the dirt, so I listened, wagging when I heard my name.

"Soon we'll be going to the farmers' market on Sundays; now, that's a fun time. My tomatoes fetch a pretty price," he said.

One afternoon I got bored with the digging in the dirt game and wandered into the barn. The mysterious black cat was long gone—there was no scent of her left anywhere, and I felt a little disappointed, somehow. She was the only cat I'd ever met whom I enjoyed knowing.

No, that wasn't really true. Though I'd mostly found it irritating, Tinkerbell's unabashed affection for me had ultimately been gratifying.

In the back of the barn I found a pile of old blankets, molding and rotting. When I pushed my nose into them and breathed deep, though, I could very faintly pick up a familiar, comforting smell. Grandpa. This was where we used to come to do our chores together.

"It's good for me, to get out, take walks," Ethan told me. "I don't know why I didn't think to get a dog before. I need the exercise." Some evenings we'd circle the farm on a well-worn path that smelled of Troy the whole way, and others we'd stroll down the road in one direction or the other. I always felt something from the boy when we passed Hannah's place, though he never stopped or went up to the house to see her. I wondered why I could no longer smell her, and remembered Carly, in the dog park, positively covered in Hannah's scent.

One such evening, as we passed Hannah's house, I was struck by something that hadn't before occurred to me: the pain I could feel burrowed deep inside the boy was very similar to what I had sensed inside Jakob, long ago. There was a lonely grief, the sense of having said good-bye to something.

Sometimes the mood lifted completely, though. Ethan loved to take his cane and smack it against a ball in the yard, sending it flying down the driveway for me to pursue and return. We played this game often, and I would have worn the pads off my feet to keep him so happy. When I caught the ball on a high bounce, snagging it out of the air like a piece of meat dropped through a fence, he would laugh in delight.

Other times, though, the dark swirl of sadness would over-take him. "I never thought my life would turn out this way," he said to me one afternoon, his voice hoarse. I nuzzled him, trying to cheer him up. "All by myself, no one to share my days with. Made a lot of money, but after a while the job didn't give me much pleasure, so I more or less quit, and that didn't give me any pleasure, either." I ran and got a ball and spat it into his lap, but he turned his face away, ignoring it, his pain so sharp it made me want to yelp. "Aw, Buddy, things just don't always go as planned." He sighed. I dug my nose after the ball, shoving it up between his legs, and finally was rewarded with a weak toss, which I pounced upon. His heart wasn't in it. "Good dog, Buddy," he said absently. "I guess I don't feel like playing right now."

I was frustrated. I had been a good dog, I had done Find, and I was back with the boy. But he wasn't happy, not the way most people were at the end of Find, when Jakob or Maya and the others would give them blankets and food and reunite them with their families.

That's when it occurred to me that my purpose in this world had never been just to Find; it had been to *save*. Tracking down the boy was just part of the equation.

When I lived with Jakob, he harbored this same dark feeling inside. But when I saw him later, when Maya and I were doing school, he had a family—a child and a mate. And then he was happy, happy the same way that Ethan used to be when he and Hannah sat on the front porch and giggled with each other.

For Ethan to be rescued, he needed to have a family. He needed a woman and to have a baby with her. Then he would be happy.

The next morning, while Ethan worked the dirt, I trotted down the driveway and out onto the road. Though the goat ranch was gone, I'd learned new scent markers on my car rides, so that finding my way into town was as easy as touring the back acres of the Farm. Once in town I quickly located the dog park, though I was disappointed Carly was nowhere around. I wrestled with some dogs in the yard, no longer afraid of being spotted by people—I was Ethan's dog, now, I was a good dog, I had a collar, and my name was Buddy.

Late that afternoon, Carly came bounding up to me, thrilled to see that I was back in the park. As we played I luxuriated in Hannah's scent, fresh and strong throughout Carly's fur.

"Well, hello, doggy, I haven't seen you in a while. You sure look handsome," the woman on the bench said. "Glad they started feeding you!" She felt tired, and when she stood after just half an hour she pressed her hands into her back. "Whew. I am so *ready*," she breathed. She began making her way slowly down the sidewalk, Carly coursing back and forth in front of her. I stuck with Carly, the two of us sending several squirrels scattering in terror.

When after two blocks the woman turned up a walk and opened the door to a house, I knew better than to follow Carly inside. I settled down on the stoop after the women shut the door, content to wait. I'd played this game before.

A few hours later, a car swung into the driveway and a woman with white hair slid out of the front seat. I trotted down the steps to meet her. "Well, hello there, dog, are you here to play with Carly?" she greeted me, putting out a friendly hand.

I knew the voice before I smelled her: Hannah. My tail wagging, I rolled around at her feet, begging for her hands to touch me, and they did. The door to the house opened.

"Hi, Mom. He followed me home from the dog park," the woman said, standing in the doorway. Carly bounded out and tackled me. I shouldered her away; I wanted the girl's attentions right now.

"Well, where do you live, huh, boy?" Hannah's hands fumbled for my collar, so I sat. Carly shoved her face in the way. "Look out, Carly," Hannah said, pushing Carly's head to the side. "'My name is Buddy,'" Hannah said slowly, holding my tag.

I wagged.

"'I belong to'—Oh my."

"What is it, Mom?"

"'Ethan Montgomery.'"

"Who?"

Hannah stood. "Ethan Montgomery. He's a man . . . he's a man I used to know, a long time ago. Back when I was growing up."

"Like an old boyfriend, that kind of man?"

"Yes, well, sort of like that, yes." Hannah laughed softly. "My, um, first boyfriend."

"Your first? Oh *really*. And this is his dog?"

"His name is Buddy." I wagged. Carly chewed on my face.

"Well, what should we do?" the woman asked from the doorway.

"Do? Oh, I guess we should call him. He lives out near the old place, just down the road from there. You sure are a long way from home, Buddy."

I'd had enough of Carly, who didn't seem to grasp the whole situation here and was busy trying to climb on top of me. I snarled at her and she sat down, her ears back, then jumped on me again. Some dogs are just too happy for their own good.

I had utter faith that Hannah would take me back to the boy and that when Ethan saw her the girl would no longer be lost to him. It was complicated, but I was doing a sort of Find/Show, only it would be up to the two of them to put it all together.

Which they did. An hour or so later, Ethan's car pulled into the driveway. I jumped up from where I had Carly pinned to the grass and ran over to him. Hannah was sitting on the stoop, and she stood uncertainly as Ethan got out of the car. "Buddy, what in the world are you doing here?" he asked. "Get in the car."

I bounded into the front seat. Carly put her paws up on the car door, straining to smell me through the window as if we hadn't been nose-to-nose for the past four hours.

"Carly, get down!" Hannah said sharply. Carly dropped.

"Oh, it's okay. Hi there, Hannah."

"Hi, Ethan." They stared at each other a minute, and then Hannah laughed. Awkwardly they hugged, their faces coming together briefly.

"I have no idea how this happened," the boy said.

"Well, your dog was in the park. My daughter Rachel goes there every afternoon—she's a week overdue, and the doctor wants her to spend a little time on her feet every day. She'd do jumping jacks, if it would help." Hannah felt nervous to me, but it was nothing like what was happening to Ethan—his heart was pounding so hard I could hear it in his breath. The emotions coming off him were strong and confusing.

"That's what I don't understand. I wasn't in town. Buddy must have gone all that way by himself. I have no idea what would make him do such a thing."

"Well," Hannah said.

They stood there looking at each other. "Would you like to come in?" she finally asked.

"Oh no, no. I need to get back."

"Okay then."

There was more standing. Carly yawned, sitting down to scratch herself, oblivious to the tension between the two people.

"I was going to call you, when I heard about . . . Matthew. I'm sorry for your loss," Ethan said.

"Thank you," Hannah replied. "That was fifteen years ago, Ethan. Long time."

"I didn't realize it had been so long."

"Yes."

"So are you visiting, for the baby?"

"Oh no, I live here now."

"You do?" Ethan seemed startled by something, but, as I looked around, I saw nothing surprising except that a squirrel had come down out of the trees and was digging around in the grass a few houses down. Carly was looking the wrong way, I noted with disgust.

"I moved back two years ago next month. Rachel and her husband are staying with me while they finish adding a room to their place for the baby."

"Oh."

"They'd better hurry," Hannah said with a laugh. "She's . . . big."

They both laughed. This time, when the laughter stopped, something like sadness came off of Hannah. Ethan's fear bled away, and he, too, seemed overtaken with an odd gloom.

"Well, it was nice to see you, Ethan."

"It was great to see you, too, Hannah."

"Okay. Bye."

She turned to go back into her house. Ethan came around the front of the car. His mood was angry and scared and sad and conflicted. Carly still didn't see the squirrel. The girl was on the top step. Ethan opened the car door. "Hannah!" he called.

She turned. Ethan took a deep, shuddering breath. "I wonder if you'd like to come over for dinner sometime. Might be fun for you; you haven't been to the Farm in a long time. I, uh, put in a garden. Tomatoes . . ." His voice trailed off.

"You cook now, Ethan?"

"Well. I heat things up, pretty well."

They both laughed, and the sadness lifted from them as if it had never been there.

{THIRTY-TWO}

After that day, I saw Hannah and Carly a lot. They came to the Farm to play more and more frequently, which was fine by me. Carly understood that the Farm was my territory, something she could hardly fail to recognize, since I'd lifted my leg on every tree on the place. I was the Top Dog, and she didn't try to challenge me, though she was irritatingly oblivious to the benefits that the natural order bestowed upon our admittedly small pack. Mostly, she just acted like we were playmates and nothing more.

She was, I concluded, just not very bright. Carly seemed to think that she could catch the ducks if she just crept up on them slowly enough, which was an exercise in pure stupidity. I would watch in utter disgust as she would slink through the grass, her belly in the dirt, moving just inches at a time, while all the while the mother duck watched her with an unblinking eye. Then a quick lunge, a huge splash, and the ducks would be airborne for a few feet, landing just ahead of Carly in the pond. She'd swim for about fifteen minutes, working so hard her body would nearly be lifted out of the water, and would bark in frustration whenever she felt she was within biting distance and the ducks flapped their wings and jumped through the air a few feet out ahead. When Carly finally gave up, the ducks would determinedly swim after her, quacking, and sometimes Carly would spin around and head back out, thinking she had the ducks fooled. I had no patience with any of it.

Ethan and I occasionally went to Carly's house, too, but this wasn't as fun, as all there was to do was play in the backyard.

The next summer, dozens of people assembled at the Farm, sitting in folding chairs to watch me perform a trick I'd first perfected with Maya and Al, which was to walk between the chairs at a slow, dignified pace, this time up to where Ethan had built some raised wooden steps so everyone could see me. He untied something from my back, and he and Hannah talked and kissed and everyone laughed and applauded at me.

After that, Hannah lived with us on the Farm. The place was transformed so that it was almost like Maya's mama's house, with people arriving for visits all the time. Ethan brought home a couple more horses to join Troy in the yard, smaller ones, and the children who came to visit loved to ride them, even though, in my opinion, horses are unreliable creatures who will leave you stranded in the forest at the first sign of a snake.

Carly's owner, Rachel, soon showed up with a tiny baby named Chase, a little boy who loved to climb on me and grab my fur and giggle. I lay still when this happened, just as I had when Maya and I did school. I was a good dog; everyone said so.

Hannah had three daughters, and each of them had children, too, so that at any given time I might have more playmates than I could count.

When there were no visitors, Ethan and Hannah often sat out on the front porch, holding hands while the evening air turned cool. I lay at their feet, sighing with contentment. The pain in my boy was gone, replaced by a serene, uplifting happiness. The children who came to visit called him Granddaddy, and each one made his heart soar when they did so. Hannah called him "my love" and darling as well as just plain Ethan.

About the only thing involved with the new arrangement that was less than perfect was the fact that when Hannah started sleeping with Ethan I was summarily dismissed from the bed. At first I assumed this was a mistake—there was, after all, plenty of room for me between them, which was where I preferred to lie. But Ethan ordered me off onto the floor, even though there was nothing wrong with the bed upstairs and the girl could just as easily sleep there. In fact, after I performed my trick in the yard for all the people to see, Ethan had beds put in all the upstairs rooms, even Grandma's sewing room, but apparently none of them were good enough for Hannah.

Just to test it, though, every single night I put my paws on the bed and slowly raised myself up like Carly inching through the weeds toward the ducks. And every night Ethan and Hannah would laugh.

"No, Buddy, you get down," Ethan would say.

"You can't blame him for trying," Hannah often replied.

When the snow fell, Hannah and Ethan would put a blanket over themselves and sit and talk in front of the fire. When it was Happy Thanksgiving or Merry Christmas, the house would be so full of people I often felt in danger of being stepped on, and

I could have my pick of beds where the children were delighted to have me sleep with them. My favorite child was Rachel's boy, Chase, who reminded me a little of Ethan, the way he hugged me and loved me. When Chase stopped trying to walk on all fours like a dog and started running on two legs, he liked to explore the Farm with me while Carly fruitlessly hunted ducks.

I was a good dog. I had fulfilled my purpose. Lessons I had learned from being feral had taught me how to escape and how to hide from people when it was necessary, scavenging for food from trash containers. Being with Ethan had taught me love and had taught me my most important purpose, which was taking care of my boy. Jakob and Maya had taught me Find, Show, and, most important of all, how to save people, and it was all of these things, everything I had learned as a dog, that had led me to find Ethan and Hannah and to bring them both together. I understood it now, why I had lived so many times. I had to learn a lot of important skills and lessons, so that when the time came I could rescue Ethan, not from the pond but from the sinking despair of his own life.

The boy and I still walked around the Farm in the evenings, usually with Hannah, but not always. I craved the alone time with Ethan, when he would talk to me, his gait slow and careful on the uneven path. "What a great time we all had this week; didn't you have fun, Buddy?" Sometimes he used his cane to smack the ball down the driveway and I would joyously tear after it, chewing it a little before dropping it at his feet for another whack.

"You're such a great dog, Buddy, I don't know what I would do without you," Ethan said on one such evening. He took a deep breath, turning to survey the Farm, waving at a picnic table full of children, who waved back.

"Hi, Granddaddy!" they shouted.

His sheer enjoyment, his love of life, made me bark with delight. He turned back to me, laughing.

"Ready for another one, Buddy?" he asked me, raising his cane to hit the ball again.

Chase wasn't the last baby to join the family; they just kept coming. Chase was about the age Ethan had been when I first met him when his mother, Rachel, brought home a little girl they variously called the Surprise, the Last One for Sure, and Kearsten. As usual, they held the baby down for me to sniff, and as usual, I tried to be appreciative—I never knew what they expected from me under these circumstances.

"Let's go play ball, Buddy!" Chase suggested. Now *that* I could respond to!

One beautiful spring day I was home alone with Ethan, napping drowsily while he read a book in the warm sunlight streaming through the picture window. Hannah had just left in the car, and, at that particular moment, our home was uncharacteristically empty of visiting family members. Suddenly my eyes snapped open. I turned and looked at Ethan, who met my gaze curiously. "What did you hear, Buddy?" he asked me. "Did a car pull up?"

There was something wrong with the boy; I could sense it. With a slight whimper, I got to my feet. Anxiety washed through me. He'd gone back to his book but laughed in surprise when I put my paws on the couch, as if to climb on top of him. "Whoa, Buddy, what are you doing?"

The sense of impending disaster increased. I barked helplessly.

"Are you okay? Do you need to go out?" He gestured toward the dog door, then pulled his glasses off and rubbed his eyes. "Whew. Little dizzy, there."

I sat. He blinked, looking off into the distance. "Tell you what, old boy, let's you and me go back and take a nap." He got to his feet, swaying unsteadily. Panting nervously, I followed him back to the bedroom. He sat on the bed and groaned. "Oh," he said.

Something tore inside of his head; I could feel it. He sank back, sucking in a deep breath. I jumped on top of the bed, but he didn't say anything, just stared at me, glassy-eyed.

There was nothing for me to do. I nuzzled his slack hand, fearfully conscious of the strange forces loose inside him. His breathing was shallow, shuddering.

After an hour, he stirred. Something was still really wrong with him, but I could feel him gathering his resources, struggling to break free of whatever gripped him the way I had once struggled to find the surface of the cold water from the storm drain, when I had the little boy Geoffrey in my teeth.

"Oh," Ethan panted. "Oh. Hannah."

More time passed. I whined softly, feeling the fight continue within him. Then his eyes opened. At first they were unfocused, confused, and then they lit upon me, widening.

"Why, hello, Bailey," he shocked me by saying. "How have you been? I've missed you, dog." His hand groped for my fur. "Good dog, Bailey," he said.

It wasn't a mistake. Somehow, he knew. These magnificent creatures, with their complex minds, were capable of so much more than a dog, and the sure conviction coming from him now let me know that he had put it all together. He was looking at me and seeing Bailey.

"How about the day of the go-karts, eh, Bailey? We sure did show them, that day. We sure did."

I wanted to let him know that *yes*, I was Bailey, I was his one and only dog, and that I understood that whatever was happening inside him was letting him see me as I truly was. It dawned on me how I might do this, and in a flash I was off the bed and down the hall. I reached up and grabbed the knob to the closet just the way my first mother had taught me, and the old mechanism turned easily in my mouth, the door popping open. I nosed it aside and dove into the pile of musty things at the bottom, tossing aside boots and umbrellas until I had it in my mouth: the flip.

When I jumped back on the bed and dropped the thing in his hand, Ethan started as if I had just awakened him. "Wow! Bailey, you found the flip; where did you get this, boy?"

I licked his face.

"Well now. Let's just see."

What he did next was the last thing I wanted. His body trembling with the effort, he hauled himself over to the window, which had been cranked open to admit the fresh air. "Okay, Bailey. Get the flip!" he called. With an awkward motion he managed to fumble the flip onto the windowsill and push it outside.

I didn't want to leave his side, not even for a second, but I couldn't disobey him when he repeated his command. My toenails scrabbling on the carpet, I bounded across the living room floor and out the dog door, peeling around the side of the house and scooping the flip up from the bushes where it had fallen. I spun and raced back to the house, resenting every second the stupid flip was keeping me apart from my boy.

When I returned to the bedroom, I saw that things had taken a turn for the worse. Ethan had sat on the floor where he had been standing, and his eyes were unfocused, his breathing labored. I spat out the object I'd brought him—the time for that had passed. Carefully, so as not to hurt him, I crept forward, putting my head in his lap.

He would be leaving me soon; I could hear it in the slowing of his raspy breathing. My boy was dying.

I could not join him on his journey and did not know where it would lead him. People are vastly more complicated than dogs and served a much more important purpose. The job of a good dog was ultimately to be with them, remaining by their sides no matter what course their lives might take. All I could do now was offer him comfort, the assurance that as he left this life he was not alone but rather was tended by the dog who loved him more than anything in the whole world.

His hand, weak and trembling, touched the fur above my neck. "I will miss you, doodle dog," Ethan said to me.

I put my face to his, I felt his breath and tenderly licked his face while he struggled to focus his gaze on me. Eventually, he gave up, his eyes sliding away. I didn't know if he saw me now as Bailey or Buddy, but it didn't matter. I was his dog, and he was my boy.

I felt the consciousness ebb from him as gradually as daylight leaves the sky after sunset. There was no pain, no fear, nothing but the sense that my brave boy was going where he was sup-posed to go. Through it all, I could feel him aware of me lying in his lap until, with one last, shuddering breath, he was aware of nothing at all.

I lay there quietly with my boy in the stillness of that spring afternoon, the house silent and empty. Soon the girl would be home, and, remembering how hard it had been for everyone to say good-bye to Bailey and Ellie and even the cats, I knew she would need my help to face life without the boy.

As for me: I loyally remained right where I was, remember-ing the very first time I had ever seen the boy and then just now, the very last time—and all the times in between. The deep aching grief I knew I would feel would come soon enough, but at that moment mostly what I felt was peace, secure in the knowledge that by living my life the way I had, everything had come down to this moment.

I had fulfilled my purpose.